ERICA M. REILLY

The Swells of Stone Harbor

This book is dedicated to my fierce and fabulous grandmothers:
Rose, Ruth, Pam, Frances, and Kay.

Mimi, you were the one who showed me Stone Harbor
and introduced me to the "Swells."

You are all missed by so many.

"For I live among the Swells, and we don't
pick up peanut shells…"

THE GREATEST SHOWMAN

Contents

Acknowledgments

This book wouldn't be here without the support of my friends and family. I am extremely grateful for every one of you.

A special thank you to my childhood best friend Ria Cooper, who took hours of her time to read, edit, and give feedback on the book.

Jim Talone, for taking the time to meet with me, answer questions, and read my novel.

To Ivy Pochoda, for her insight and editing skills; Brenda Chando, for our long walks and friend therapy; Brett Russo, for offering her experience writing and publishing; Bonnie Raley, for her amazing photography skills; Anthony Nepi, the best contractor who gave advice on electrical work (anything I got wrong is my own doing); and everyone else who offered support and guidance.

A special thanks to my incredible friends and family, especially my mother Mary Jane and mother-in-law Cathy, for reading the book and giving me valuable feedback.

Thank you to my children Bowe, Samantha, Parker, and Tori for letting me write while I ignored all of your snack requests.

And most of all, thank you to my husband Brett for always believing in me. Without you giving me the time and space to sit down and write, I never would have finished this novel.

Chapter 1

April 12

It starts as a thumping noise that won't stop. Over and over, the sound of something bumping up against another.

Margo hadn't been able to sleep, feeling anxious and unsettled about the upcoming season at her gym. Worries about finding the right summer staff, keeping member enrollment high, saving money, and solving the mystery of ALL those missing spa towels have been keeping her awake.

If she can't make The Plank a success this summer, all of the time and effort she spent there will have been a waste. And then what will she do for a living? She *needs* this job. For so many reasons.

She's too restless to stay in bed. She needs air.

Margo pulls open the sliding glass door to the deck and pads down the wooden stairs to the water.

She's standing on the dock in her bare feet when she hears the noise and makes the connection. There's a boat slapping against wood, the gentle waves from Snug Harbor pushing it up against her bulkhead.

It isn't hers.

She doesn't own a boat, only a small kayak that is still safely stored against her cottage's side. When she looks across the bay to the soft lights of the Stone Harbor Yacht Club, she knows immediately that something isn't right.

The last thing she expected to see when she stepped outside was a bunch of empty sailboats drifting out to sea.

A few of the sailboats are upside down, which puts them at risk of sinking in the murky water. Others are floating away to open water. They should all be safely stored on big metal racks.

Holy shit. They're going to lose them all.

Running back to the house, she grabs her cell phone off the charger. The first person she calls is Tyson. She doesn't think to get anyone else - maybe the Police Department or the Coast Guard? Just Tyson. He'll know what to do.

He doesn't pick up at first. Dammit! She's going to need to keep calling him until he does. Tyson has always been a deep sleeper.

When he finally answers, she's getting frantic. "Tyson! You have to get over here!"

"Margo? What's going on?" It's a legitimate question for a 3 AM call. "Are you okay?"

"I'm fine. But someone tossed a bunch of the club's sailboats into the harbor. I need you!"

"The boats?" He's still not catching on. His voice is thick with sleep. "They're in the water?"

"YES! And they're all floating away. Just get dressed and get over here."

Margo hangs up before giving him a chance to waste any more time. Her next call is to the Stone Harbor Police Department. *They* get the Coast Guard. And the Fire Department.

Tyson lives in a small condo less than ten blocks from the Stone Harbor Yacht Club. At this time of night, it won't take him long to get there. There's no traffic this time of year. Most of the homes around hers are still empty, quietly waiting for their summer residents to return.

She needs to do something. She gets a rope and ties the boat to her dock for the time being, then grabs a pair of sneakers and runs over to the club. Although it's directly across from her on the water, she has to go around the perimeter of homes on the bay to get there on foot.

Margo is already at the club trying to grab pieces of equipment that will help catch them by the time Tyson rolls into the parking lot. The police cars and fire trucks are on the way. She can hear their sirens as they approach the marina. Tyson doesn't wait for them to catch up. He jumps out of his truck to join her.

"The boats are spreading out all over the bay." She points to her dock. "I managed to secure one of them back at my place."

Sunfish are the smaller sailboats used by young sailors at the yacht club. Even though the boats are small, they're well-made. And expensive.

"How did they fall into the water?" he asks. She knows he's trying to get an idea of what happened. Still sleepy, he runs his hands through his thick head of hair.

"I'm not sure." Why would she know? "I couldn't settle, so I stepped outside. I found one banging against my dock."

"They were all tied down when I left," Tyson tells her. "There's no way the rack could have toppled over. It's too heavy. And I always make sure it's secure before I leave."

He's bending over and shedding his clothes as he talks, getting ready to go in the water to save them. Tyson has the build of a swimmer: tall, lean, and lanky. He came prepared with a suit underneath his sweats.

Margo bites her lip. Does this mean she also has to get in the bay? She really doesn't want to.

Besides the fact that it's the middle of the night, it's also the middle of April. The Atlantic Ocean hasn't warmed up from the long winter. The water must be *freezing*.

"Good morning, guys." She's spared from getting wet by the arrival of Quinn, one of the town's year-round firefighters. He offers a brisk hello and quickly takes in the scene from the parking lot overlooking the water.

"We have a dive team on the way," Quinn tells them as he rubs his hands together. "We'll need to get these boats out of the water before we lose them for good. If any are damaged, they're going to sink fast." He starts taking off his shoes to join Tyson in the Snug Harbor Bay.

"Margo spotted them," Tyson explains quickly. "I'm counting at least five that I can see. We might have lost a few more."

They leave their clothes in a pile and walk down the slope of the floating dock that stores all the club's sailing gear. It's about 30 feet long and attached to the club's bulkhead on the east side of the water. Sailing equipment is scattered around the area.

The dock is set at a 45-degree angle that connects it to a flat section for guests to stand on while getting in the water. That part of the dock is about ten feet wide and maybe 30 feet long, with two ladders going into the bay.

More people arrive at the yacht club. Some show up and dive right in, while others pull out some of the smaller watercraft from the ramp area to fan out over the water. A Coast Guard boat approaches with a spotlight on, searching the pitch-black marsh.

Margo has a basic understanding of how the Stone Harbor Yacht Club's fleet operates, but no one knows it like Tyson. He's been working there since he was a young summer counselor at the sailing camp. She steps out of the way.

Several divers swim around trying to tow in the boats, which aren't easy to catch. At least the sails aren't on them, or they'd be all the way out to the marsh by now. The rescuers need to keep the boats from drifting away and getting lost forever. Or sink to the bottom, causing all sorts of problems for other boats and watercraft.

A crowd stands around on the dock, looking uncertain about what to do to help. A few others point flashlights towards the bay, offering light to the swimmers. Margo bets they're considering just how much they want to help out. You could still catch hypothermia in the water at this time of year.

She eyes the familiar sight of the two-story club perched over the marsh. It's normally an iconic landmark in town, with it's pennant flags flapping atop the massive flagpole. Tonight, lit up by fog lights and flashing cop cars, the building looks downright eerie.

She wishes whoever did this would have been more considerate and tossed the boats off the docks in early September. The water would be the ideal temp then.

Margo isn't surprised to see Tyson and Quinn are working together. The pair swim over to the nearby residential docks surrounding the bay. They know every house around Snug Harbor. The docks go out pretty far from their bulkheads and often have rigging attached to the sides. There's a good chance some of the boats drifted and got snagged on the residential lines or floated under a dock.

"Over here!" Tyson calls out.

She watches two other people in the water swim over to his location. They've caught another one! A crew helps pull the boat up onto the residential landing. Lucky for them, Sunfish are pretty light. They probably only weigh a little more than 100 pounds.

Sunfish are popular beginner sailboats for a reason. They're hard to tip over because of their Lateen-style rigging and shallow hulls. They are beautiful pieces of equipment. Top-of-the-line boats are so well made that even older models retain their value.

Beginning sailors start on Sunnys and Optis, officially known as Optimist Dinghies, before moving over to the individual Laser Radial or double-handed 420 Class racing boats. The Sunfish, which have been the most popular for beginning sailors for years, are starting to be replaced by Optis and Lasers.

But no sailors are present. Summer camp hasn't even started yet. They won't begin until the last week of June.

The divers start coming out of the water. They've been pretty lucky. In less than an hour, most of the boats have been tracked down. One was on its way out to Muddy Hole Island before getting snagged by the Coast Guard's boat. It could have been lost forever in the sludge of the marsh.

Things begin to slow down as the Sunnys are reclaimed. Stone Harbor's Police Chief Ed Walsh pulls out a bullhorn to get their attention. "Everyone out of the water!" he blares. They've been at it too long. Even with short breaks, someone could still freeze quickly.

Tyson swims over to one of the ladders and pulls himself up onto the landing. He's still with Quinn. The pair have an easy rhythm from years of swimming and surfing together.

"Someone cut holes and tossed them over," Tyson says to Quinn. "If ten boats are damaged, you're looking at more than $50,000 to replace them." He runs his hands along the seams of the boats on the large dock to assess the damage.

Margo doesn't know how he can see anything. Most of the homes are still empty, sitting dark along the water. They don't offer the same amount of light as over the summer.

"Let's tie this up and figure out what to do with it tomorrow," Quinn suggests. "No one's going to be able to move these back until the morning."

Tyson agrees. They make their way over to Margo, who hands them their clothes. Tyson pulls his sweatshirt over his head, and they head back to the club parking lot.

She recognizes most of the people who are there helping out. Locals who stay on the island year-round.

Helpful volunteers hand warm towels to Tyson, Quinn, and the other divers. The chief announces they're officially calling off the search for the night. No one argues.

As the crowd disperses, Margo spots her co-worker Banksy. He's quietly talking to a man on the other end of the docks. He looks cold, his dreadlocks still wet from the water. There's a wet towel draped around his shoulders.

Banksy has been helping Margo prepare for the upcoming summer at The Plank, the boutique gym and spa she manages. He has a knack for fixing all their gym equipment. A new arrival to town, he also works part-time at the yacht club helping Tyson manage the fleet.

Banksy sees Tyson and heads over to greet him. "I don't know how this could have happened," Banksy says. He shakes his head regretfully. Margo wonders if he's worried he did something wrong.

"They were stacked when we left," Tyson reassures him. "It isn't our fault. Someone got to them." He tells Banksy how he found jagged gouges and holes in the hulls of some of the boats. "It looked like they were trying to sink them."

"I don't know who noticed and called the department, but we're lucky they did before the boats drifted out to the marshes," says Banksy. "It would have been a hell of a time finding them then."

"It was me," Margo says. "I woke up to find one of them near my dock, and then I saw the others."

Tyson looks out at the bay. "I still don't know how someone got access to them. We had them safely secured."

"You better hope so," Quinn says helpfully.

Margo shoots him a look. "They better not blame you," she says. "And don't even think about blaming yourself." She links her arm through his and rests her head on his shoulder. Margo knows him better than anyone. He's going to take responsibility, even though none of it is his fault. But that's how Tyson is.

Quinn rolls his eyes. He's all fired up, hopping on the balls of his feet. He isn't a bit tired. He's used to being up at this hour from working 24-hour shifts at the firehouse.

Ed walks over to them. "Thanks for stepping in tonight," the chief tells them.

"What do you think? Someone told me they were shot at, but I didn't find anything," Quinn offers. "No bullet holes."

"Bullets?" Tyson asks. "No way. There are holes, but they're not round like a gunshot."

Quinn shakes his head. "I heard some of the officers discussing it. They must have seen it on one of the other boats."

"You're telling me that someone used a gun? In Stone Harbor?" Margo has a hard time believing it. This isn't something that usually happens around here. The most significant crimes on the island are stolen bikes or drunk vacationers. Maybe a lost dog. A fight over a parking spot. Nothing like this.

"We're not sure of anything right now," the chief says. "Someone would have had to have heard gunshots if they were shooting at so many boats."

"They could have used a silencer," Quinn points out.

Tyson looks back at the club. "I know they were fine before I left. I'm positive. Someone messed with them."

Banksy agrees with him. "They were all good, man. Laid out on the racks."

Ed shifts his weight without responding. Margo can tell he's not going to tell them what he's thinking. "We'll know more tomorrow. Not much we can do now, when there's not enough light to inspect the boats."

There's movement on the club's dock. Someone's found another boat. From their spot, they can see the Sunny but can't hear what the divers are saying.

A kid pulls it onto the landing. He's young, maybe in his late teens or early 20's. Margo is pretty sure she's seen him working at the Seven Mile Hotel, one of the more expensive places to stay on the island.

The chief walks over to investigate. "What's your name?" he asks.

"I'm Benjamin," he answers shyly, then ducks his head. He doesn't say anything else as he steps back to give them space to inspect the sailboat. She doesn't try to engage him in conversation. He doesn't seem like he's the type who wants to attract attention.

This boat is the most damaged by far. The mast has been snapped off. Angry scratches are scored across the hull.

There's no replacing this one. Its sailing integrity is gone.

It's so unreal. Margo has no idea why someone would do this to a rack of Sunfish. They're not even the nicest boats at the club. Someone was either really angry or had a major bone to pick. Not to mention, they would have needed a lot of strength to damage that many at once. Even with help, that would take heavy lifting. And this late on a Sunday night? The whole thing seems off.

Was someone angry they couldn't get into the club, with its four-year waitlist? Nursing a grudge that they lost a race in one of the summer regattas? Or could it be a group of rowdy college students? There are too many possibilities to run through in the middle of the night.

"Let's get here early tomorrow," Tyson tells Banksy. "We have a lot of cleaning up to do." The parking lot is a mess.

Margo looks around. It feels like every member of the Fire and Police Department is here. She's confident they'll find out who did it eventually. The officers are probably looking forward to looking into it. They finally have something to investigate in this sleepy beach town.

Regardless, nothing is getting solved tonight. Tyson offers to give

Quinn a ride back to the firehouse.

"We have a team from North Wildwood coming over in the morning to process the evidence," Quinn tells them. "We also got a hold of the Commodore. He's not in town but he's flying back tomorrow."

The Commodore is a volunteer but prestigious position at the Stone Harbor Yacht Club. He runs the place, deciding on all the events, policies, and programs for the members. There's also a Vice Commodore. And a Rear Commodore. Margo isn't sure what *that* guy does, but he's at all the club's events.

"I'm so glad I'm not one of the employees here," Quinn jokes as he nudges Tyson's arm.

"Yeah," Tyson agrees, shaking his head. "They're screwed."

Chapter 2

April 14

Tyson Vandenbraak stands on the dock of the Stone Harbor Yacht Club watching the sun disappear over the marsh. He's been working 10-hour shifts over the past couple of days, trying to get everything back to normal after the night of the damaged boats. Even though he's been enjoying this view for years, it never gets old.

It may be the fact that the town is surrounded by the beach and the bay, so the water is never far from any point of view. Or it could be the way Stone Harbor is perched on the Atlantic, a barrier island separated from the wetlands by a coastal channel of water.

It really doesn't matter why. For Tyson, Stone Harbor sunsets can't be duplicated anywhere else. He was born and raised here. The small island is located less than 30 miles south of Atlantic City and 10 miles north of Cape May, the final exit at the tip of Southern New Jersey. It's only accessible via bridges that link it to the mainland and neighboring towns.

Stone Harbor was even the setting for a major television series, The Shallows. The show gave a few young heartthrobs the start of their acting careers. His hometown became famous in the show's opening credits that showcased the historic downtown and pristine coastal shoreline.

It had been a major hit. Fans still came to take photos from some of the more iconic scenes, including the Harbor Square Theater and Coffee Talk, where the cast of teen actors filmed.

For him, Stone Harbor is home. He's never lived anywhere else. He and Margo grew up as part of a small group of year-round residents who remain on the island after Labor Day, when Stone Harbor unloads its summer high of 20,000 visitors and dwindles to a population of maybe 800.

From the deck of the yacht club, Tyson spots Margo sitting off her little dock across the bay. He raises his arm and waves. He knows, without needing to be asked, that she's open to company. She can usually be found there, looking for inspiration and enjoying the view. It's her favorite spot.

Margo doesn't like being alone for long. She never misses a party or turns down a fundraiser. For her, the more people there are around, the better.

That's not his style. Stone Harbor can feel comfortably isolated in the off-season. Most of the beach houses sit empty with their lights off and outdoor items stored away for the winter. Bud's Market is closed, so he has to drive ten minutes off the island to the Acme in Cape May Courthouse every time he needs groceries.

If he feels like going out, Atlantic City is a short ride away. And New York is just a few hours up the Parkway.

Tyson doesn't need much more than that. He's the opposite of Margo, content to be in his own company. He might go away for a trip, take a few runs from the East Coast to the Virgin Islands, or venture out on a deep-sea charter a few times a year. But he always comes back to Stone Harbor. Other than getting laid every once in a while, he has everything he needs right here along these three miles of shoreline.

Which reminds him that it's been a while. He's mentally calculating how long when he hears a loud tearing sound.

"Oh, shit!" Banksy yells.

Tyson quickly swivels around. Banksy's torn one of the covers of the boats.

Damn it. Tyson recognizes it immediately. This one belongs to Al Conwell, a former Commodore of the club and current member of the board. They don't need this kind of hassle right now.

Each cover is stitched with the name of the boat's owner, and the older looking the cover gets, the more seasoned the owner looks to everyone at the yacht club. It's one of those little things that Banksy wouldn't have known was important unless he'd been there a long time.

"I don't know what happened." Banksy shakes the cover. "It must have dried out. The thing had no give."

Tyson crouches down to inspect the canvas. It's an older cover, but he should have allowed for that and been more careful. The covers aren't cheap.

It happened under his watch, so Tyson will take the fall for it. A company is coming out tomorrow to fix the hulls and repaint the Sunfish. Maybe they can take a look at the cover as well? He has a feeling the cover won't be that easy of a fix.

They got lucky, for the most part. The majority of the boats didn't look as bad in the daylight as he had feared. The worst of the damage had been a few spots that had been cut with some kind of sharp metal object.

There was no gun involved, despite the rumors. The police thought someone had made the holes with an electric drill, and then flipped the rack of boats into the water.

Every boat was fixable except for one: Roger Elliot's Sunfish. It was the most damaged by far. As the owner of the swanky Seven Mile Hotel and a swath of businesses, he's one of the most important men in town. He can also be an asshole.

A long-time member of the yacht club, Roger wasn't happy to learn his treasured sailboat was a complete loss. It was a shame, because they could last for more than 40 years if well-maintained. But there was no way to fix the broken mast and the wide holes on the side. The foam blocks had been completely soaked and ruined the integrity of the boat.

Tyson doubted the man had taken it out for years, but Roger stored it at the club for sentimental reasons. It was the boat he'd learned to sail on.

Tyson had been the one to make the call to let him know about his beloved Sunny. He was still reeling from the conversation, and now it looks like he has to make yet another phone call. He isn't looking forward to being reamed out again.

"Don't worry, I'll take care of it," Tyson tells Banksy. How can he blame him? Banksy is still new to the sailing scene. He moved to Stone Harbor from Queens on a whim and is still learning how to maneuver around the gear.

Banksy has a lot to pick up about being on the water. Tyson still doesn't regret hiring him. He'll figure it out eventually.

Tyson just wishes it was another member's cover. The Conwells are not a flexible family. And dinghy covers aren't something he wants to deal with right now when they're on the clock to get all the gear ready for the sailing season. With all the boats in line for repairs, the yacht club's sailing camp season is in jeopardy. No camp would mean a lot of angry members.

He'll make it happen. Tyson doesn't take his responsibilities lightly. Most people might peg him as an easy-going sailor, but he has his ambitions. They just aren't the same ones most people have.

One day, he's going to own a top-of-the-line boat and create a fishing company that charters guests along the Jersey Cape. It will be different from the usual touristy crap. He'll show clients the hidden spots that only locals knew about and stay away from overfished areas to help with conservation.

Once they arrived back on dry land, Tyson would dazzle them with a three-course dining experience using the fish they'd caught that day prepared by his buddy Ray, one of New Jersey's most innovative chefs. It would be a trip they'd never forget. A charter to compare against all others.

He just needs the collateral to buy his first boat.

And then buy another one. *And* find a crew. Easy.

Tyson sighs. With his current savings account, he's a long way from getting that charter boat in the water. He helps Banksy up from the landing dock.

"We did well today," he tells Banksy. "We can regroup at 7 tomorrow."

"Except for destroying that cover," Banksy says with a shake of his head.

"Don't worry about it. Let's get a beer," Tyson offers. "We deserve one."

Chapter 3

April 15

Margo picks up a box of scented creams to restock the front of The Plank Athletic Club and Spa's front display. She's thrilled they've been selling out of this line, even in the off-season.

The seasonal summer highs and extreme winter lows are what Margo loves the most about where she lives. There's a full distinction to every season that makes each one unique; something special to enjoy that the other months don't have.

It also means that her current job as manager at The Plank Athletic Club and Spa goes from tranquil to *demanding* as soon as Memorial Day strikes.

Everything has to be ready when the wealthy Swells come to town. They're the chic part-time citizens of the town with the richest taste and most expensive needs. To them, money is no object. Unlike the Bennies, out-of-town guests that usually come in to New Jersey beaches for the day, drink on the beach, and head home at night. They might also be called Shoobies, a derogatory nickname for visitors who used to come in on trains with their lunches packed in shoeboxes.

The town jumps to attention as soon as the trickle of people enjoying the early spring weather becomes a long line of traffic backing up past the bridges every Friday in the summer.

For now, she has four or five solid weeks until the population begins to increase. A brief lull before the chaos. Stone Harbor Public School is still in session, and the summer hires have yet to come on board.

"Did you reorder the Bover bath salts?" Sandy asks.

"Last week," Margo confirms.

It's going to be a big year. Years of working at The Plank are finally coming to fruition. If she finishes one more successful season, her boss has agreed to let her invest in their second location.

Sandy Cohen is planning another branch in Avalon, and Margo hopes she'll be able to get in on the ground floor. Owning a small percentage of a growing company at 30 years old is a big opportunity for her.

"I couldn't do it without you." Sandy grants her a rare smile.

Margo hopes that's the case. After years of working, she is finally becoming known for her artwork, too. She learned to carve wood sculptures when she was a kid. Her grandfather was a carpenter by trade, and taught her everything about woodworking. Her work has been gaining traction online, and some of the local boutiques have started carrying her line.

She's even getting requests to do larger, private commissions from some of her wealthy clients. She welcomes all the extra work. Living in Stone Harbor isn't cheap!

Margo realizes that most people don't have the opportunity to live on the water. The home she lives in was passed down to her parents by her grandmother, who raised Margo's mother when prices were much, much lower than they are now.

When her grandparents lived here, you could earn a decent wage and have a hope of buying a home with a water view. Now, many of the old "saltboxes," the smaller framed cottages with two stories in the front and one story in the back, have been torn down to make way for seven-bedroom estates with separate guest houses.

The buyers aren't getting a bargain, either. Margo recently saw a small beachfront cottage with three bedrooms and two baths that sold for $10 million.

It can be unsettling to see some of the familiar houses she's passed by for years become an empty lot overnight, just waiting to be built on and framed out by a new generation of owners. Lots are more valuable than homes, so the easiest way to find your dream house is to knock down and rebuild. Especially if it has waterfront views.

Her grandfather had been one of the original bay clam diggers, a seasonal occupation he supplemented with handyman work around the island. At some point, Rip had been in the homes of most of Stone Harbor or Avalon, their sister town next door. Together, the towns make up Seven Mile Island, the small stretch of land nestled along the Jersey Cape.

When she was a child, Margo followed him on different house calls and errands to the local Ace Hardware. She tagged along as he diagnosed plumbing problems and offered estimates for small projects.

Rip was fair and reliable, often helping to fix something while asking for little in return. As a result, she was treated as one of the little darlings of the town, with all the perks of free doughnuts at Maryanne's Bakery, extra scoops of ice cream at Springer's, and free rounds of mini golf at Pirate Island.

From Rip, Margo learned carpentry. How to choose and handle a piece of wood, learn to follow the grain and work with it to reveal what lies beneath. He gave Margo her first chisel and helped add to her toolkit every year, patiently showing her tips and techniques and helping fix her first early mistakes. With Rip's help, she built her first workbench. She was instantly hooked. It only grew from there.

The season of hibernation has shed its icy grip, and Margo knows she's about to lose her precious free time. Winter is when she does most of her carving. She takes most of her inspiration from the beach and bay, creating ringed bowls and serving pieces, carved wooden ducks and delicate ospreys, wooden bangles, and hoop earrings. By August, almost everything will be sold, and she'll begin thinking of her next pieces to carve over the coming months.

The warmer weather also means her big brother will be coming back to town. Eddie blows in every summer to surf a few waves, see a few friends, and work a couple of shifts before ducking out again. The schedule suits him. He's never liked the winter season here.

She doesn't like living alone, but what can she do? Her parents retired to Arizona, so they don't make the trek back to the East Coast often, and they never stay for more than a week when they visit. Despite growing up here, her mother has always preferred the dry heat and mountains to the water. Margo has never understood why.

She watched a crew working on the boats at the club this morning. A couple of police cars were also parked in the lot. The cops have been there for days, trying to piece together the events of that night. So far, they have nothing.

Margo feels for them. And is seriously glad she's not dealing with it. It's Tyson's problem.

If anyone can handle it, Tyson can. She's known him since they were kids at Stone Harbor Public School, with its small class sizes bringing them together year after year. Ty's been in charge of the club's sailing activities for the past three years.

They both worked there as camp counselors when they were teens. But Tyson stayed. He's always known his way around water. He runs the club's summer sailing camps and regatta races and maintains the fleet of sailboats, powerboats, and kayaks. This means he's always busy. They sail Sunfish, Laser Radials, Optis, and double-handed 420

Class sailboats. The club also owns a Flying Scot.

Margo texts him, *Are you around for a drink later?* He usually is. She knows he's been swamped trying to clean up the mess from that night. She still can't come up with a reason why someone would have dumped all those boats into Snug Harbor.

She needs to do some work of her own. Margo opens her laptop and pulls up a few saved emails in response to her job postings. There's a group of resumes she has yet to review for summer help positions.

The Plank prides itself on its personal training and coastal spa offerings. Their clientele is high-end and used to getting *exactly* what they want when they want it. Most of their guests are used to the most chic trends in personal training and nutrition. They only go to the most exclusive professionals shared by word of mouth in the social circles of Manhattan and Philadelphia's Main Line.

They're always looking for the next big thing. It seems like they never stop trying to improve themselves, whether it's Ozempic or fillers, buccal fat removal or powdered brows.

On the other hand, this *is* the beach, and people also come here to relax. She does her best to make it accessible. No judgment.

Look at herself, for example. She doesn't spend a lot of time getting ready and probably needs a haircut. She can usually be found in leggings and a Plank workout tank, her hair pulled back into a high ponytail. Half of the time, she's covered in sawdust from whittling pieces of wood.

Between carving commissions for clients and managing a health center, she's up early and goes to bed late. And as the sole year-round resident, she maintains the beach house and dock herself.

Her grandfather taught her enough about home repairs that she could repair drywall or rewire an outlet. He would have been disappointed if she'd called a plumber for something he'd shown her how to do a thousand times.

Margo misses Rip most of all. It can get lonely living in the house by herself. Even with friends nearby, carving is a solitary activity. Eddie can't arrive soon enough.

Margo pulls out her first resume. Tish Jones, from Hoboken. She has an impressive background in facials and low-grade IPL treatments, which would come in handy when clients wanted to remove the brown spots and lines from too many days in the sun. She recently graduated from cosmetology school and has a few gaps in her resume, but she looks promising.

Definitely worth an interview. She puts that one to the side, then flips through a couple more. She dismisses a few potential candidates. Not enough experience, major career changes, or worrying lapses in employment.

Chelsea Richards is coming back for another season at the front desk. A college student at Clemson whose family has a place in Stone Harbor, Margo knows Chelsea can be a bit much sometimes. But she's friendly and reliable, two traits needed for her position.

There are a couple of college students looking for work in the summer. She'll reach out to them as well to see if they could fill the hourly positions or be on her backup list when someone is sick or on vacation. They have a small year-round staff for the lighter fall to spring season.

"Did my three o'clock show yet?" Tony asks as he walks by her desk. "I didn't see anyone."

Tony and Hank have been personal trainers for the past few years. They each come with an established clientele, even if they couldn't be more different. Hank has been with his partner for years, but she has to have a talk with Tony about inappropriate relationships with gym members every single season. She's hoping she won't have to again this year.

Their part-time maintenance person, Banksy, has already started.

If she's short on staffing for a few shifts, she knows her brother Eddie will fill in, but he's never been interested in committing to a regular schedule.

There's also marketing to be done at the nearby hotels. The Plank offers free day passes to guests at The Reeds, Icona, and Seven Mile Hotel. Jax and Adrienne run the studio classes and also hold sunrise yoga and boot camp sessions near the beach.

Things are looking up. If Margo can finalize her crew by the first week of May, she'll be ahead of the game. She decides to send out some emails to set up interviews.

Tyson texts her back that he needs a rain check. *You wouldn't believe how many times I've been yelled at today*, his text reads.

She has plenty of work she needs to do anyway. One more season under her belt as General Manager. She tells herself that everything will work out just fine.

Chapter 4

April 16

Tish grips the steering wheel. She knows nothing about her destination, and her stomach is a ball of nerves. The double espresso latte she just finished on an empty stomach doesn't help with the jitters.

She passes through sleepy towns where discarded boats and cars have been piled up next to some of the homes. Some houses are completely abandoned. One home even has the roof torn off, with the items in the attic open to the elements. A chair dangles over the house's edge, ready to fall at any moment.

Tish passes produce stands bursting with Jersey tomatoes and sweet corn, along with tiny post offices and vintage antique stores. It's a relaxing ride. She doesn't know what to expect next.

She eases through the lights and turns onto Stone Harbor Boulevard, a long stretch of road flanked by water on both sides.

The homes here are perched in one long row along the marshland. Some are so close to the water that it seems like they're about to topple into the canals behind them. The owners take advantage of their easy access to the Atlantic with wide decks and long docks.

Tish grips the steering wheel as she crosses over the 96th Street

Bridge that grants visitors access to the island. The suspension bridge rumbles under her tires. She passes by a little station where the bridge operator raises the bridge for larger boats to pass underneath and then lowers it once they've passed through. Fishermen stand along the walkway, casting their lines into the water.

She's in Stone Harbor! She opens the window, and the smell of saltwater fills her nose. It feels right. For the first time in a long time, she's doing something just for herself. And that is a very good thing.

"You can do this, Tish," she tells herself as she brushes her hair off her face. "This isn't your first new start."

Courage doesn't come easily to Tish. She was raised in a small river town with two older brothers protecting her throughout childhood. Her hometown of Frenchtown, New Jersey, is a tiny hamlet along the Delaware River where everyone knew or was related to someone.

When she applied and was lucky enough to be accepted to her prestigious cosmetology school, Tish decided to branch out from Frenchtown and try New York City. Who didn't want to live the "Sex and the City" life?

It was a good experience. But the reality wasn't as glamorous as she'd expected. Far from it. She'd felt overwhelmed trying to make it in New York and felt like she never quite fit in. She never had enough money to go out to nice dinners or plan trips with friends. So, she took odd jobs and found herself spending more time as a nanny than a student. Not what she had planned.

She's always loved skin care, facials, and new treatments. There's something magical about making someone feel good about themselves. It makes you happy, too.

This interview is her first shot at doing what makes her happy. People have taken advantage of her way too often. Tish is always the one asked by total strangers to watch their things or keep an eye on grocery carts when they have to run back for another item. But she is learning to stand up for herself. Turn over a new leaf. And Stone Harbor looks like the perfect place to do so.

She cranes her neck to see the blue water tower from Stone Harbor Boulevard. It's beautiful. There's open space, flowers, and trees, along with other things she missed in New York. It's only a few hours away, but Stone Harbor is as different as could be from where she'd been living.

Tish really hopes the interview works out. If it doesn't, she tells herself she'll chalk it up to an experience that didn't work out. She can deal with it.

Besides, she has no doubt that the manager Margo, is going to be a snob. Thinking she knows everything about prestigious skincare. Subsisting on green shakes and ionized water.

Tish could just picture her: a sleek brunette with a sharp bob and meticulously arched eyebrows. Used to working at the most prestigious spa and gym in this wealthy enclave, always getting her nails done and every spot of facial hair lasered off.

It honestly doesn't matter what Margo is like. Tish is going to do her best to impress her. Because she really wants to be a part of this community.

It's spread out before her, the grand multi-million-dollar houses on the water. The cute downtown with local stores and restaurants. No chains here, just smart boutiques full of home décor and clothing shops. There's even a movie theater with a vintage marquis showing the newest releases.

Picture perfect.

Tish pulls into a parking spot on 96th Street and gets out with her portfolio pressed against her chest. The Plank's sign is featured prominently along the main drag. She walks past an open construction site and opens the front door.

The club itself is stunning. Wide plank flooring in light oak, soft lighting, and oversize windows. State-of-the-art workout equipment, exercise studios with techno lighting, a zen yoga and barre studio. They haven't spared any expense in outfitting the space.

Margo St. James isn't what Tish expected, either. She doesn't look like the manager of an exclusive athletic club. She's way too friendly, for one. And awfully young.

"Hi Tish! It's so great to meet you."

Margo's light brown hair is pulled back in a side braid, and she's wearing a black tank top and leggings paired with white Chuck Taylor Converse sneakers. She looks like she could be applying for a summer internship.

"You're Margo St. James?"

Tish would never have pegged her as the General Manager of one of the area's most luxurious spas. She's also disarmingly sweet, flashing Tish a warm smile as soon as they meet.

Margo takes her around The Plank. "There's an entire wing for spa and skin care," she says as she points to where they're heading. "Two facial rooms outfitted with facial steamers, microneedling devices, IPL, and peel treatments."

"Wow. It's so much bigger than I expected."

"We have some of the latest in skin rejuvenation lines to help with wrinkles and sun damage," Margo tells her. "You would be the main aesthetician, with two other part-time helpers who would be called in as needed."

Tish nods, soaking it all in. They head to the yoga area. The studio is outfitted with dim lighting and a Buddha figure to meditate on.

"This is converted into a Pilates or barre room when needed. And then there is the main attraction, a float pool and hot tub area." It's ringed with light blue and white tile.

"It's gorgeous," Tish says honestly.

Margo flashes her another smile. "We have a small café that serves freshly squeezed juice, smoothies, and energy drinks. There's an area with high booths and low tables scattered around for guests to relax and recharge."

It's edgy and gorgeous, the counters lit from within so they radiate light. Tish has never seen a gym this fancy in her entire life.

Margo introduces her to Hank, one of the head trainers at the gym. He's seriously ripped. "Great to meet you, Tish."

He tells her that he'd been a professional boxer before moving to Stone Harbor. "When I'm not personal training, I lead outdoor boot camp classes. You should join us."

Tish doesn't have the heart to tell him she's not into HIIT. "That sounds fun."

"We have two more trainers returning to The Plank next week," Margo tells her. "Jax and Adrienne will run the yoga and pilates studio." The Plank offers classes on the beach from early June to late August.

She meets Banksy, who works at both the Yacht Club of Stone Harbor and The Plank. Basically, he fixes anything that needs to be fixed. Like Tish, Banksy is also an expat from New York. He's thrilled to have someone who lived in the city on their team.

"Any questions, let me know," he says with a smile. "I can tell you the best spots to get a real slice of pizza."

She talks to a few other employees and regulars at the gym before they go back to Margo's office. Tish's palms began to sweat. She really wants this job. She can see herself here, finishing up work and then taking a walk on the beach. Making friends and creating a life for herself that she can enjoy.

Margo's office is just as stunning as the rest of the place. Lucite and brass curtain rods, floor-length curtains, a white desk, and striped navy chairs. There's a gorgeous carved wooden tray loaded with stacks of coffee table books. A huge abstract painting streaked with arcs of blue and light pink is hanging on the wall behind the desk. It ties all the colors in the room together.

Despite the obvious glamour of the club, Tish wonders if she can take Margo seriously. What kind of a manager could she be? She seems way too young and laid back for such a big management role.

In all fairness, Tish is used to people dressing to the nines in New York. Margo's vibe is much more casual.

"It's still early in the season, so we don't have a big crowd today," Margo says, offering her a mug of coffee. She doesn't ask how Tish takes it. She would have said cream and sugar.

"The regulars are usually here from eight to eleven most mornings, and then we have a late afternoon to early evening rush." She walks back to her desk. "We're also looking to expand our spa offerings to include eyebrow and eyelash treatments."

Tish hands her a copy of her resume and takes a deep breath. "I've got plenty of experience in the field. And I just finished my last semester of school to become a certified medical aesthetician."

She takes a sip of the coffee. It's actually matcha tea. Tish tries not to spit it out. Who drinks this stuff?

"I see that. You graduated at the top of your class and have stellar recommendations from your teachers."

Margo pauses, picking up the sheet of paper. Even her hands are classy, long fingers with unpainted nails. Tish is starting to feel even more anxious.

"It says here you were a nanny before." She pauses to read the bullet points. "Did you decide you wanted to work in a different field?"

"I helped out a family and got caught up."

"Hmmm. Enough that you stopped working in the field completely." It's not a question. It's a statement.

Suddenly, Margo doesn't seem so inexperienced anymore. She has more bite to her than Tish had expected.

Tish swallows a lump in her throat. "I started out babysitting part-time and then…" She shrugs. "They didn't have anyone else, so I stepped in. It wasn't my first choice. They just kind of took over my life."

She knows it doesn't look good that she'd paused some of her schooling to care for the kids. What can she say? She's a pushover, something she is currently working to change.

This is the beginning of the new Tish. She'd already taken the first step when she quit her nannying job and started applying elsewhere. A few years ago, she would have never had the courage to even drive to this interview.

It isn't impressing her prospective boss. Margo arches an eyebrow. "Listen, I'll be honest. Your work history is a little all over the place. We need someone to develop this part of the spa, a member of the family who will become known by word-of-mouth to all the regulars here. Not an hourly employee."

Of course, Tish knows that. That's why she's here.

Margo continues without allowing her to interrupt. "Build your brand, become a part of the Plank brand. I need to know this isn't a summer job for you. We need you to commit to living here year-round."

"Yes, I know. And I really want this opportunity. I want to move here, become a townie." Tish flushes. "I didn't mean it that way."

"No, I get it." Margo grants her a smile. "I'm a born and bred townie."

She pauses to read her resume one more time before she sighs. Tish is squeezing her hands together.

Margo finally shakes her head. "Okay, I'm going to take a chance on you." She puts the paper on her desk. "Don't blow it."

"I won't, I promise!" Her hands are cramping with excitement. "I won't let you down."

"I called around, and everyone who's worked for you had high praise about your work ethic. But this is your first time working full-time in the field. There's going to be some very tough customers to please. Major pains in the ass. You're going to have to work with them."

"When can I start?"

This earns Tish an actual grin. "Right now? At this point in the year, we need everyone as soon as possible. We have only a few weeks until the town is packed with the summer people." Margo laughs. "We call them the Swells. You'll learn why."

She reviews Tish's salary and job expectations. "I know it's not a ton, but you'll be making excellent tips. Our clients are extremely generous. And you'll also get a percentage of any product lines you sell."

"No, that's fantastic. I'll take it. I can start next week." Tish pauses. "Any idea where I can find a place to live?"

"I'll set you up with a realtor who specializes in off-season rentals. You can probably house-sit any of these beachfront mansions in the fall and winter. For the summer, it's probably going to be tough. If it doesn't work out with her, come back to me and I'll find you something."

"Thank you soooo much," Tish gushes, then stops. She needs to act professionally. "You won't regret it."

Margo nods. "We'll see how it goes."

Tish's new manager has a pretty solid take on how to run a business. Margo might look like a 70's supermodel, but she acts like a 90's supermogul.

Tish respects it.

"I'll be in touch. Welcome to the team."

Tish walks out of the spa, elated. She can't wait to tell her family. There's a ton to do to move everything in one week, but she's ready for it. This has been her dream for so many years, and she's finally within reach of it.

Her new life begins now.

Tish starts walking down the street, then turns. She's already lost. Where did she park her car?

96th Street is a long stretch of wide sidewalks with businesses on either side. Cars are parked in angled parking spaces stretching the length of both streets. She'd been so anxious this morning that she hadn't paid attention to where she'd parked.

Spotting a fudge shop, Tish decides to treat herself. It's been a really good morning. Summer is officially underway.

It's going to take a while to find her car, anyway.

Chapter 5

April 19

The Plank has been buzzing about the damaged sailboats. What happened and who they think could have done it. It's all anyone can talk about for the past week. The biggest news this spring. And the police have no leads to date.

"Margo!" Chelsea spots Margo as soon as she walks into the gym. She flies around the corner, running to pounce on Margo with a hug.

Margo softens. "Hey, Chelsea. Did you have a great year?" You can't help feeling protective of Chelsea. She's so young. And energetic. *So energetic.*

Chelsea is in her second summer working the front desk. Even though she's a seasonal hire, she's been able to start sooner than most students because she goes to college in the South and finishes up with school a little earlier.

"Fantastic," Chelsea squeals. "It sounds like a lot has been going on here, too. Can you believe what happened to those boats?"

"I know, I know. It was a crazy night."

"You were there? Tell me everything." Chelsea grabs her hand. Margo knows she's thrilled to be getting first-hand information.

"I actually found them," Margo admits. "One of the loose ones drifted over to my dock."

"Wow," Chelsea breathes. "Did you see anyone around? Hear anything?"

Margo shakes her head. "No. I think they were long gone when I saw the boats all over the bay."

"That's so cool, that you can see the Yacht Club from your house. You are *so* lucky to have waterfront property. Even if your place isn't very big."

Margo smothers a smile. She knows Chelsea doesn't mean any harm. Stone Harbor *is* one of the richest towns in the state. It's hard not to see all that wealth on display. Chelsea is one of the only people in her sorority with a summer job, and she's told Margo that it's not easy to swallow working when her friends have unlimited credit cards.

"Who do they think did it?" Chelsea asks. She's wiggling with excitement.

"They don't know anything yet." Margo roots around in her tote looking for her calendar. She always has it on hand. Even if she did know what happened, there's no chance she's telling Chelsea anything. The girl can't keep a secret to save her life.

"I heard ALL the boats were in the water," Chelsea tries to get Margo's attention again. "Shot up. And there's like ... thousands of dollars of damage."

"No, no." Margo shakes her bag out. "It wasn't as bad as any of that. Just a few small holes."

"Margo? Can you please focus? I need to let my followers know."

Seriously? "I don't think there's any news I can tell. Especially to your *followers*, as much as they're waiting for updates. But *def* no bullet holes." She pauses. "Also, there were only ten boats. They were tossed in the water, but most of them were fine."

Chelsea rolls her eyes. "Bullets sound so much better. More

dramatic."

"Totally," Margo nods in sympathy. She's doing her best to keep a straight face. Chelsea is taking this way too seriously.

Margo already had to talk to her about doing *her job* and staying out of everyone's business last year. She'd hoped another year in college would have made Chelsea a bit more mature and a little less likely to spread rumors, but it doesn't seem to be happening.

Before Margo can have a talk with Chelsea about it again, one of their regulars walks in. Liz is one of the town's most successful realtors. It's her job to keep up with the latest happenings.

Great, another gossip. Margo tries not to roll her eyes.

"Girls! So happy to see you. Have you heard any new updates?" Liz knows where Margo lives and that her best friend is Tyson. She's not dumb. She's going right to the source.

"Morning, Liz," Margo responds. "Yeah, it's been pretty insane." She wonders how soon she can get out of this conversation.

"I figured you were there. Utter insanity. To think they shot someone."

"Wait, what? Shot someone? Who said anything about that?"

Liz waves her hand. "Oh, I don't know. I just heard there were gunshots. I figured someone got hurt."

"Someone was actually shot? Who?" Chelsea squeals. This is major.

Classic Liz. "No one was shot," Margo replies firmly. "They thought someone shot the boats to sink them. But they didn't find any bullets."

"Then what happened? How did they sink?"

"They think they tried to put holes in them with a tool of some sort, but weren't successful, so they tossed the rack over. But that's not official. They're waiting for an analysis team to look them over today."

"I think bullets sound better," Liz sniffs.

Chelsea nods in agreement. "It totally does."

"Well, one of the boats was a total loss, so at least you have that going for you," Margo says with a shrug of her shoulders. She reminds herself to stay calm and agreeable. She's going to be hearing about this police investigation all week. She's sure the gossip will get out of control.

"Oh, Margo, I can't make it in until 11 tomorrow," Chelsea tells her. "I forgot I had a dentist appointment."

Seriously? Taking off without any heads up?

Chelsea knows Margo isn't going to fire her, with it being hard enough to find summer help. But now Margo is going to have to find someone to fill her morning shift. It will most likely end up being herself. Coming in on her one day off.

"I'm going to head to my office," Margo tells them. That way, she'll be able to see what's going on but stay apart from it. Between Liz and Chelsea, she's already had her fill of small talk for the morning.

Things are falling into place, but Margo still needs to line the rest of her staff up. Organize a list of substitutes to fill in when her full-time employees take vacations or sick leave. Finalize the hours for the summer. Line up a full-time boot camp instructor. And get some of them to start taking her seriously. For once.

Chapter 6

April 20

Tyson feels a sharp tug on his line and automatically begins reeling it in with his pole. The movements are second nature to him. He's been casting a line since he was four years old. He keeps the tension steady as he winds the line tight and pulls it out of the water.

Quinn stands a couple of feet away on the public dock at 83rd Street. He doesn't comment, just stands there with his own pole in the water watching Tyson pull in his catch. He knows he doesn't need any help. They've been fishing together for way too long.

Still, his friend can't help being nosy. He leans over to check on what Tyson is reeling in. It's a small black sea bass, not large enough to keep. Tyson takes it off the hook and lets it back in the water.

"So, what's going on with those damaged Sunnies?" Quinn asks.

Tyson heaves a sigh. "Not much. The police tried running fingerprints, but there are so many people using those boats every day." He baits his hook and casts it out again. "There are always members coming in and out of the club. The police said that makes it pretty much impossible to get a valid print."

Quinn nods. "And most houses are still empty, so they probably don't have any eyewitnesses besides Margo."

It's a calm Thursday morning, ten days since the incident. Stone Harbor Yacht Club's Manager has reached out to every member who was affected, letting them know the club would take care of all the damages. Even still, some of the Swells griped about the hassle.

Roger Elliot's Sunny, which one of the local kids had found, was a confirmed total loss. The marina offered to salvage some of the parts, but Roger wasn't interested. He had other boats that were much bigger and flashier than a little sailboat. But he still lashed out at the club for leaving the boats out (*where else would they put them?*) and threatening to revoke his platinum sponsorships for upcoming events.

"I still think it was a bunch of high school kids," Quinn says. "Some of the guys on the force agree with me." Tyson can't dismiss his opinion. As a firefighter, he usually has more inside knowledge of what's going on in town. Quinn pulls his rod up and shakes it. Nothing is attached.

Tyson has already caught and released three fish. It just isn't Quinn's lucky day.

"I'll be glad when they figure out who did it," Tyson admits. "Most people have been understanding, but we still got a few nasty comments from some members." He doesn't name any names, although it would be easy to.

Quinn grunts in understanding. As locals, they share a common distaste for the wealthy summer renters while understanding they're essential to the economy. Some of the richest residents aren't too bad. And some of the up-and-coming ones are the worst.

They keep fishing for another half an hour, content not to speak without it being necessary. Just as Tyson is about to wrap things up, Quinn gets a tug on the line.

"Holy shit, it's a big one!" Quinn yells.

He's not going to insult his friend with an offer to help, but Tyson can see Quinn is struggling to hold on. It's strange - Quinn is always lifting at the gym. He shouldn't be having issues.

Tyson crouches down on the dock to try and see what's giving Quinn such a hard time. There's no way it's a fish. Something big enough to give Quinn a run for his money wouldn't be swimming in these shallow waters.

He starts to make out its shape as Quinn pulls it up and out of the water. It's covered by dark, stringy pieces of sea grass. Tyson leans in closer.

It's a small duffel bag.

"What a catch," he teases Quinn, who shrugs it off.

"Maybe there's money inside. Or diamonds."

"As long as it's not a body part."

Quinn pulls the bag up and over the dock, where it lands with a splat. It's not a big bag, maybe two feet long and a foot wide. Water gushes out of the bag.

Quinn looks over to Tyson. "Do we open it?"

Tyson nods. "Yeah, let's do it." He goes back to his truck to get a pair of leather work gloves. They have no idea of knowing what they're about to touch.

He walks back to the dock. Quinn hasn't moved a muscle. He's just standing there, staring at the bag. Tyson hands him the gloves.

"Oh, no way, man. You do it," Quinn backs away with his hands up.

"And I'm supposed to trust you to run into a burning fire," Tyson tells him.

"I know what to expect with a fire. This could be anything."

"Fine," Tyson agrees. He pulls on the gloves and lifts the bag to check its weight. It's not heavy. He decides to go ahead and unzip it, pulling the sides apart.

Quinn leans over his shoulder. Together, they peer into the contents. Long pieces of metal. And a saw.

A saw? Tyson shakes the bag to make sure there isn't a body part inside. You can't be too sure.

Nothing. He sighs in relief. Not even one finger.

"They're drill bits," Quinn says as he picks one up. Now that they know what's inside, he's back to being his cocky self. "And a saw. Why would someone toss them in the bay?"

"You don't know if they did or this fell in," Tyson answers. "But I'm going to take them to the station. There's a chance they could have been used to sink the sailboats."

"I'll go with you," Quinn says. "It's not like I caught anything else all day."

They pack up their fishing equipment and head over to the police department to share their catch.

Chapter 7

April 21

In the middle of a manicure, Sabrina realizes she doesn't like the shade. It's too light. She prefers darker pinks, and this is showing as a pale pink color. It's not even *close* to the nail dip she requested.

"Excuse me," she says to the nail technician. "This is all wrong. I need you to redo it."

Damn it. Why does she have to do everything? Now she's going to have to have them soaked and polished off before getting the color she TOLD the nail tech she wanted. It's so frustrating.

This is the difference between New York City and the Jersey Shore. Sabrina usually has a driver take her up to Manhattan, but she didn't have time today. Lunch went later than expected. She had to cancel her bi-weekly appointment in the city and make one in Avalon instead.

Now she's seriously regretting the decision to change nail spas. The tech tries to convince her that it's a pretty color, then turns to speak to one of her co-workers in another language.

"Yeah, no," Sabrina tells the tech. "Do it over. And please speak English."

One of the women next to her gasps. Several heads turn in her direction.

"What?" she asks. People these days.

If someone were to ask Sabrina Elliot why people generally disliked her, she would have told you it was because they were jealous. That's what her Daddy said. They wanted her wealth, looks, and privilege. When they realized they were never going to have what she had, they held it against her. Every single time.

Quite frankly, Sabrina found it exhausting. Her relationships never lasted long. She would become friends with someone or start dating a guy, and then out of nowhere, they would ghost her. With no explanation! Never to be seen from again.

It wasn't her fault she was so damn lucky. She worked for it, didn't she?

Sabrina knows she is a *very* successful interior designer. She is in charge of the decorating budget for every one of her Daddy's companies. It is a lot of work to oversee the decor for his hotels and other business ventures.

She does have a team that picks out and measures for art, light fixtures, and furniture. They create a mood board with a color palette and fabric patterns, then get an estimate of the cost for all the materials. Order all the samples and lay them out for her to approve. Once everything is ready, she reviews and tells them yes or no.

That takes valuable time.

Among all her father's businesses along the coast, the Seven Mile Hotel is her favorite. The hotel is so luxurious that even Oprah stayed there for a vacation. Really. Oprah. Sabrina got to meet her.

She has had the opportunity to meet a lot of famous celebrities and athletes, politicians, and actors over the years. It's one of the perks of owning a five-star hotel. And just another reason everyone is so jealous of her.

There was one time she was fooled by a celebrity imposter. A young production assistant told her he was an actor in The Shallows, a major TV series that was filming there. How was she supposed to know he wasn't? That had been embarrassing when she posted pics of them all over her Instagram account.

It doesn't matter. That was so long ago. Right now, she's more worried about looking perfect tonight.

Sabrina is going on another date with Mac, the gorgeous architect from Cape May. He might be a small business owner now, working on residential renovation projects. But she has big plans for him. With her connections, she sees him becoming one of the largest developers in the tri-state area.

She'd known she would sleep with Mac the instant she met him. Even though he's as good-looking as she is, he doesn't seem to realize it. And he's kind. When she tells him about her problems, he doesn't act disgusted, like so many of her previous boyfriends did. He listens to her.

They've only been going out for a few weeks, but she knows this has potential. He told her he wasn't interested in anything serious. After they had sex together, she knew he'd change his mind. It had been incredible. Life-changing.

Together, they're going to be a power couple. They're going to have such gorgeous babies. Even more beautiful than she and her brothers were. Sabrina's mother had doted on them before she passed away.

Sabrina frowns. She doesn't want to think about that. Losing her mother had been the worst thing that had ever happened to her. Her family had never been the same. Her dad didn't know what to do with her, so he sent her off to the Westtown School, a co-ed boarding school in Pennsylvania.

She'd been so lonely there, missing her mom.

Since Westtown School was a boarding school, its student population comes from nearly 20 different countries and towns all across the United States. Most of the people she met there live really far away. It didn't make sense to try and retain those relationships after she graduated, so she didn't. Why bother? They're of no use to her anymore.

She's never fit in around Stone Harbor. Because she only visited in the summer when she was out of school, they never welcomed her into their tight-knit community. She might not be a Shoobie, but she's definitely not considered a local.

It's fine. Sabrina is used to being alone. She's never had a best friend or a close cousin, little sister, or family friend. There's never been anyone to confide her deepest secrets, laugh at her old outfits, or swoon over a crush with. Her mother would have been her closest buddy if she hadn't lost her when she was young.

Don't feel bad for her. Never feel bad for her. Those are old memories. It was a long time ago. Now she's grown up and back, living with her father at their beach house in Avalon. Building her interior design business. Dating the gorgeous and talented Mac.

She's excited to see him tonight. They're going to an upscale Victorian-style restaurant in Cape May. Champagne and candlelight. He was going to ask her to make it official. She just knows.

That's why her nail color had to be perfect! Doesn't the nail technician realize this?

"No, not that color," Sabrina tells her after the first coat of the dip powder is applied. "Let me see the board."

She has to do everything around here.

Chapter 8

April 24

The biggest issue with running a business in Stone Harbor is that you only have three months to make the most of the high season. Despite needing to pay the rent, utility, and operating expenses over the course of the whole year, the restaurants and boutiques have a limited number of days to meet their profit goals.

Come September, the population drops to fewer than a tenth of its summer residents before shedding more and more people each week, until one day, it's winter. And no one's around to spend money.

Sure, you have a few pop-up events like Savor September, the Thanksgiving and Christmas parades, or Stone Harbor Shiver (where locals jump in freezing cold water in freezing cold weather; don't ask why). But for the most part, a lot of places have to shut down during the off-season to cut down on the cost of staffing and operations.

It adds a sense of urgency, as well as some excitement, Margo can admit. Especially when a new place opens, and everyone takes bets on its longevity.

Margo loves what she does, but it's stressful as hell. Nothing can go wrong. With such a short window, you need to have your best face forward. A simple snag as small as a one-week delay in supplies could cost you the ability to make a profit for the entire year.

And that's why she's currently freaking out.

She's standing with Chelsea at the front desk, looking over their list of active members. "I wish we had more daily activity," she confides. "It seems low."

"Well, it's not even May yet," Chelsea consoles her. "It will happen." She glances up at the sound of hammering. "They're at it today."

Margo rolls her eyes. "They're supposed to be almost done." The construction work next door was slated for completion by May 1. It's a major overhaul of an older restaurant that is going to be remade into a flashy new restaurant.

Margo already saw the plans when the owners appeared before the zoning board, and she has to admit the design looks incredible. Which isn't surprising, considering who they are. They have a few other high-end restaurants at the Jersey shore.

This one will be their biggest launch yet. It's being called Fourth & Bay. The drawings showed a large oval waiting area with a two-story gallery overlooking the main dining area. Huge black aluminum windows outfitted with wrought iron trim.

Front doors that were unlike anything she'd ever seen, sliding open to bring in the outdoors. Margo had even heard the owners tell the board that there was going to be a long, flaming firepit spanning the length of the dining area. They plan to host private events upstairs on the rooftop terrace and balcony area.

The restaurant was being built to impress, which was happening with the boutique hotels, stores, and resorts that had opened in the past decade. They were a far cry from the Mom and Pop stores or local sandwich shops where she shopped to make up most of her meals. Or the town's Wawa, which she frequents on a daily basis.

Fourth & Bay was going to be a gorgeous place to see and be seen when it was done. The problem was, it was so custom that the entire project had stalled with supply chain delays.

Two-story aluminum windows weren't in stock at the local glass company. They had to be custom-built by trained artisans who lived in obscure, hard-to-ship-to areas.

Interior fire pits that spanned the length of the wall had to be fitted with special anti-inflammatory safety devices to ensure the fire didn't get out of control. And on such a big scale, they had to be retrofitted to meet the parameters of the space.

This was what the construction guys had told Margo when she checked in. It had already been one delay after another, which was why the restaurant wasn't going to be done in time. Since the new place shares a wall with The Plank, this is a major problem. They only have one month until summer arrives.

Margo is sick of hearing the constant hammering and loud thuds of construction. Her office is on the same side of the shared wall, so she's been treated to the noise even more than other areas of the gym. She doesn't see any of her guests enjoying a relaxing seaweed treatment with the sounds of metal clanging in the background.

"I've tolerated it for months, but enough is enough." Margo has never been a pushover, and she isn't about to start now. "I think it's time for a personal site visit."

"Do it," Chelsea encourages her. "Find out what the hell is going on over there."

"Fine, I will." Margo goes back into her office and grabs her bag off the back of her chair. She walks out of the lobby, waving at a few regulars as she turns the corner to the noisy spot next door.

The sidewalk is clear except for a light sprinkling of sand across the concrete. With so much foot traffic in town, they have to keep the walkway open for pedestrians. It's a town ordinance. But the entrance is still under construction. She's walked by it ten times a day and personally seen how slowly they're moving.

A big piece of plywood is propped against the entrance, keeping the elements out of the gaping hole. There's a black and white contractor's sign with "MacIntyre Group" that's been proudly displayed for weeks, despite their lack of progress. The firm isn't based on the island, but she's seen their trucks around town.

Taking advantage of her slender size, Margo squeezes under the gap and enters the main reception area.

There's no one in sight. Someone has to be working somewhere in this drafty building, right? She's heard their hammering all morning.

They must be upstairs. She heads towards the staircase, taking stock of the space. It only riles her up more.

There is no freaking way this restaurant is going to be done in time. The way it currently looks, she doesn't even think it will be done by the end of summer, much less the beginning of it. This is going to be a problem.

Margo sighs in frustration. Make that a HUGE problem.

"Hello? Anyone there?" She calls out.

It's too loud to be heard over the shunting noise of a nail gun. She doesn't want to startle any workers and cause someone to lose a finger, but it's past time for a serious talk.

Margo might not look like she could rip shit up, but appearances are always deceiving.

She pulls the plastic covering back and climbs up the stairs, taking care not to brush past the open wiring. The fact that the electric is still exposed isn't a good sign. She knows every step of wiring and electrical installation from Rip. As her grandfather would have said, there wasn't "an ice cube's chance in hell" that the restaurant would be ready in the next few weeks.

The second floor looks even rougher. A well-built guy dressed in faded jeans and a gray t-shirt is crouched down, stapling pieces of trim around the windows.

Margo pauses to give him time to finish. He wraps up the last piece before turning around to grab another. Spotting her, he screams. Loudly.

"What the fu-....!"

"Sorry! I didn't want to scare you."

"I almost shot you!" He pants and puts the staple gun down on a ledge.

Since this is a wild exaggeration, Margo doesn't bother to respond. She just stands there with her arms crossed, waiting for him to calm down.

His chest is still going up and down, but he shoots her a friendly smile. "Sorry about the near miss. Didn't expect anyone to show up like that."

The hell with it. She throws up her arms. "Why are you still working on drywall? You should be almost done."

"Couldn't be helped." He's still trying to catch his breath. "I'm not even supposed to be here today, but I'm trying to move things along." He pauses as a thought strikes. "Wait. Where are you from? The township?"

"No, I'm not from the township." She does a slow turn to inspect the room. "Although they should be called over the state of this place."

"Then who are you?" he asks.

"I'm the manager of the lifestyle center next door."

"Gotcha." He pauses, then shoots her a careless grin. "Lifestyle? What's that even mean?"

Look at this guy trying to be funny and defuse the situation. Margo's sure that women just eat him up. Green eyes flecked with brown, a shaggy head of dark hair, and a day's worth of stubble across an elegantly masculine face. His features shouldn't have worked so well together, but even she has to admit they do. They really do.

"Yes," she answers without a hint of a smile. "It's a lifestyle gym and spa. Devoted to *relaxation*."

"I've seen your sign." He looks at the tool in his hand. "And I get it. We definitely need to catch up on our schedule."

"By weeks."

"Do you want to pitch in?"

Okay, he was late *and* clueless. "Uh, not really. I have a job. I manage people." She looks around. These projects usually have a bunch of people working on-site, but he's the only one there. "Speaking of, where are *your* employees?"

He shrugs. "We ran into a lot of delays. Supply chain issues, labor shortages, building code violations, you name it. I'm not normally here, but I'm trying to get it done quicker."

Margo flicks a glance at one of the walls. "You should consider hiring a new electrician."

"Yeah, why's that?" he responds.

"Those receptacles are at different heights, and that light switch is too far away from the doorway."

He takes a closer look and realizes she's right. "Well, trade in those Chucks for some steel toes and help me fix it."

"It's really cute you actually believe that. But I don't have the time. Because of you, my clients aren't going to be able to enjoy a relaxing facial when someone is hammering nails next door. We share the same wall." She knocks on it for emphasis.

His eyes narrow as she continues berating him. She *knows* she's being bitchy but can't control it. "I'm ready to make a call to the town about this."

He sighs. "I do know, and I'm sorry. That's why I came in today."

He holds out his hand to shake. Margo ignores it. She doesn't need an apology; she needs him to take action.

Something needs to be done. They can't be in full construction mode all summer long.

"Our landlord told us this project would be finished by the end of spring. And you're nowhere near being done."

"It's a damn shame," he agrees. "I know how frustrating it can be."

He doesn't seem the least bit affected by it. This pisses her off even more.

"Are you the foreman?" Seriously, who *is* this guy? She can't tell if he's trying to be funny or just started day drinking.

"Oh no, I'm Mac. I own the company."

So he was the Mac in the MacIntyre Development Group. She'd always thought those big firms were owned by a bunch of older men in suits, not someone in work boots.

"MacIntyre. That's your last name, then. What's your first?"

"That's a secret," he smiles. "Only my mother and I know."

She decides to drop it. It sounds like a line he's said several times before.

Even though her questions aren't going anywhere, Margo presses on. She needs some resolution, and he doesn't seem to be taking her seriously. "Why are you the only one? What happened to your company?"

"They're working on a home that needs to be done on a tight deadline. So right now, it's just me." Amiably, Mac moves around her and reaches for a drink from his cooler.

"Want a soda? Banana muffin? They're very good muffins. Just picked them up this morning."

No, she doesn't want a drink. Or a stupid muffin.

She wants the hammering that goes on all day, every day, to end. It was bad enough when she thought she only had a few weeks to go. But this project looks like it's going to go on for months.

Margo narrows her eyes. "I'm going to complain to the town council."

He doesn't seem worried. "Can I come with you?"

"You want to come with me?" He keeps catching her off guard. Nothing about this situation is what she'd expected.

"Yeah. It'll be fun. We can spend more time together. I'll bring the coffee and donuts."

"You'll bring the…" No, she wasn't going to partner up with him. Why does he keep offering her food? "You can meet me there."

"That works. Let me know what time."

So now she is going to show up with him to complain about his project. Margo recognizes the ridiculousness of this situation.

"When do you honestly think this project will be done?"

He smiles at her innocently. "Any day now."

"Mmmm, I'll bet. Listen, I'm not an angry woman who likes to go around yelling at people. I just need you to prioritize this project, so my clients aren't turned away from the gym or spa this summer. You know it's our big season."

"Absolutely. I'll get more men on this today."

She starts to feel bad for giving him a hard time. Maybe he isn't so terrible. He's trying. Reluctantly, she holds out her hand. "Thanks, appreciate it."

He holds it but doesn't let go. "Can I buy you coffee? Or a drink?"

"I don't have time for a drink. Go back to work," she tells him. "Stop slacking off."

"Then stop interrupting me." Mac turns back to the wall.

Unbelievable. If she had more time, she wouldn't have let him off that easily. He has way too much charm for his own good.

Margo has another interview arriving in ten minutes, so she gets out of the construction zone as quickly as she can. She has a feeling she'll be arguing with him again soon enough.

Checking her watch, she curses. She's already late. This freaking project.

Chapter 9

April 24

Mac puts a hand to his chest. That's it. He's done for.

His dream woman appears out of thin air, and he barely has a chance to figure out why she's standing there before she's gone again. She didn't even tell him her name.

She just waltzed in, took him completely by surprise, and tore into him as elegantly as anyone he's ever encountered. Even noticed his electric was out of code. Then very politely told him to go to hell when he offered her a baked treat. Before he could even think of a clever way to respond, she was already out the door.

Well, he knows where to find her. She said she works at the gym next door. The *lifestyle* gym. Easy enough to find an excuse to run into her again.

Just think, their businesses have been sharing a wall for months, and he's never seen her. Hasn't even run into her once. But then, one day, a project runs over schedule, and he gets to meet his dream girl.

Mac isn't surprised he hasn't seen her before. He doesn't work on 7 Mile Island that often, and even less frequently on new commercial construction. He only took this project as a favor for an old friend.

Not to mention that up until recently, he had been dating someone. It was casual, but it ended a few days ago. The breakup hadn't gone over well.

It's probably too soon to meet someone else. But what could he do? It was fate. Mac isn't worried that his mystery woman didn't seem as impressed with him as he'd been with her. He'll win her over eventually. He just needs some time.

Whistling, Mac gets back to nailing the trim around the window. He'd better get to work, or she'll be back to lecture him again.

Not that he would even mind. She could yell at him all day. Those sharp hazel eyes, that gorgeous tawny hair, the clever way she showed how pissed she was without saying a word.

She has long bangs. He hadn't even known he had a thing for long bangs until he saw them on her.

Mac needs to find out more. Where she lives, what her interests are. Does she like dogs? Because he'll get one. Cats? He'd consider it. He'll even get a hamster if it will make her forgive him for the noise level on their job site.

Even though he lives off the island, he's in Avalon and Stone Harbor enough to get to know most of the faces of the year-round residents. One of his best friends lives in town. He'll ask Quinn. His buddy must know her. She's hard to forget.

"Mac? You up there?" Two of his crew members are back.

"Second floor," he confirms.

He needs all the help he can get. With everything they have going on right now, they're stretched thin, working overtime and odd hours to finish up.

It's a shame the mystery woman wasn't around to see he has more than one person working on the space. Now he has three. See? Already tripling his workforce.

The other project the firm is working on is a huge beachfront house where the owners are expanding with yet another addition and a larger pool house. While it isn't his style, he doesn't argue with the firm redesigning the $30 million home.

If someone wants to build another wing to their summer house, then he will build it for them. And make sure the specs are up to the highest standard.

Mac wasn't born into the construction business, but he made up for lost time almost as soon as he discovered real estate development.

His mother, a historian and vocal preservationist, would have cut him out of her life if he'd made a career out of tearing down buildings to replace them with new ones. So instead, he chose to focus on renovations and restorations, working with architects and craftsmen to create custom homes and businesses.

He grew up in Newburyport, Massachusetts, a historic seaport with a rich maritime heritage. The site of the first "Tea Party" rebellion against the British. He respects the past and would never want to be part of erasing it.

That's the other reason Mac settled on historic renovations. He specializes in updating homes without having to tear them down. While it can be a bigger headache (original window sashes) and almost always cost more than a new build (uneven floors), in the long run, his clients are the ones who realize it was worth the effort.

The MacIntyre Group works all over the Eastern Seaboard but primarily focuses on New Jersey, New York, and Connecticut. His firm rehabs the grand houses of the past whose new owners want to update them while still keeping them historically accurate.

It's a lucrative business, which is why he's rarely home at his place in Cape May, a town known for its whimsical houses sitting along the water. Unfortunately, there's not a major need for his work in most of Avalon and Stone Harbor, where homes are torn down instead of remodeled. He's not in this area often.

He'd toured and bought his house in Cape May because its bones appealed to him, and it reminded him of some of the classic homes in Newburyport. As a contractor, he could see its potential. But he still hasn't given it the attention he should have. He's been so busy over the past few years that he hasn't had a chance to bring it back to what it deserves.

There's also the obvious fact that it's way too big for just him to rattle around in. A problem that's easily solved when his three brothers and sisters come to visit. With all of their kids. At once.

He's 34 years old and independent. If he meets someone who he hits it off with, he usually dates briefly. He had his heart broken a long time ago. They were young, but he still refers to Ruby as his first love. That had been years ago. Too many years.

No one had made that kind of impact on him until he found himself being yelled at by a gorgeous green-eyed gym manager. That spark. *Where have you been?* Mac wanted to ask her.

He turns to watch his foreman climbing the stairs. Silas doesn't say anything while he inspects the work they'd done that day. He's a man of few words, which is why they get along so well. Mac usually has too much to say.

Silas bends down to check on an outlet. "Getting there," he says.

"Yeah, we are." Mac is trying to be positive, even though they're weeks behind schedule. "I need to run some errands. I'll be back this afternoon."

"Will do," Silas nods. He doesn't ask why.

"Can you check out those receptacles? And the light switch? It's too far away from the door frame."

"You're right," Silas answers. "Good thing you caught it."

That confirms it. Love at first sight. Mac cleans up the space and heads for the stairs. It's time to sign up for a gym membership.

Chapter 10

April 27

It's been a few days, and Margo still feels guilty for how she behaved at the construction site. It had been stupid to flip out on a guy just trying to finish a job. Once again, acting first and thinking about it later.

She isn't a big fan of confrontation unless it's absolutely warranted. Yes, she realizes she came off like a major brat. But she couldn't help it. She was *hangry.*

Tish gets it.

"Don't let it bother you," Tish hands Margo a dark chocolate graham cracker. It's her third. "Anyone would have been put out. It's been a constant nuisance."

They're sitting at the front desk on a lazy Tuesday afternoon. It's Tish's official first day. Only a week and a half since her interview, and she's already at The Plank. True to her word, she found a place to live and started working right away. It gave her time to learn the ropes before the crowds arrived. The gym isn't that busy yet. Give it a month.

Margo already knows she made the right choice in hiring Tish. She's perfect for the position. And so easy to confide in. "It has, hasn't it? You think I wasn't that terrible?"

The chocolate is definitely helping. Margo reaches for another piece.

"There's just so much to do right now. I've got to finish all these interviews, get our marketing materials out, finalize the prices, and firm up the class schedules. Not to mention all the promotions we have going on. We're going to need all the help we can get. Our clients aren't going to appreciate all the construction noise." It was too much.

"Absolutely." Tish finishes another Graham cracker and hesitates. This is supposed to be a healthy living space. Was having a fourth one too much? She's always trying to lose the last ten pounds, but then something like this comes up and derails her diet.

Margo doesn't seem like she's pausing on the chocolate any time soon, so Tish decides to go ahead with another one. They're just too good.

"What was he like?"

Hmmm. How should Margo answer? She has to be a little honest. Chances are, Tish would run into him at some point. If Margo fails to mention the way Mac's Henley shirt had been open wide enough to show off those incredibly superior pec muscles, it might seem a little suspicious.

"You wouldn't be disappointed if you swiped right," Margo admits.

"Ooh, really? I was thinking he was an older developer. Someone from a third-generation family business."

"Nope. He looks like he came out of Hallmark casting."

Tish laughs. Now she needs to look him up. "Then he can develop my property any time."

"Oh, Tish, it's not funny. He thinks I'm an absolute bitch!" Margo pulls her hair back into a messy bun. It's getting way too long. She makes a note to make an appointment in the next week, before the bridge traffic makes it impossible to book a time.

"Then give him a free guest pass. He'll get over it."

Margo changes the topic. "Tony should be here soon. I'll introduce you."

Tish cocks her head. "What's he like?" she asks. It's always better to get the lay of the land before meeting her future co-workers.

"Tony? He's a phenomenal trainer. He can transform bodies, but then he has a tendency to date those same bodies as soon as they're up to his speed." Margo rolls her eyes.

"I could use some toning myself. Haven't been to the gym in months."

Margo feels the need to give some advice: Tony should come with a warning label.

"Have him give you a mini-session, but watch out for his pickup lines," she says. "He's a really charming guy, and you're new here. He'll be all over you."

Tish nods agreeably. "Gotcha. I'm not looking to date anyone I work with. I just need some help with my form."

"Hank is amazing in that respect." Margo nods to where he's setting up free weights for a client. "I'd have him show me a routine, if I were you."

Margo hopes for the best. There's a chance they'll all get along with no drama. She hopes so, because she's seen gym romances happen way too many times. It never seems to end well, and then you're stuck working together in an awkward situation. That's what happened last year, when Tony dated The Plank's former pilates instructor Julie.

She shudders at the memory. It was not a pretty breakup.

The object of their discussion sails in with a gym bag under his arm and a fresh smoothie from the café. He's wearing a deep cut muscle T-shirt and a pair of low shorts. Tony likes drawing stares. He figures he has an obligation to advertise his own hard work.

He has no inhibitions at all. Catch Tony eyeing himself in the mirror doing squats? Filming his workout routine? He isn't the least bit embarrassed.

Margo has to admit Tony has grown on her. He *is* harmless enough. He just wants to have a good time. And every season, he makes sure he does.

Since last year's flame, Julie, isn't coming back this summer, Margo knows Tony will be on the prowl for a new seasonal romance. She just hopes Tish isn't going to be it. There's something earnest and vulnerable about her. Margo finds herself taking Tish under her wing, even though they have only just met.

"MARGOOOOOOOOO!!!!" Tony yells from a few feet away. Grabbing her around the waist, he lifts her up for a fierce hug.

He does give the best hugs.

"You fabulous creature. How do you get even more gorgeous every year?" He puts Margo down, swooping his hair back with his hand.

"Are you ready for me?" he asks playfully.

"I've been waiting all month," Margo answers truthfully. Because Tony *is* fun. He's her busiest and most successful trainer. She needs him more now than ever, as the spa and health center continue to grow.

Hank comes over for a fist grip, back slap greeting. He and Tony are happy to see each other. They haven't worked together since last September.

Tony says he can't handle the cold, so he flies down to Miami in November, where he spends the winter months training wealthy housewives desperate to keep the pounds off in the year-round bikini weather.

Of Cuban-Italian descent, he's loud, bright, and bold. He's also as dependable as a migrating bird. As soon as the weather warms up, he's back up North at The Plank. When the fall months shift to winter weather, he travels back down South. Margo can't blame him.

"Tony, meet Tish," she says by introduction. "She's going to be heading up the spa as our lead facialist."

Tony grabs Tish's hand and doesn't let go. "I'm thrilled to meet you," he says.

Margo can tell Tish is slightly dazzled. She shoots him a warning look. "Tish *just* moved here, so she's still new to the area." And we don't want to lose her, she thinks to herself.

His canines gleam. "Extraordinary. You must tell me all about where you lived before." In less than two minutes, he's guiding her away from the watchful eye of their manager.

Well, Margo warned Tish. What happens next isn't up to her. Tish is a grown woman.

Hank shoots her a commiserating grin. He knows Tony's methods. He and his husband Jack have been happily married for several years, so he enjoys watching the entertainment from a careful and amused distance.

"I know, I know," Margo answers Hank's silent question. "I told her."

"It never matters," Hank says as he pulls out free weights for his next client's session. "They always fall for him."

She shrugs. "Personally, I don't get it. He's way too over the top for me."

"He makes them feel good about themselves. Sometimes, that's all it takes."

Hank is the most well-adjusted (and adorable) trainer she's worked with. He and Jack are polar opposites. Jack runs one of Stone Harbor's most popular bars. He stays up late partying. Hank puts health and fitness before everything. Still, it works for them.

Margo decides to switch her focus to other items on her "to-do" list. Chelsea is coming in for yet another HR session, and she's only been working there for a few days. She's a smart and reliable employee, but Margo has already had to pull her aside a few times for her personal commentary.

Margo doesn't think the girl means to sound like a complete asshole, but Chelsea is just way too blunt. The other day, she told a woman that she needed to put down the fork and start coming to the gym four days a week to lose weight.

Margo had to talk the guest out of quitting her membership by bribing her with a free spa day worth over $500 in perks.

Then, while checking in an older man at the front desk, she let him know that working out in jeans was the funniest thing she'd seen at The Plank. Since Bruce isn't a fan of spa treatments, Margo had made Chelsea write him a lengthy apology note. She isn't sure if it worked. He hasn't been back.

Normally, she would have fired Chelsea, but staff positions have been really hard to fill this summer. None of the candidates she's interviewed seemed to have much interest in customer service. She is stuck with the double conundrum of a clientele that expects elite service and a staff that considers it a fun summer job.

Chelsea rushes in a half an hour late. "Margo, you should have seen the traffic!"

There is not one spot of traffic yet. She also knows Chelsea is staying fewer than 15 blocks away, on 82nd Street. Still, Margo knows she is adjusting to working after college hours, so she gives her some slack.

Margo reminds herself that it's very hard to find summer help. Especially good ones.

"Let's get started." She hooks her arm under Chelsea's and leads her to the office.

"The first thing we need to do is respect our clients' feelings. That means not mocking them for their weight, clothes, or appearance."

"Even when they absolutely need to be told?" Chelsea asks.

"Yep, even then."

"I get it, Margo. Totes positivity all the way."

From the office, Margo can see Tony leaning into Tish's personal space as she stands there rolling up a load of white spa towels. Whatever he's saying is making Tish blush.

"The jeans thing was pretty funny though."

"Mmmm." Privately, she agrees. But she can't say that. Who knows what Chelsea would say next? Margo doesn't have that many gift certificates left.

She takes the college student through customer service expectations, with Chelsea checking her phone the entire time. It isn't easy to keep her focused. It doesn't help that the hammering is picking up again next door. She can barely talk over the noise.

No one is manning the front desk while she is working with Chelsea. Margo spots someone walking in and look around. Seeing no one there to greet them, they walk right back out. Great. Margo's sure she'll hear about that tomorrow from her boss, Sandy.

She earns her yearly bonus based on the growth of the club. She needs that bonus to pay her share of their expansion to a second location in Avalon. They also need a solid membership base. This all means that right now, it's essential for them to do all they can to retain and boost their numbers.

"Margo?" Hank yells to her. "There's someone on the line calling to freeze their membership."

Margo sighs. Damn it. Her optimism is fading fast. This is already shaping up to be a long, frustrating summer.

And it hasn't even started yet.

Chapter 11

May 1

"I'm glad it's working out. We should be able to schedule our final walk-through next week." Mac ends his call with a happy client and grabs his things to leave the office. He's meeting a friend for drinks at Fred's Tavern.

He's been juggling multiple residential and commercial projects since the beginning of the year. Supply chain issues and custom orders have delayed quite a few more installs than he had planned.

Luckily, most of what he needs is either in by now or he's convinced his clients to pivot towards a new design that works better with readily available materials.

His crew has been amazing. They've worked overtime to get projects completed and adopted new skills to adapt to changing product lines. Mac knows he owes every single one of them big time. He might not have a lot of guys, but each one of them is a highly skilled member led by his right-hand project manager, Silas. The guy doesn't miss a trick.

The restaurant is actually coming along. Mac hasn't taken a single day off from work since January. He's been so crazy that he had to. He's exhausted, but it has helped out in the long run. They're finally making real progress. The flooring is installed, the bar is finally in place, and the plumbing work has just been approved by the inspector, Robin Metcalf.

All in all, it's been an extremely successful year. Judging from the number of calls he's been receiving about upcoming projects, it looks like next year will be a solid one as well.

They've weathered the big storms in redevelopment and renovation work. He's surprised himself by learning he enjoys solving the problems that crop up, finding ways to resolve them, and keeping his clients happy.

In fact, even with all the delays, the biggest challenge he's had this winter hasn't been a customer or another contractor.

It's a former girlfriend. A trendy interior designer who still isn't happy with the way things turned out in their relationship, which is why she's currently trying to make his life a living hell. She's doing a damn good job of it, too.

As the only daughter of Roger Elliot, Sabrina Elliot is used to life going her way. She's been raised in wealth and privilege, with two much older brothers and a father who openly adores and spoils her.

Cherished, rich, and beautiful. All of this was great for Sabrina. Not so great for Mac. When the person you are dating expects to be put on a pedestal even though she hadn't necessarily climbed there on her own, it doesn't make for a smooth relationship.

She'd been late to a funeral because she was getting her hair extensions done. Another time, she made him change their dinner reservation because she had a "blowout emergency" (her words).

Mac never figured out everything she had done, but he did know she was on a complex schedule for hair, nails, and lashes. Those appointments were non-negotiable; never to be moved or canceled.

Why had he ever thought it was a good idea to get involved with her? He'd been an idiot.

When he finally realized it wasn't working out, Mac thought he'd done a good job ending things at dinner. He explained why they weren't a good fit without pointing fingers. He hadn't cheated on her or gone and blabbed about their problems to everyone on the island. He'd tried to let her down as gently as possible, and in person, too. Honestly, he hadn't thought they had even been that serious.

Sabrina didn't think the same. She'd flipped out on him in front of the entire restaurant, tossing forks and sobbing hysterically. He didn't know what to do. Apparently, she'd thought Mac had chosen that restaurant so he could ask her to take the next step in their relationship. Instead, he'd broken the whole thing off.

It had caught him off guard. He'd figured they were both keeping it casual. Sex and dinner. Nothing else had been promised.

Mac had known they were nothing alike. But she'd been so damned persuasive, showing up at job sites with coffee or calling him for a late-night hookup. She was actually nice to be with when she relaxed and let her guard down a little. Still, he'd known they weren't the right fit. He didn't expect it to last. And that was even before he met his mystery crush.

After a long discussion and several awkward hugs, he felt they'd ended things amicably. But he hadn't considered that Sabrina wasn't used to being dumped.

She wanted Mac, and she was used to getting what she wanted. When he didn't change his mind and come running back to her, she decided it was time to punish him.

It had started out as a minor issue. He got a few messy calls and voicemails in the middle of the night, accusing him of using her for sex.

He ignored them all. Which had been dumb.

In less than two weeks, things began to escalate. A couple of his crew members got phone calls telling them not to come in to work that day. It had taken him hours to convince them otherwise, costing him a half day of work.

An order from their window and door supplier was canceled. After losing the deposit, he had to start all over again, pushing back his timeline.

He didn't have any way to prove it was Sabrina, but he didn't have any other enemies on the island. There was only one person who had an ax to grind. A reason to be pissed off right now.

He took some of the blame for it. No one liked being dumped. So once again, he ignored the drama and hoped she'd get the message that he wasn't interested in playing her games. This wasn't high school.

Yesterday, Mac got a visit from the town's building inspector again, who told Mac she'd been tipped off that their company was doing illegal plumbing work. After losing a full day for Robin to check out and approve all of the work, he was told that the "anonymous" tipster was someone he might know. *Might* have dated.

Coming after him was one thing. But coming after his business and his reputation was another. It seemed to be escalating more and more with every week he stayed away from her.

Mac realized he needed to do something to keep her from destroying his life. But he didn't know how.

He walks into Fred's and gets a seat at the bar, where he fills in his friend Quinn.

"Mac, I told you not to get involved with Sabrina Elliot," Quinn tells him, shaking his head. "She's always been a pain in the ass."

He plants his elbows on the bar. This area of Fred's Tavern is spread out in a wide rectangle. The length of the room gives guests as many seats as the space can fit. And sometimes, that's still not enough space. From the ceiling hangs a vintage Budweiser light with Clydesdale horses on the shade. The dark and cozy bar is one of the busiest in town.

It's also open year-round, with live music on weekends that draws a solid crowd. There's also an attached liquor store that is one of the only places to buy alcohol on the island.

Fred's has been a Stone Harbor mainstay since opening in the 1930's. Their line of T-shirts and other gear is famous, giving the wearers bragging rights when they're spotted on trips around the globe.

Mac picks up his beer, turning it around in his hand. "I wasn't thinking. She just kept coming at me. Told me it would be an easy, no-strings thing. She knows how much I'm gone on projects. I'm never in Cape May."

"Probably would have been," Quinn agrees. "But then you turned her down. She's not used to that."

"I get that she's pissed off. But coming after my company? Again and again? It takes balls."

Quinn nods. "Not sure what she'd expect you to do after that. It's not like you're going to come back to her." Quinn is philosophical. As a firefighter and a local, he's used to the various personalities in town.

Stone Harbor and Avalon benefit from New Jersey taxes on the big mansions, but because they don't have a lot of year-round residents, they don't need to fund a large school budget to go with it. This means the town council has more money to spend on government projects and employees.

Avalon is building a new fire station, and Stone Harbor has just finished a new lifeguard building and a two-story, state-of-the-art library. Mac doesn't begrudge them the money. They have to spend it somehow.

Being a firefighter is a solid gig. Quinn works long shifts but then has a few days off in a row. Most of the firefighters have side jobs. Quinn helps Mac out on projects when he needs an extra set of hands. He also has a nice fishing boat that Mac likes to help himself to when Quinn allows him. Or even sometimes that he doesn't know about.

"I can't have her sabotaging what I've built." Mac runs his hands through his hair, which is always slightly perpetually in need of a trim. "She won't stop. It's like she's out to destroy me."

"Have you talked to anyone in the police department?" Quinn knows all the cops on the island.

"I talked to Sergeant Betty. She told me I don't have anything to prove it's coming from Sabrina."

"Can they pull her phone records?"

Mac shakes his head. The conversation is making him feel even worse.

"They don't have a warrant. I can't just accuse her and have her phone turned over. Technically, she hasn't done anything wrong."

Quinn pauses to say hello to a patron walking past. He knows everyone. Mac picks up his cell and holds it in his hand, considering his options.

What if he called Sabrina? Offered to take her to dinner? He knew he could charm her back into his life. After a couple of dates and a few more sleepovers, he'd be able to gain access to her phone and find a way to prove it was her. Some real proof, not just hearsay.

It's tempting. He's itching to prove his innocence. But he can't go through with it. And when he finally does break up with her, which he would have to do eventually, she'll just go back to her old tricks. It would be pointless.

Not to mention he's intent on asking out the brunette who he's pretty sure is the most perfect creature on earth. Even if she despises him.

It's been weeks, and Mac hasn't seen her again, even though he's tried to be as noisy as possible so she comes to yell at him. He hasn't run into her once. He hopes she didn't quit, or he'll never find her.

Most of the time, he's 25 minutes away in Cape May or wrapping up projects in either Stone Harbor or Avalon.

Mac doesn't even know if he has that long before she disappears again. Or what she would say when he asked. What if she's not around next year? Or wasn't even here anymore?

Come to think of it, he doesn't know anything about her besides the fact that she works in the gym next door. She could be married. With kids. He shudders at the thought.

"Quinn, do you know the manager at the Plank? A brunette with bangs?"

"Ah," Quinn sighs, holding his beer to his chest. "The foxy Margo St. James. Who doesn't know her? She's a townie."

That surprises Mac. "Really? She's from here?" That means she wasn't going anywhere.

"Oh yeah. Third generation or something like that. She's an artist, too. A lot of her work is in the stores around town. She does private commissions for the Swells."

"I had no idea. She looks like she's from the West Coast." She's so badass.

Quinn nods amiably. "I can see that. But she's born and raised. Lives here year-round. Over on Snug Harbor Bay."

So she was only a few blocks away from them. Fred's is on the main drag of 96th Street. Yeah, he definitely can't get back together with Sabrina. He's juggling too many renovation projects. There is no way he could date two women. Besides, it isn't his style.

"I'm going to marry her," Mac tells Quinn.

His friend isn't fazed. "I'm sure, buddy. Good luck with that." Quinn toasts Mac with his beer, then tips it back. They order food and settle in, waiting for the live music to start.

Chapter 12

May 3

More and more clients are coming into the gym each day. The season is officially on track. The Swells are backing up traffic, walking against the lights, and double-parking at beach entrances. It's what they do.

Chelsea is now full-time, manning the front desk and commenting on every single person who walks in the door. She's pissed off two members this week so far.

Hiring Tish has worked out even better than Margo expected. She'd been right to go with her gut and offer Tish the job on the spot.

She watches as Chelsea checks in a new member, Sara DiCecco. The new mom is currently home on maternity leave with her baby. She told Margo she was desperate to lose the weight she gained while pregnant, to which she'd tried explaining it took a while to get back into shape and not to do anything drastic. Chelsea nodded, then signed up for a set of 20 personal training classes. So much for easing into it.

Tony walks up to greet his newest client for their training session.

"Sara, looking gorgeous today. Let's go get you set up." He leads her away, his hand planted at the top of her butt.

Margo hopes she doesn't have to give him another talk about client/trainer relationships. She wonders who his client is after Sara. She goes to pick up her calendar, but it isn't there.

Shit. She had been in such a rush this morning to get to work. She must have left it at home.

Even though Margo uses her phone for reminders, she's still old school with a paper agenda book. She feels insecure without the notes she always keeps with her. It's where her online passwords are written down, because who could remember them all?

Margo heads to her office, still rooting around in her bag, looking for her calendar. It might be somewhere else.

After several minutes of rummaging through her drawers, she comes up empty. She even crouches underneath the desk to look around the floor. She finds her favorite lip gloss, but not what she was looking for.

She should run home to see if she'd left it there. One of the best parts of her job is her commute, a quick four-block walk. Especially now, since they're fully staffed. She decides to go back home to find it.

"I'll be right back," she tells Chelsea, who nods without looking up from her phone.

"No probs," she answers.

Margo pulls open the gym's front doors and briskly walks down 96th Street, darting around the occasional pedestrian out for a leisurely stroll. She doesn't want to be away for too long.

This late in the spring, more and more summer visitors are showing up to get their homes ready for the summer season. It almost seems like they're unpacking their cars, then heading immediately to the gym for a workout.

She turns the corner, passing by a home design store, and then continues past the Episcopal Church and Stone Harbor Elementary School. She has a brisk walk-trot thing going that seems to be working.

Her calendar is on the kitchen counter, right where she'd left it the night before. The back door to the deck is wide open. Did she leave it that way? She must have been more out of it this morning than she realized.

She tucks the calendar under her arm and then makes sure she closes and locks the door behind her. It only took a few minutes.

Making her way back along Third Avenue, she ducks around people moving slowly down the street.

She knows pretty much everyone by sight. Crowds are still at maybe 30 to 40 percent of what the population will be in another few weeks, so Margo is able to bob and weave in and out of the benches and street parking posts with ease.

The contractors are some of the worst offenders with their street parking. While they are leveling houses, installing windows, and putting up cedar shake siding, their large trucks and heavy equipment block driveways all over town. She darts around a sawhorse that has been set up to keep pedestrians out while the sidewalk waits to be laid in concrete.

She's just about home free when she spots a familiar face. There's no time to duck and hide.

"Margo." Sabrina Elliot is standing on the sidewalk in front of a breakfast spot. "So nice to see you."

"Oh, Sabrina! Hey!" Now she has to stop walking too. Ugh.

What is it about Sabrina that Margo particularly dislikes? Sabrina has never done anything to her. In all honesty, she's always been pretty nice to Margo. She always comes over and says hi when she sees her at a party, and she's never rubbed in Margo's face the fact that she's a trillion times wealthier or more glamorous.

Maybe Margo is just being petty. Sabrina had dated her older brother Eddie one summer when he spent a lot of time with a group of their mutual friends. Every time Margo hung out with them, she told herself she would never do it again. It was so uncomfortable.

Luckily, she didn't have to. The relationship ended quickly. Eddie had told Margo it wasn't serious, but then again, nothing was with him. He dated frequently and indiscriminately, often with more than one person at the same time. That's Eddie.

But why does she avoid this girl? Is it just that Sabrina seems so fake? Or her voice is just too high-pitched? Margo *hates* fake high voices. You always have to respond in the same vocal range, or you sound like Eeyore.

"I still can't believe it," Sabrina squeals. Her eyes narrow, then open again. "Did you hear?"

Of course, Margo has heard. Everyone on the island knows by now. It just shows how out of the loop Sabrina is.

But wait! What is Sabrina talking about? Her circles are definitely way more exclusive than Margo's. It could be a scandal she knows nothing about. Didn't she date someone from The Shallows?

"What do you mean…"

"The boats! I never thought someone would target the yacht club. OUR club!!!" Sabrina says in top vocal fry mode.

Even though she knows she shouldn't, Margo can't help it. Her voice *is* a tad higher than normal when she responds.

"I KNOW. I can't believe IT." Ugh. She winces at herself. She sounds like she's squealing.

"Nothing like this has ever happened here! To us!" Sabrina's voice rises even higher.

Right. As if being a WASP should keep you from ever experiencing hardship. Margo swallows the retort and comes up with the vaguest response she can muster.

"Totally. Yeah, it really sucks. Hope they figure out who's behind it." There. She did it. Her voice is at a normal level again.

"Well, of course they're going to find out." With her hands perched on her hips, Sabrina exudes elegance even while she radiates aggravation at the current situation. "I mean, could you ever? They think it's someone from out of town." Sabrina shudders. "My boyfriend told me they're scouting the area to see if anyone caught it on camera."

Margo can't help herself. "Who's your boyfriend?" She asks.

"Well, he's not technically my boyfriend. We're on a break," Sabrina responds. "He's from Cape May."

"Oh, I love that town," says Margo. She's still trying to be friendly. For some reason, she suddenly feels bad for Sabrina. She tries *so hard*.

"Yeah, he's not from around here. It's like these guys. No one in this zip code is going to sink a bunch of boats at the yacht club," Sabrina says. "They'd be blacklisted forever. Unless it was the Avalon Yachties as a prank?"

While Sabrina rattles on, exasperated, Margo gives her a silent study. Sabrina's hair extensions have been freshly blown out. Her makeup is impeccable. She'd bet her beach cruiser that Sabrina has lip fillers.

Still, she does look fabulous. Maybe it's time for Margo to pay a little more attention to her own grooming. Or at least, stop air-drying and actually take the time to do her hair. Get a mani to help with all the small nicks and calluses from carving basswood.

"Are you coming to our Memorial Day Party?" Sabrina asks.

Margo considers it. There isn't a good reason that she doesn't like Sabrina Elliot. She actually does feel bad for her, losing her mom. She remembers going to the viewing as a little girl and seeing Sabrina crying there, all alone next to the casket. It was terrible. When Margo tried to hug her, Sabrina pulled away.

Right after, she was sent away to boarding school, and no one heard from her. When she came back, she was different. Never fit in with the rest of the locals.

Margo feels like a jerk. She should have more sympathy for her. "Sure, why not?" The Seven Mile Hotel's event at the Stone Harbor

Yacht Club is one of the biggest parties on the island, held to celebrate the opening of the summer season. They have a really good spread. And it's right next to her house.

Nodding and smiling at appropriate intervals, she loses a few more minutes before she can catch a break in the conversation. She finally ends their conversation with a quick air kiss, telling Sabrina she has to get back to The Plank. Which she honestly does. She's been gone too long.

Margo hurries back to 96th Street, dodging more people on the sidewalk as she races back to the club.

Chelsea is perched on the front desk, actively gossiping with Tish and Tony. Cardboard boxes of new workout gear and branded hats that must have just been delivered are piled up around her. The boxes are just sitting there, right in the path of guests. Apparently, no one has thought to put them away or even just move them out of the way.

"C'mon, guys! Find something to do!" Margo yells as they see her and scramble away to gossip somewhere else.

Margo sighs. They're never going to be ready in time for the season.

Chapter 13

May 10

Tish isn't sure if she's reading Tony's signals the right way. It's so hard to tell, and it's been so long since she's been interested in anyone. It's starting to drive her completely *crazy*.

He's a flirt by nature, but she thinks he's interested in more than playful banter with her. He actually takes the time to ask about things going on in her life and check in on how she's doing. He even stopped by to help out when she moved into her new place.

She thinks he's super cute. He's always dropping in at the spa for a mint or to tell her about one of his clients. And he seems genuinely interested in hearing about her past life as a nanny and what it was like living in Hoboken.

They've known each other for a few weeks by now. If she doesn't say something soon, they'll solidify into friends, and she'll miss their chance for something more.

She's too nervous to flat-out ask him on a date. Tish needs to know if he's as interested in her as she is in him. It's also a tricky situation since they work together. If something goes wrong, it would be a disaster to still have to see him each day.

Tish *craves* someone to confide in. The uncertainty is killing her. But who? She just moved here. She doesn't have a close enough relationship with anyone yet where she can confess her secret crush.

Margo seems like she'd be a good listener, but she's the boss. It would be an awkward position to put her in. Chelsea is too young. And blunt. She'd give Tish's secret away without even realizing it.

Her friends back home don't know what he's like, so they can't offer any valid advice. They would also dismiss him as a seasonal fling since he doesn't live here year-round. They've all seen how frequently long-distance relationships bust up.

Everyone else she knows at The Plank is a client. It wouldn't be professional to confess her feelings to them.

So here she is, stuck without a shoulder to lean on.

Tish sighs. Why is she always so unsure of herself? She wishes she could be as confident as some of her coworkers. Margo and Chelsea are so effortlessly *poised* and *secure*. They never seem to doubt themselves.

She's always been a little self-conscious, not sure of her place in the grand scheme of things. If she were asked, she'd say there was nothing remarkable about her. Tish doesn't have anything to set her apart from the next person. No special talents or hobbies. Quitting her job and moving to Stone Harbor was the bravest and most remarkable thing she's ever done.

She really needs to confide in someone. What about Hank? He seems like the most level-headed person out of everyone she's encountered so far in Stone Harbor. He has a stable relationship that has been going on for years.

After thinking it over for a few days, Tish decides to confide in him about her crush.

"Hey, Hank. Can I ask you a question? What do you think of Tony?"

"No. Absolutely not," he replies.

The denial isn't that harsh. It's delivered with good humor and a touch of empathy. He crosses his absurdly ripped arms as he does it, his warm smile and golden skin making him too adorable to get mad at, even if she wants to. It's like he can't be a part of her love life drama but feels bad denying her the satisfaction of spilling her guts.

"But why?" Tish exhales in frustration. Everyone she knows *craves* gossip. Wasn't it why *The Real Housewives* were all so famous in the first place?

Maybe it's her. She certainly isn't glamorous. She's been called cute, but there's something about her that shows through when she starts dating someone. It's almost as if she broadcasts the fact that she's willing to settle for someone. Anyone. Even if he isn't that special.

It's so disheartening. There aren't that many people to date in this town in the first place, much less at a spa, and she's facing the same obstacles that she experienced in Hoboken. Maybe even worse.

"Hank, I NEED you," she practically wails. She fully realizes this is pathetic.

"Listen, I may be gay, but I don't want any part of this drama," he says. "It's never a good idea to hook up with someone at the gym. Especially someone you work with."

"I just need a little guidance," she begs. Tish feels desperate.

Hank stares at her sympathetically with his deep brown eyes. "You know I'd love to hear all about it. But trust me, it's better not to get involved."

And with that, her favorite coworker pats her shoulder with sympathy. If he weren't so damn nice, she would be mortified.

Ugh. There is no one else to talk to. It's too late anyway. Her 11 o'clock is 15 minutes early.

Kirby is a mom of two and extremely angry with her husband, Jacob. Apparently, he's never around and leaves her to take care of everything. The renewal package is her latest attempt to get back to her old self.

Tish knows her client's skin will look fantastic once she is done cleansing and extracting, but she doesn't think Kirby will be any happier.

The poor woman constantly looks angry and exhausted. She works for a private venture firm based in Connecticut. It's remote work, so she decided to stay in Stone Harbor at her family's summer home to have more space and support away from the city. All she talks about is the fact that her husband is no help. She absolutely despises Jacob. Tish has been working there for less than a month and knows all about it.

"Kirby!" Tish greets her client with a hug and a fresh glass of mint water. She wishes she had something stronger to offer.

"Hey," Kirby says as she gratefully takes the cup from Tish and follows her into the treatment room.

Tish tucks her personal thoughts away and begins prepping Kirby's skin. She makes small talk, asking about Kirby's kids and listening to her vent about the amount of work she's juggling.

"I'm so over him, Tish," Kirby tells her. "I feel like it's over. Therapy hasn't helped. He won't change. All we do is fight."

Tish is a romantic at heart. "But you loved him once. Maybe you're just going through a phase? You're both juggling a lot."

Kirby snorts. "I juggle and he sits back. He's never around. All he does is play golf with his friends. He told me he's going to leave and not come back."

"Who's watching the kids now?" Tish asks. They're both too young to be left alone.

"He is today," Kirby says begrudgingly. "But that's because he's been away all week." She'd told Tish that both their families spend the summer season there. They have for generations. That's how they met and fell in love.

"Well, that's something at least," Tish says encouragingly as she rubs the knots in Kirby's neck.

"Enough about Jacob," Kirby declares. "I'm done with him and his drama. Did you hear about the boats at the yacht club?"

Tish nods. "Everyone has by now."

"Oh, really? So, you know that they found out what happened?"

No, this was new. "They figured it out? The boats were definitely shot with bullets?"

"No." Kirby laughs, disbelieving. "They were drilled. Someone took the time to carve out holes in the base of each of the boats."

"It must have taken hours. Unless there were a bunch of people doing it."

"Some guys found the tools they used to damage the boats while they were fishing. Reeled them up in a duffel bag," Kirby tells her. "They're interviewing all the employees and anyone who's been there the past couple of weeks. They think it was done little by little, and then one night they were all tossed in."

Now this is major gossip. Tish can't wait to tell her co-workers at The Plank. Who would want to ruin so many Sunfish? She'd heard they caused tens of thousands of dollars in damage. People were irate.

"Do they have any suspects?" Tish asks.

"Not that I know of. The only reason I heard this was because of my mother-in-law. Soon to be *former* in-law. The council members were talking about it."

That was right, Tish remembers, Kirby's mother-in-law is on the town council. Tina Martinez. Kirby has complained about her before. According to Kirby, Tina is a big deal but a pain in the ass, too. But then again, Kirby isn't a fan of anyone in the Martinez family right now.

Kirby flinches as Tish begins to apply the peel. "Wow, that burns," she says.

"Just for a second, and then it should go away. Hold still just a second longer."

"Okay, ummm…. So, what was I saying?"

"Drill holes. In the bottom of the boats."

"Right. They're actually doing fingerprints on the tools now because it's considered criminal mischief in New Jersey. They used electric drills and saws to sink the sailboats." She waves her hand. "Okay, it's feeling better."

Tish doesn't want to sound callous, but she really needs to hear more. The peel can wait. "Do you think they could face jail time?"

"Oh, I have no idea. But yeah, I guess so. If they find out who tossed the tools."

"You're going to want to have this sit for ten minutes to activate. I'll be right back."

Tish quickly backs out as casually as possible. She can't wait to tell Tony and Margo. She isn't telling Hank *anything*. He can hear it from someone else.

Chapter 14

May 12

Mac is knee-deep in paperwork. He's been trying to get a subcontractor to step in to help the crew finish up the restaurant as close as possible to their Memorial Day deadline. It's going to cost him, he knows. Probably double the pay to get the guys working overtime and weekends.

In the end, he probably won't even make much of a profit on the project. But this is a personal connection, and he has a professional reputation to maintain. If he wants to secure any jobs on 7 Mile Island in the next decade, he knows he can't risk negative reviews.

He shifts forward to prop his elbows on the desk and rubs his eyes in frustration. He's exhausted from working 14-hour days. So is his crew. They can't keep up with this pace. No matter how he slices it, he needs to find a solution fast.

Mac knows he needs to do it. But he's dreading the call.

He HATES groveling. And this is going to be a deep knee grovel.

There is no one more connected on the island than Sabrina's father, Roger Elliot. He owns one of the nicest hotels, half a dozen businesses, and a few of the most successful restaurants in town. He also enjoys close relationships with several of the area's biggest building and construction firms.

Mac needs Roger's help, but he isn't happy about asking for it. Not to mention, he knows Sabrina's father isn't too happy with him either. If Sabrina isn't happy, Roger isn't happy.

That's a lot of unhappy people.

Mac decides to let go of the past messed-up things Sabrina has done. Be a bigger person and all. It isn't her fault she's so spoiled. And the Elliot family is one of his best chances for getting the restaurant to open on time.

Mac calls the business office line, and Roger's assistant, Linda, picks right up. It's almost as if she'd been expecting his call.

She's not particularly friendly. "Mac? He's going to have to call you back," she says and hangs up.

Mac doubts that Roger is that busy. Linda is incredibly sharp. She knows everything going on in the area, as well as how to handle any thorny issues. She's going to give her employer advance notice about someone he might not want to talk to.

"Thanks, Linda," Mac says to the empty line. He rests his elbows on his desk again and runs his hands through his hair. Who else can he call for a favor?

There is a huge amount of contract work to be found at the Jersey shore - if you are decent at your trade. New homes are constantly being built, old ones torn down, or even raised on higher platforms to protect against future storms or rising floodwaters. Contractors needed all the help they could get.

This is custom, detailed work. Mac needs the best.

He shoots Quinn a text. A lot of the firefighters have side gigs when they aren't working their shifts, and Quinn has tons of contacts on the island. He might know some people who are available to work.

There is no way Mac is going to get out of this hole without some help. He's scrolling through his contacts, trying to come up with names, when his phone rings. It's Roger Elliot.

"Mac!" Roger bellows. "What can I do for you?" He sounds friendly. That's a good sign.

Mac knows that Roger is well aware that he dated Sabrina. He even had dinner at the Elliot's beachfront home.

What he doesn't know is whether Roger has been privy to what went down between Mac and Sabrina. That he broke up with Roger's darling daughter and made her upset. It would make a huge difference when he asks Roger for a favor.

Might as well get it out. Fortune favors the bold. "Thanks for the call back. I'm pretty sure you're aware I'm adding on to the house on 53rd Street. I'm also rehabbing a new restaurant space in town."

"I heard about that. Congratulations." Nothing in Roger's voice suggests he's holding a grudge.

Mac relaxes and plows along. "The thing is, I'm spread thin. We're low on guys and tight on schedule. I need both projects done by Memorial Day."

There's no response, so he keeps talking. "I was wondering if you knew of anyone with a good set of hands that could help out."

Again, no response. Mac's heart starts beating faster. He suddenly feels very uncomfortable.

Finally, a sigh. "Mac, you know I think the world of you and your family." Roger had actually dated Mac's mother in their college days, something Mac doesn't like to think about. Ever.

Mac waits for him to respond, not wanting to interrupt.

"I'm aware that you and my daughter had a relationship, and it hasn't gone in the direction where she'd have liked it to."

The understatement of the year.

"I just don't think I'd feel comfortable lending you some of my men. I heard there's been some quality concerns about the work being done."

The deep gravel of his voice doesn't sound very sorry.

"What do you mean? Those complaints were bullshit, and you know it."

Roger clears his throat. "That's not what I was told."

Christ. Sabrina is still spreading rumors all over the island. He starts to feel real flickers of panic mixed with anger.

"Listen, Roger, I take offense to that statement. Our firm takes pride in the work we do. We're known for it." His voice sharpens.

Everyone always thinks Mac is laid back and easygoing. Which is true, he is. Until someone goes too far. And then he's lethal.

The gossip and the canceled supply orders. Big enough problems for someone with a razor-thin margin. But then, when it didn't succeed in damaging the status of his projects, "someone" made a call to Robin, the building inspector.

He's tired of being taken advantage of because he isn't connected in high circles. He wasn't handed his firm. He built it from the ground up, working his ass off in construction every day since the beginning of high school.

Mac learned every technique for laying drywall. Every method for filling mortar gaps or replacing vintage trim before he went to school to study architecture and historic preservation. He can look at every single house on the East Coast and tell you when it was built, down to the decade.

Maybe he's not a huge developer, but that doesn't mean he doesn't take pride in his work. He's done being pushed around.

"Roger, I'm going to say this one time and you won't hear me say it again, but I will stand by it for the next few decades," he says. "I have a reputation that I have lived and worked for. And it's being trashed by your spoiled rotten, pain in the ass daughter. One more time. ONE more time and I'm telling everyone what really happened. I won't say it again."

There's silence on the other end.

Mac knows he's caught Roger by surprise. He doesn't give a shit. Sabrina's a spoiled kid who has been given everything she wanted. And now that she hasn't gotten her TOY, she's deliberately destroying his business and everything he's put into it.

Still no answer. The extended pause on the line doesn't make Mac cave. He knows it's a tactic all the asshole bigwigs use.

After a long silence, Roger finally responds. "I'm sorry you feel that way. I can assure you that Sabrina had nothing to do with it. I am concerned by you bringing her into this."

"She brought herself into it. It's just the first time she's been called out for it."

"Careful what you say about my daughter."

"Same goes. And hey? Sorry about your boat." Mac ends the call. He'll probably regret it later, but hanging up on Roger Elliot feels so damn good that he doesn't care. Forget the Elliots. There has to be another solution.

His cell pings with an incoming text.

I've got a couple guys who would be interested, Quinn says. *Me too. But I get double.*

Mac rubs his chest in relief. His heartburn is going away.

Thank God for Quinn coming through, because Mac's going to need every connection possible going forward. He's already burned one bridge today.

It was worth it. The Elliot family has caused him enough problems. He isn't stepping back anymore.

The next time he hears anything about Sabrina trying to sabotage his business, he's going right to the source. The girl needs to grow up. And he's just the person to help her out with that.

Chapter 15

May 14

Quinn finishes a double shift at the fire station. Nothing happened, like usual. Just a lot of meal prep, equipment checks, and weight lifting. He's one of nine full-time firefighters who handle emergencies. But with less than a thousand people currently on the island, there aren't that many for them to handle.

He gets into his truck and starts driving back to his parents' house in lower Avalon. Yes, he still lives with his parents. Do you really think he could afford a mortgage in this town?

He cruises past the main shopping drag on Dune Drive. At this time of night, Quinn has the street to himself. He's driving past The Preppy Palm, whistling along to some Olivia Rodrigo, when he notices a few lights on in one of the stores. Every other store is completely dark.

Quinn brakes suddenly, his truck coming to a shuddering stop. He catches a glimpse of shattered glass. A broken storefront door.

What the hell?

The Gables, a boutique art gallery and gift store, has either been broken into or pretty badly vandalized. The entire front glass entrance is gone. A gaping hole out to the sidewalk.

No alarms are going off. Either someone forgot to set them, or the store doesn't have any installed. Probably the latter.

He grabs his phone and jumps out the door, making his way to the bright striped awnings that normally welcome shoppers. Shards of glass crunch under his boots.

He doesn't see anyone around. They could already have fled, taking off on foot or by car. He was too late.

He puts in a call to the emergency line. "It's Quinn Kearney. I've got a break-in at 24th and Dune. The Gables."

"I'll send a car out right away," the dispatcher promises. He wonders if he should wait for backup or go in.

A few moments go by as he stands under the awning, shuffling his feet on the broken glass.

Oh well. He's never been patient. Pushing out a breath, he ducks under the metal bar of the door and steps into the new opening created by the perp. All the lights are on, giving him a clear view of the space.

There's no one there. They must be long gone.

Whoever was there left behind a huge mess. Shelves have been cleared of their inventory. Displays are toppled over, with broken items all over the floor. The checkout area is in shambles. Frankly, it's a shitshow.

From the display signs, he can tell what's now missing. Framed prints and artwork by some of their local artists. Jewelry and trinkets, pricey skin care products.

Pieces of driftwood, bowls, and serving trays are broken and strewn across the tile. Quinn doesn't recognize most of the artists' names, but one sticks out. Margo St. James.

Interesting. He'd just been talking about her to Mac.

He checks the register. The drawer is still shut, so he doesn't think anyone messed with it. Even stranger.

He walks all the way to the back storage area. It doesn't look like anyone spent much time there. Maybe they got spooked and fled.

There's a door that serves as the fire exit to the back parking lot. It's closed, but there's a cold pocket of air left behind. They probably got out that way. Less chance of anyone spotting them.

Quinn shoves the push bar of the fire exit door and strides out to the lot. Maybe he'll get lucky and find something they dropped on their way out.

It's the last thing he remembers before he's knocked out cold.

* * *

When Quinn comes to, he's surrounded by the Police Chief Ed Walsh and Sergeant Betty Niell. They're crouched around him, pressing an ice pack to his head.

"What the hell?" Ed booms out. The chief is so *loud*. It's killing his skull. "I can't believe you went in alone. You know you're not supposed to do that."

Quinn winces. At least Betty feels some sympathy for him. "How are you feeling?" she asks in the softest tone he's ever heard her use. "There's an ambulance on the way."

They're in the Gables storage room. Quinn's lying flat on the ground. He tries to sit up, but the chief pushes him back down.

"Just wait," Ed says. "Don't get up. The ambulance will be here in a minute."

Betty holds up her fingers in standard concussion protocol. Quinn doesn't have time for this. He pushes her away.

"I'm fine. I just got knocked out. Did you see what happened?" Quinn asks.

"We got here just a couple of minutes after you called it in to dispatch," Betty says. "We must have just missed them."

"They probably struck you with whatever they were using to trash the store," Ed offers. "I'm thinking it was a baseball bat."

Now that's a fun thought. "They didn't get anything from the register, but they did a fair amount of damage. Especially to my head."

"Not much damage they could have done there," the chief says. He doesn't sound concerned. "Did you see anyone in the area when you were driving past? Before you saw the broken glass?"

"No," Quinn answers slowly. "I was just driving home from a shift when I came across it. Most of the stores are dark, so I noticed the lights on right away."

The sounds of ambulance sirens pick up in volume as it approaches. Great. He's sure his fellow EMTs are going to have a field day with this. They pause to wait for two of them to make their way back to the storage area.

Despite his objections, they tell Quinn he has to go to Cape Regional Hospital for an evaluation.

"It's standard protocol," one of the EMTs tells him. They get the stretcher and start loading him on it. One of them is busy taking his blood pressure.

This is so embarrassing. He doesn't want to go to the hospital. He needs to help figure out who did this. To him and the store.

Now that medical help is here, the police lose interest in Quinn and begin checking out the damage to the store. Sergeant Betty is taking photos of the evidence and making notes on a pad. Chief Ed is near the register area.

"We'll need to place a call to the owners once we find out who they are. We can have them take stock of what's missing or damaged," she tells the chief. "They're not going to be happy."

"Who would be? They probably just got ready for the summer, and now they have to replace their door and order more stock," Ed says. "Tough spot to be in right now."

"Yeah, they're screwed," Sergeant Betty responds. The comment makes Quinn think of Tyson. He'd said the same thing to him just one month ago.

"Chief, this must have something to do with the boats," he says. It feels like someone is trying to deliberately ruin the upcoming season. But why would anyone want to? It was the best time of the year. No one hated the beach. Unless they were freaking psychos.

Ed doesn't respond for a bit. He just looks around. "Don't worry about it. You just focus on getting better. Do you want me to call your parents?"

"I'll do it," he says with a sigh. He's now strapped to the stretcher. They're taking him to the hospital whether he likes it or not.

"Really, I'm fine." He says. They don't answer as they load him into the back of the ambulance. "Can you please not use the sirens?"

They agree not to. As Quinn rides along to the medical center, he can't stop thinking about why the store was vandalized.

It was such an angry act. Whoever it was could have chosen to come in and steal some money, take some items. But to break all that art? Something that couldn't be easily replaced. It felt like rage. Exactly what they did to the boats.

Who was seriously pissed at Sunnies and woodwork? And why now?

It's not an answer they're likely to get tonight. He knows officers are going to come in and tag the evidence, take prints of the front door, and canvas the neighborhood. See if anyone could have heard or seen something.

Quinn bets the owners are not going to be so happy when they wake up and learn their business is in tatters.

He feels terrible for them. Five minutes earlier, and he could have caught the suspects in the act.

And to think he had just been moaning that nothing ever happened around here.

Chapter 16

May 16

Tyson might not be the best person to give advice, but he's all Margo has right now. It's the only reason why she's pestering him while he works the dock at the yacht club.

"I can't stop thinking about what happened to Quinn," she says with a sigh. "Who attacked him? And why? And how could they do that to the store?"

Tyson nods. "I feel bad for Martha. She's owned the store for years."

"Sweetest lady ever. Never did anything to anyone." Margo tucks her legs underneath and sits on them. "I promised to help in any way I could. I just don't have much inventory left, right now." She's been spending all her time on a large commission for the Seven Mile Hotel.

"Means you're selling a lot." Tyson knows what to say to make her feel better.

Still, they have two weeks until the start of summer, and things already seem way off. Everything feels different. For the first time, she's making sure she locks up and turns her outdoor lights on before heading to bed. Checking to make sure everything is how it should be before leaving for the day.

She and Tyson went to see Quinn at his house. His parents were so upset that Tyson teased him, he was going to be grounded for the rest of the summer. Luckily, after one more day of rest, he'll be cleared to go back to work.

Those are the big things, the deliberate harm affecting those she loves. But then there are all the other little things, the ones that take up day-to-day life. An order of white spa towels gets delivered to the wrong business in another state. A stair climber keeps burning out. Someone left a nasty Google review about their Monday morning HIIT class. They're small, but they're unexpected and take up a lot of her time and effort.

The Plank's owner, Sandy Cohen, had stopped by the day before to address some of the issues. *I'm not too thrilled with the way things are going,* she'd told Margo. If Margo doesn't get Sandy's support, there's no way in hell she's going to become a part-owner in their next venture.

Sandy had promised that Margo could be an investor in their second location. The problem is that she needs $30k to do it. It's why she's been working so hard, carving extra pieces and taking commissions. Any little bit helps. And now some of that inventory is gone. Smashed to pieces on the floor of The Gables.

Maybe she can still make it. She's banking on the bonuses Sandy hands out in September if they have a profitable season. She *needs* that extra five grand.

She thanks her lucky stars every day for Banksy. He can fix anything. And she has Tish, who keeps booking new clients via word-of-mouth recommendations. Her class instructors Jax and Adrienne have been killing it with their beach workouts and yoga classes, too. But it's still a lot to juggle.

She doesn't know how Tyson manages all of it. He's been busy polishing up the boats that were saved, dealing with angry yacht club members, and doing his regular job of getting everything ready for the season. Managing the sailing schedule and prepping for sailing camp.

Al Conwell did NOT take the tearing of his boat cover well. But what did you expect from a Swell? They didn't like anything disrupting their lifestyle.

The cost of a new cover is coming out of Tyson's paycheck, although he never said anything to Banksy about what happened. Actually, he didn't tell anyone about it.

Of course, Margo had heard it from Chelsea.

She knows Tyson is swamped and likely irritated with all the members and their nonsense, but he doesn't mention it. He just keeps working. Never complaining. That's always been his style. Things never seem to bother Tyson like they do other people.

Margo's brother Eddie is the same way. Everyone else might panic, but he stays the same unflappable person. Sometimes it helps, and sometimes she finds the lack of reaction to be extremely annoying.

She needs a friendly shoulder to lean on. Tyson is open to listening to her issues, but he doesn't really *react*. Give her the kind of response she needs. The *drama*. But he's the best she can do at the moment, so she's working with what she has.

"I feel like I have to teach every single person how to do something that they should have been able to figure out themselves," she says with a sigh. "I don't have any time to make new pieces."

Tyson nods with sympathy. He's organizing the roping. She takes that as a sign to keep complaining.

"Tony is likely sleeping with, if not one, then two or three people at the Plank. And Chelsea can't keep her mouth shut. She might be the biggest gossip I've ever met. Even more than Stacy was, back in the day." An old classmate of theirs in high school. Stacy couldn't keep a secret if her life depended on it.

He grunts. "Yeah, she was always in everyone's business."

Margo pulls her legs up and wraps her arms around them. Tyson responds to the least important thing she mentioned.

"That's not a real answer. You're not paying attention."

Tyson looks up. She can tell by his face that he's struggling to recall what she said. "Sorry. You know this isn't my thing."

"Ugh, I need someone to talk to. You're the worst girlfriend ever."

He shrugs his big shoulders amiably. "I do what I can. Why don't you talk to one of your actual girlfriends? Here or the ones from college?"

Margo had attended Northwestern University in Chicago. She'd done the whole sorority thing, the keggers and the parties hosted by sports teams. She still talked to her college friends, but in all honesty, didn't see them often. They were scattered all over the country: Dallas, Cleveland, and Charlotte. It made it hard to get together. It wasn't like they could drop by each other's places after work. Sometimes she doesn't feel like calling them because it takes so long for everyone to catch up on their lives.

"They don't get it. They're all in these corporate ladder careers in the city, and I'm back home in a shore town. They think I have a summer job."

Tyson nods in understanding. He had also gone a decent distance away for school, to the University of North Carolina. She knows he feels the same way about desk jobs. He's always been driven, but he isn't interested in working in an office either.

"They don't see how important it is to me," Margo continues. "Getting equity in a company. Becoming an owner."

"I know," Tyson answers. "Just because I'm not working on Wall Street doesn't mean I'm washed up."

Their friends are all going the big company route or going back to grad school. Grinding, demanding jobs that require ten-hour workdays. When you never see the light because you're stuck in front of your computer all day.

Not for Margo. Never for her. She needs to make her own schedule. One that accommodates time for her art as well. She loves the freedom of running The Plank.

Margo sighs, uncrossing her legs. She knows she's whining. Tyson doesn't have a problem with anyone.

Time to move on to a new topic. "What do you think about the break-in? Any idea who would have done it?"

"I know a lot of people who probably wanted to hit Quinn at some point, but no one has ever had a problem with Martha."

"I still can't believe how much they trashed the store."

Tyson bends down to hook a line. "I just don't know what they were hoping to do. A lot of the pieces are original. It would be hard to resell them. Doesn't seem worth it."

"Yeah, I know. Maybe someone has a grudge or a bone to pick."

"With a gift store? It seems strange."

"I know. But first the boats and then the Gables. It's weird," she says with a shrug. "And it seems personal. Poor Quinn."

"Yeah," Tyson agrees. He doesn't need to say any more. She knows what he means.

He checks his progress. Most of the rigging is inspected, accounted for, and sorted. They're going to need all of it when the boats come out of dry storage and are put into the water.

By now, the sun is going down. Tyson pulls a quarter zip up over his head. "Want to grab some dinner?"

"Why not?" They leave the club and go to Margo's place so she can change out of her work clothes. Tyson makes himself at home while she gets dressed, and then they head to the Stone Harbor Pizza Pub. It's an easy spot to grab a bite.

The fully stocked bar is L-shaped and opens to a dining area with whitewashed brick walls. A green turf patio area with oversized umbrellas and clear glass railings offers one of the best views of the bay.

The pizza pub feeds into The Reeds next door. Both businesses benefit from the flow of customers staying and eating at their establishments. It also helps boost the number of guests who come to town off-season and are looking for somewhere to eat

On the other side of the hotel is Buckets, a casual restaurant with colorful seating overlooking the water. It's the perfect spot to grab a margarita while the sun goes down. They usually open in the middle of April and have a steady business until late fall.

The Reeds has one of the best spots on the corner of 96th Street. Its grand front entrance flanks the corner, while the back entrance is known for spectacular sunset views. There's also an upscale outdoor restaurant with huge canopies and chic seating arrangements.

It's very much a scene as soon as summer hits, and there are hour-long wait times. But right now, in the off-season, they should be able to grab a table without a problem.

They spot Chelsea sitting at the bar as soon as they walk in. She looks thrilled to see them.

"Margo!" She squeals and runs over to give a hug. Since they just saw each other while closing the gym, Margo simply smiles and gives her a squeeze in return. Only Chelsea.

The downside of a small town is that you run into everyone you know, all the time. She sees enough of Chelsea at The Plank. She doesn't need to share a drink with her after hours. But she's the manager, so she has to at least try to act friendly and professional.

"Hey, Chelsea," Margo greets her. "Grabbing something to eat?"

Chelsea rolls her eyes. "Yeah, long time no see. I just couldn't wait to catch up with my friends from the Watering Hull." Her vocal fry is tough for Margo to listen to.

Chelsea is friendly to everyone, but she's so energetic that it makes Margo feel ancient. Chelsea has only one speed: rapid.

"Tyson! How are things at the yacht club? Are the boats fixed?" She's probably hoping for a new update.

"All good," he says with a smile. "Everything's back up and ready to go."

That's all Chelsea is getting out of him. Tyson has never been a fountain of information. He isn't about to start now.

She turns to Margo. "I'm so glad I ran into you. I was wondering if you found those keys."

"What keys?"

"The keys to the Plank, of course. The missing ones."

Margo looks at her blankly.

"Oh, I didn't tell you?"

"No," Margo responds slowly. "Are you telling me you lost them?"

Chelsea doesn't seem to be too concerned, but she isn't making eye contact. Margo isn't sure if Chelsea feels guilty or if her tiny attention span is already forcing her to move on to the next thing.

"Yeah, a while ago," Chelsea answers. She's twirling the ends of her blunt-cut bob while gazing at the front door to see who else is going to walk in.

"Why didn't you tell me?" She grabs her arm to make her look at her. "Chelsea, this is serious. Anyone could use the keys to get in." She knows she's getting angrier by the minute.

"I thought you knew." Chelsea's voice is plaintive.

"How would I know? You didn't *tell* me."

Chelsea snaps her gum, her eyebrows raised. "It wasn't a big deal. What would anyone take? A bike? There's not much they could move out of there. It's heavy."

"It doesn't matter. They could damage the machines. Steal the spa equipment. Make off with our products." Margo is too stunned to even yell. "I can't believe you didn't say anything, especially with what's going on in town right now."

Chelsea starts to look worried. "I'm sorry. I meant to tell you, but you've been so busy you haven't had a chance to talk."

"Come to me with something like this *immediately*. I've got to get someone to change the locks."

Tyson starts scrolling through the saved numbers on his phone. "I know somebody."

They leave the pub without saying another word to Chelsea. Margo's hands are clammy. They move quickly. The gym has been a sitting duck all this time. What if something has already been stolen?

Tyson calls Banksy. He doesn't pick up, so Tyson leaves a message

Next, he tries the only locksmith they know in the area and goes straight to voicemail. No one is around.

Margo is now angry enough to wish she had fired Chelsea on the spot. "What an idiot," she mutters as they walk toward the main entrance.

The club shuts down at six every night. There isn't much of a call for late workouts or spa appointments. Everyone gets their sweat on in the morning or by the afternoon.

She's lucky they ran into Chelsea. There was no way of knowing when Chelsea would have notified her about the missing keys. It sounds like they've been gone for *days*.

If someone had broken into the club with a missing set of keys, Margo would be out of her job and out of the five years she'd invested in becoming part-owner. Especially after her last disappointing visit with Sandy. She doesn't need the headaches that the yacht club or council members are dealing with right now.

Margo knows she locked the front entrance when she was closing up. She grabs the handle of the door. Thankfully, it's still locked. No one has tried to get in.

Yet.

She uses her keys to unlock the door, and Tyson walks in with her. She turns on the lights and checks out each area. Everything looks normal. The treadmills are off, the bikes are standing, and the weights look racked and wiped down.

The two facial and massage rooms are fine too. She checks the spa. All good there.

She's inspecting the windows in the back when she hears voices and heads back to the reception area. There's someone else standing there, talking to Tyson.

It's Mac. Mr. Not-so-helpful contractor. "What are you doing here?" Margo asks in a not-so-friendly tone.

"I got a call. I can help. I know how to change out locks."

"I got his number from Quinn," Tyson tells Margo. "If Quinn says he's good, then he's good."

Whatever. She'll take what she can get. It's already 9 p.m. Most contractors or locksmiths are off the clock by now. And she's sure she won't be able to sleep tonight knowing someone could simply walk in at will using their own set of keys.

They need to get a better security system. She's brought it up to Sandy before, but she was never interested in fixing the broken one they still have. It will be one of her priorities tomorrow. Sandy needs to stop worrying about the bottom line so much.

Margo sighs. "Thank you."

Tyson starts explaining the situation to Mac, so Margo walks back to her office for one more look. Something is nagging at her. She can't figure out what it is, but it feels like something is off.

She shut her computer down and organized her desk before she left. She always does this. They have member information and credit card numbers on file, and she can't risk them being exposed. It could get The Plank in a lawsuit if she didn't protect their information.

Something isn't right. She gets a tug of a memory of what the desk looked like before she clocked out.

Her MacBook isn't in the same place she left it. It's on top of a set of folders, not in the center of her desk. And one of the wooden bowls she carved that she uses to store paper clips and rubber bands is on her bookcase, not the drawer she always keeps it in.

Margo walks over to her pile of job applications. Her calendar book? Has it been moved, too?

"Hey, Margo?" Tyson interrupts. He's standing in the doorway.

Damn. She lost her train of thought. There HAD been something else, something she was just about to discover wasn't right. But now, she's unsure what it was.

"Yeah?"

"We finished changing the locks. Mac's going to make new sets of keys for everyone, but you might want to come in early tomorrow to hand them out before anyone gets here."

"Okay, thanks." She says it absently. She's still trying to get a grip on what happened. Someone was in her stuff. It makes her uneasy. What were they looking for?

Tyson touches her arm, something he's done a million times. He looks worried.

"What is it?" she says, arching a brow. She's not used to seeing this kind of expression on him. He's not easily bothered by anything. Ever.

He pulls his arm back and puts it in the back pocket of his jeans. "It's nothing." Margo isn't going to say anything until she does some more digging herself. She doesn't need her boss to know that someone was in her office. It might be cowardly, but she isn't ready to tell Sandy. And everything else looks fine. Nothing was damaged or stolen. She's going to write it off as a mistake and check around tomorrow.

Mac walks into her office. He looks back and forth between them, as if he'd caught them in the act. "Am I interrupting?" he asks.

"What? No, not at all. Let me pay you for your time." She grabs her purse off the desk.

"I owe you. I've ruined your season," Mac says with a grin. "This lets me make up for it."

No. She can't let him do that. "Why don't I take you to dinner? I have to find some way to repay you."

Mac shakes his head. "I'm good. But thanks."

Well, she has her answer. That was pretty clear. He's not interested in going out with her. She heads over to the reception area to give herself some space.

Mac stays for a few more minutes, talking to Tyson and being his usual charming self, then leaves. She wonders where he's off to in such a hurry. Not that it matters why he's leaving. Either way, he made it clear that he doesn't want to go out with her.

It's probably for the best. She doesn't need to start anything two weeks before the season begins. She has enough on her plate, doesn't she?

"You ready?" Margo asks Ty, her best friend. The one who's been with her since the first day of kindergarten. Her safe place.

He gives one last look around. "Yeah. We're all set."

By unspoken agreement, neither one of them is in the mood to go back to the Stone Harbor Pizza Pub. Margo offers to grill something up at home, which Tyson quickly agrees to.

They head back to her house. Margo can see from the street that there's a light on in her little kitchen. She knows she turned it off before she left. Is someone there? She thinks of the damaged boats and break-in. Her office, which had definitely been rummaged through. What the hell is happening?

She gives Tyson a look. He knows her too well. He just nods and puts his hand to his lips to be quiet, and they sneak around the back.

The family room of her small cottage has a sliding glass door that opens onto the back deck. It can be squeaky, but it gives a good view of the interior when the blinds are open. They gently walk across the boards, careful not to make any loud sounds. Margo leans forward to peek inside.

Her brother is standing in front of the oven cooking something in a pan.

"Eddie," Margo and Tyson say at the same time. He's back.

Margo decides not to worry about someone being in her office. It was probably the cleaning crew.

She opens the sliding glass door and steps inside. It looks like summer is officially here.

Chapter 17

May 21

It's been five days since Eddie moved in. This means there are surfboards stacked on the side of the house, wetsuits drying in the outdoor shower, and damp towels hanging on the line.

It's pretty easy to see where his priorities lie.

Margo can't blame Eddie. In fact, no one has ever blamed Eddie. Since he was born, he's coasted through life with an easy smile and a lack of commitment to anything binding. College? One year. Jobs? Seasonal. Long-term relationships? About a month.

He'd been a standout high school athlete and was scouted to play lacrosse at the Division 1 level by colleges, but he didn't have the focus to commit to the training and practices that would have gone along with it.

He was offered a promising career as a financial advisor to the affluent members of their community. All he had to do was get his bachelor's degree and pass a few certifications. That never happened.

He simply doesn't care about material things the way most people in their area do. He doesn't need a nice car or a big house or a demanding job. He just wants to live life on his terms.

Their parents gave up trying to convince Eddie to settle on something – anything – permanent. He's a free spirit. Or lazy, depending on who you ask.

If Eddie's in town for the season, Margo will have an amazing summer with happy hours on the beach, quick trips to Atlantic City, and nights out at the Icona dancing to local cover bands. In the fall, though, Eddie will be off again.

She accepted a long time ago that no one was going to change her brother. He would always do what worked for him. Some people called it selfish, others said it was putting yourself first – going for what you wanted out of life and not caring what others thought. To her, it's just how Eddie has always been.

She does still feel some resentment, though. He can still disappoint her when she calls and doesn't hear back for days. But when he is home, there is no one she'd rather be around.

It's early when she gets ready and walks up the street to open The Plank. Eddie is still sleeping in the second bedroom. She'd been up late carving a new piece, a three-tiered serving tray for a picky client. It will help pay a healthy chunk of her bills and earn money towards her investment in the next Plank franchise.

She knows she needs to replenish inventory at the stores that carry her line. Especially The Gables. It feels like the pressure is always there to create more work. Even something she loves can be stressful sometimes.

Despite getting to bed after midnight, she still rises earlier than her brother. The sun is streaking pink and yellow across the sky. Seagulls squawk as they find food to fight over. Mornings are warming up now. She doesn't even need the hoodie she's brought along with her.

It's the morning shift for her today. The majority of their clients come in each morning between 6 and 7 to work out before heading to the office. And then there are the class junkies, who only exercise to guided yoga, pilates, barre, and HIIT sessions taught by Jax or Adrienne.

The Plank has a new member, much to the delight of several women and a few of the men. Mac is at the gym nearly every morning, sweating away. You might catch him running, rowing, or lifting free weights. Sometimes he sits in the café, returning emails and catching up with guests.

The gym had an opening for a new member after Chelsea's comments had caused them to lose Bruce (the one with the jeans). The apology letter hadn't worked.

She arrives at work and sits behind the reception desk. Most of their clients are regulars, like Rafael and Tina Martinez, who consider The Plank part of their daily routine. Tina likes to get her Stairmaster session in before she heads over to the Stone Harbor Borough building. She's had the same schedule three days a week for years.

Rafael is retired but remains a morning bird. He was one of the founding members of the Stone Harbor Museum. Tina has been a council member for decades after retiring from her teaching career. Together, they're two of the town's biggest advocates. Margo knows they'll show up in the next hour or so, like they always do.

Liz the realtor is usually there to greet Margo as she opens up. Hank trains Liz on Tuesdays and Thursdays. It gives Liz a chance to hear what's going on in town.

Liz is savvy that way. You just never know who might be moving or deciding to upgrade their beach house. Trainers and hairdressers often have the inside track on their clients' life changes.

Tony usually has a packed schedule full of female members. He came in early to open the gym for his current client, Sara DiCecco. She's completing a series of squats with a pair of dumbbells in her hands. Her face is sweaty and flustered.

"Good, good," he encourages her as she goes through the motions.

He's sweeping his palms across her thighs as he makes her dip deeper into the squat.

"This huuurrrtsss," Sara moans, wiping her face with a towel. Her dark brown hair is pulled back into a ponytail, but the new bangs she'd given a try were always getting soaked with sweat.

"Summer bodies are made in the spring," Tony tells her.

Margo rolls her eyes. Sara is dead set on getting her pre-baby body back. She's now one of his best clients. She hopes Sara isn't paying Tony for anything else.

There are others she knows by name but isn't particularly close with. They want to come in, get their workout done, and leave for the day. It suits her just fine.

Margo unlocks the door and switches off the alarm, a newly installed feature just a few days old. The best part of the new alarm is that she can run it through her phone. If she ever forgets to turn it on, she can go on the app and do it remotely instead of having to run back to the gym.

Technology these days.

She also decided to put a camera near her office door. She turns it off when she leaves for the day. She doesn't tell anyone about it. It's her own little secret.

Margo is still a little miffed by the way Mac dismissed her so easily. She could tell he was interested, at least initially, and just when she realized she was interested back, he turned her down.

Go figure.

She'd learned a little more about him, which was funny because a month ago, she didn't know he existed. After a few discreet questions, Margo found out he had dated Sabrina Elliot for a while. Wealthy, gorgeous, and connected. Sabrina was the poster child for the Swells.

Maybe Sabrina's more his style. Margo can't fault him for that.

Thinking of Sabrina reminds Margo that she's supposed to attend

Seven Mile Hotel's annual cocktail party next week. The Elliot's Memorial Day party is THE event that opens the season.

She wonders if Mac was at the event last year. As Sabrina's date.

Okay, enough. Margo wonders if she could talk Eddie into it. There is no way he owns anything halfway decent to wear. But with his charm, he could show up wearing only a pair of board shorts, and the ladies would love him anyway.

It is frustrating, but what can she do? He's her darling older brother. She's adored him since she was born. She makes a mental note to ask him.

Tish walks in, positively glowing. The beach life suits her. She's lost that stressed, pinched expression she had when she interviewed. Now, she has some color on her face.

"Hey, Margo." Tish stops at the reception desk. She's wearing black and white spa scrubs with the Plank logo embroidered on her chest.

Margo smiles back. She looks at the bookings on the screen. "Hi, Tish. You've got a busy day. And a lot of repeat clients."

"I know. It's been great."

"It's all you. We've more than doubled our spa treatments with you here."

"Aw, thanks. I love everything about this place. I'm learning so much, and everyone has been fantastic to work with."

Tish is so radiant that anyone looking at her would want to do what she's doing. Margo wonders if Tish has met someone or scored a waterfront rental. You don't get that happy working, even if you like your new job.

"How's the adjustment been so far? You're settling in well?"

"Oh, yeah," Tish nods. "Really well. It's like living in paradise here." She has a smile in her voice. "I meant to tell you that I can't stay too late tonight. I have to leave around four."

There's definitely a guy. Margo is willing to bet her next paycheck on it.

"Sure. Let me know if there's anything I can do to help you get set up. I just restocked your towels."

Margo watches as Tish walks back to the spa area to get ready for her next client. She's absolutely coming out of her shell. The Tish Margo had met had been run down, anxious, worried about what others thought of her. This Tish is poised and confident.

And lucky. At least someone is getting some around here.

Tony walks in fifteen minutes later. He's always getting some. Margo doesn't ask because she doesn't want to know. He would be all too happy to tell her.

"Tony. Your day looks pretty busy."

"Oh yeah, I have BIG plans today." Even the way he talks is full of innuendo. He's so damn cheesy. Margo tries to keep a straight face, but what does she know? His clients seem to soak it up.

"I'm out of here around four, so I'll start setting up soon."

Tony and Tish? No way.

They are so different. Tish is a quiet people-pleaser. Tony is the walking example of a Don Juan with a Napoleon complex. Margo doesn't see it. He likes to date the women he trains. Still, they're both leaving at the same time.

Well, to each their own. Margo has already warned Tish about the history of Tony's quick flings, even if it won't matter. No one wants to be told to stay away from a romantic prospect. And as the manager, it will be best if she stays out of the situation entirely.

They're both adults. They can handle it. And if nothing is going on, Margo will look like an idiot for butting in and saying something.

Mac walks through the front door. "Morning," Margo greets him as she scans his membership tag. Polite. Professional.

"I have good news. You're going to be happy to hear the restaurant is on track to open in a couple of weeks."

"I saw the job postings in the *Seven Mile Times*." She doesn't say anything more.

"We're finally getting to the finish line." Mac could have told her he was basically living at the restaurant next door. He hired an extra crew on top of the two already working there to get the flooring and electric done. A team of painters is there now, their trucks parked out front spanning the street. But he doesn't.

Because it's one of the newest Stone Harbor businesses, Margo knows it has the potential to be the hot spot of the summer. She's just grateful the hammering is almost done. Her head can't take the pounding for another week.

It's been less than a week since she's seen him. The last time he was at The Plank, she'd overheard him tell Hank that he'd been coming in at different times, based on when he could grab a quick workout.

Since it seemed like the work at the restaurant was almost done, she was prepared to cut him slack. Besides, he looks good. The way he fills out the simple light blue T-shirt he's wearing. And his hair looks recently cut - shorter on the sides but longer on top. It doesn't look like he has any product in it.

Get a grip, Margo. Stop thinking about his hair gel.

"Well, I'm happy for you. Everyone's talking about the place."

He gives a friendly nod and walks to the weightlifting area. Whatever.

Chelsea isn't in yet. Today, she'll run the front desk at 11 and stay later to help close up. Margo doesn't fully trust her after the missing key incident, but she's all Margo has on staff right now.

Tina and Rafael Martinez walk into the lobby. Right on time. She's been expecting them.

"Have you heard anything else about what happened at the Gables?" Margo asks.

"What a disaster," Tina sighs. "I don't understand the motivation for all these incidents. They're still working on it."

"It's like someone is messing with our island," Margo answers.

"We can't say they're related. The police are still investigating both incidents. But yeah, it's been a rough start to the season." Ever the politician, Tina isn't going to make a statement for the record. She'll keep her thoughts to herself.

The woman is smooth. Margo respects this approach, but she does love to hear what's going on. And Tina knows *everything* that's happening in town.

Rafael had been on the council before Tina, back in the days when they were raising their young kids. Margo knew he'd been asked to resign his post. She had heard rumors of a mishandling of funds, but there had never been any confirmation of what had happened. It was substantial enough for him to resign, but apparently not to have any charges held against him.

Tina stepped in and took his seat after a special primary election was held, and she won the vote. She's now the Council President and Chair of the Recreation & Tourism Committee.

Their daughter-in-law Kirby is always booking spa appointments, but it doesn't seem to make her any happier. She also doesn't seem to be a big fan of their son.

Personally, Margo can't imagine that Rafael is capable of doing anything that terrible. Or at least, doing it intentionally. He'd recently retired as a community college professor, and she'd heard him tell another gym goer that he was still hoping to teach the masses the virtues of the Renaissance era.

She's distracted by their next client, Sara. Margo is pretty sure the young mom is about to make a serious mistake. She's been coming in and training with Tony regularly. Every time Margo passes the pair, they're giggling like a new couple. She has seen the flush of excitement on Sara's face, and she's pretty sure it isn't just a post-workout glow.

Sara's husband isn't around much, and she's obviously enjoying the excitement of a flirtation. Margo just hopes they stop there. She doesn't need the drama of Tony sleeping with TWO women at the same gym.

Especially when she isn't getting any herself.

Chapter 18

May 21

Eddie makes plans to meet up with Tyson and Banksy for a few drinks at The Watering Hull. He's picked up a few shifts at the surf and watersports shop, giving surfing and sailing lessons. It's a great gig. Since he's one of the most popular instructors with the kids, he can choose when he wants to work. It allows him to pay his fair share of the bills with Margo.

He may be comfortable living like a college student, but Eddie is generous to a fault. It's probably the main reason why he never has any money. A lack of funds doesn't bother him. He figures if money isn't supposed to buy happiness, he may as well use it up.

His morning was perfect. A big breakfast, a paddle boarding session, and some fishing off the dock. Then drinks with a couple of buddies. Why didn't everyone enjoy themselves like he did? It's the best.

Tyson and Banksy are going to show up around six after finishing up their shift at the yacht club. Eddie has grown up with Tyson. As townies, they basically lived at each other's houses over the years, spending every free moment on the water surfing, swimming, or fishing. Smuggler's Cove had even let them store their crabbing boat there before it was sold and knocked down for more condos. That still gets him.

Margo had always been the infuriating sister until she finally grew older. She can still be pretty annoying, though.

It's odd being back and seeing how much has changed since last summer. There is so much construction on every block. New homes are being built as old ones are knocked down. Even the homeowners who want to save the older houses are having them raised up another level to help with flooding.

Stone Harbor's bay and beach streets often take on water during high tide. They have for years. The main street has been underwater more times than anyone wants to admit.

The town is in what seems like an endless cycle working to bring in sand and preserve the dunes. They're in a constant battle against Mother Nature and rising water temperatures.

He knows there have been some major concerns. Stone Harbor Point, a designated conservation beach at the top of the island, lost a huge swath of sand. Drops of more than ten feet from the entrances to the beach. Wooden steps with open space beneath them from massive amounts of erosion.

The town recently brought in trucks, dredge pipes, and heavy machinery to fight against erosion and save the beach. They slowly dredged sand from the ocean to refill the lost shoreline. A huge ship was docked at sea to monitor the hundreds of thousands of cubic sand coming through the pipes. It's been a massive project.

It also came at an enormous cost. But what is their other option? To lose their beach? It was the reason 7 Mile Island existed in the first place.

Eddie's been traveling for nearly eight years since graduating college. He spent time living in Costa Rica, Panama, Hawaii, and California, but Stone Harbor has always been home.

What if it is time to start figuring out where he wants to finally land? He's always thought that he'd come back eventually. Maybe it's finally the right time.

"Eddie!" Tyson shouts, walking across the bar. He grabs Eddie and gives him a hug. Ty always looks the same - tan from the constant sun, his shaggy light brown hair and Croakies slung around his neck.

Tyson has to lean down to hug Eddie. It still pisses Eddie off that he stopped growing in eighth grade. Eddie is built like a brick tank, solid and low to the ground.

Tyson introduces him to Banksy. They click immediately. For starters, at least he's at eye level with Eddie. Banksy was born in the Dominican Republic before his family moved to Queens. Living in Spanish-speaking countries for a few years gave Eddie a little fluency in the language.

They grab a few beers and sit at the bar overlooking Harbor Square. It's the perfect night: 75 degrees, slightly breezy but warm.

"What's new on the island?" Eddie asks.

"Aw, man, so much drama lately. You'd never believe it," Tyson answers, shaking his head.

"I still can't believe Quinn got clocked." Eddie takes a pull from his beer.

"Wouldn't be the first time."

Eddie laughs. "Are you getting a lot of heat at the club?"

Tyson nods. "Yeah. We're still getting the Sunnies and Optis fixed. People are moving on to Lasers, too. I've been trying to get the new sailing instructors certified for at least Level 1 Small Boat Sailing."

"Same old bullshit." Eddie worked at the club before he was fired for not showing up.

"We had a wedding over the weekend," Tyson adds. "The mother of the groom was so upset her son was marrying this girl that she cried during the entire ceremony and then left the reception in their limo."

Banksy nods. "It was bad, man. She wouldn't stop bawling. She was really loud."

"Ouch. I won't tell you about my day then." Eddie had enjoyed a large breakfast at Uncle Bill's Pancake House and then did some fishing and paddle boarding. Took a nap, woke up, and showered to meet them for drinks.

"What did you do?"

"Helped Margo fix up some things around the house." What they didn't know wouldn't hurt them.

"How long are you in town for?" Tyson asks.

"I don't know. I'm starting to think I might stay for longer than usual. See what it's like in the fall. Maybe even the winter."

"Stay here?" Tyson looks surprised.

"Yeah. It's about time." He knows that's not what Tyson was expecting. His friend looks happy about it, though.

The decision feels right. He shoots a quick smile at a server he remembers from a past gig at one of the local bars. Hopefully, he'll find a good opportunity at one of the businesses in town. He figures his sister and friends know enough people to land him a few interviews.

It will all work out. He doesn't stress about it. That's the way he is, though. He never does.

They watch a waiter wind her way around the tables with a full tray of food. The Watering Hull has a laid back, surfer vibe. It's one of the busiest places on the island, especially on a Friday night.

It doesn't take long to run into people they know. Tyson is a mainstay at the yacht club, so everyone wants to stop and talk to him. They ask his opinion on the wind conditions, the Flying Scot Sailing Fleet, an upcoming regatta, or the sailing schedule. Ty knows the answer to every question.

It doesn't matter who walks up to him, from wealthy businessmen to young kids. They all want to talk to Tyson. Even Banksy chimes in about current water conditions. Looks like he caught the sailing bug, too.

Not Eddie. He finds himself growing bored with the small talk. He spots a curvy brunette sitting at the end of the bar by herself. She isn't obsessively checking her phone or hiding behind a menu, just simply resting at the bar with a smile on her face.

He likes her confidence. He decides to walk over to her side of the bar.

"Hi, I'm Eddie," he says as an opener. Short and direct. Like him.

"Oh, hi." She flushes. "Nice to meet you. I'm Tish." She tucks a strand of dark, curly hair behind her ear. She has great energy. Like he could ask her anything. She isn't wearing a ring, but she *is* wearing a really pretty sundress with thin straps.

"Are you in town for the weekend or the summer?"

"All year. I just moved here for a job. I guess for a while at least."

This is promising. She isn't leaving. He sits down at the empty stool next to her. "That's great. I'm living here too. I grew up here, actually. Where are you working?"

"The Plank?" Tish answers. "I work as a facialist at their spa."

"Really? Do you know Margo St. James?"

"Of course. She's my boss."

"She's my sister." Eddie doesn't know if that's going to work in his favor or not. He hopes Margo hasn't talked about him. This beautiful girl will think he's a bum.

"What a small world. Margo is terrific. I didn't know she had a brother."

This is good news for Eddie. It will give him a chance to impress Tish, then let his sister tell her he's unreliable. He knows he's cute, in a non-threatening way. Light blue eyes, a decent body, confident in his approach. Casual. He's wearing a Hawaiian shirt, shorts, and a pair of flip flops.

All goes to plan. They talk for another few minutes before he asks for her number.

He notices she seems unsure what to do. Debating if she should give it to him. He wonders why. Because he's Margo's brother? Or is she already taken? He has no idea she's about to meet another guy for a date. Who's already 20 minutes late. And still hasn't called.

Tish goes for it.

"Sure. Let me give it to you." She types her number into Eddie's phone.

Eddie takes his phone back and shoots her a dazzling smile, his dimple showing. "I've got to get back to my friends and order some apps. But I'll be in touch." He can tell Tish is interested.

As Eddie walks away, he sees Tish check her phone. He smiles. He already texted her with his number, asking what her schedule is like next week.

Chapter 19

May 24

Mac is so close to the finish line. This restaurant project is all he can focus on. If he can just get this final building inspection approval today, he'll have the Certificate of Occupancy he needs so badly. If he doesn't, they'll have to wait another few weeks, and the grand opening will be delayed again.

The restaurant space has already been cleared for fire, plumbing, and electrical zoning from the Office of Code Enforcement. Right now, County Inspector Robin Metcalf is in for one last review before allowing the restaurant to begin operating. She's circling the second floor with her clipboard and camera while he has a silent panic attack downstairs.

If he wraps this last one up, he can turn the keys over to the owners, Ryan and Kyle, so they can begin planning the opening night party. He knows the couple wants to throw a huge bash to celebrate.

Tables, bar stools, and chairs have already arrived and are being set up around the space by the staff. One of Wilmington and Stone Harbor's hottest design teams is currently hanging clever works of art and colorful chandeliers.

The inspector has already talked to them about where everything will go. It looks like she is okay with all their selections. Mac really hopes so.

The space is vivid and bold. In the circular lobby, tall swings hang from the second-floor ceiling, letting guests sway as they wait for their tables. Bright wallpaper, neon hashtag signs, and a living wall of plants and flowers make it Instagram swoon worthy. There's even a low-level gas flame wall that travels around the perimeter of the dining area.

It isn't Mac's personal style, but he has to admit it's fun. Edgy. The younger generation will eat it up. Ryan and Kyle named the restaurant Fourth & Bay, a nod to Ryan being the fourth child and Kyle growing up living on the bay.

It's going to open to the public in just a couple more weeks, if Mac gets the COO. Reservations are already fully booked for the next two months. Which is why he's absolutely screwed if he doesn't get the final permit in time.

Robin walks down the stairs and meets him at the bar. She sets her clipboard on top. He struggles not to peek at it.

"Okay, then. We just need you to add handlebars to the bathroom to make it ADA-compliant. And make sure there's a rope clipped to the bottom of the swing, so people don't veer too far out. Once you get those finished, we're all set." She hands him the clipboard to sign off. "I'll come by tomorrow and hand you the approval when I see that's been done."

A flood of relief. He got it! "Fantastic. Thanks so much, Inspector. I'll make sure those are done today."

Mac stretches his hands behind his head, looking around at the space. "I'm not going to pretend I'm not glad this one's all wrapped up."

"I heard you were working around the clock," Robin offers. Then she adds, "I'll admit I didn't think you'd finish before Memorial Day."

Mac laughs. "I didn't either." He lets the inspector out after thanking her once again for fitting him into her busy schedule.

He's done it. Although he isn't alone, he doesn't care. He raises his arms up in victory, shouting, "Hell, yes!"

He circles the space, satisfied with the work he and his team have accomplished. It might have *been* rushed, but it doesn't look rushed. He loves the feeling of a completed job. Now he has some free time. He's going to try again with Margo; see if she'll consider going out with him. He hopes he didn't fuck it up already.

"Not too shabby." Mac doesn't have to turn around to recognize the voice. He's heard it enough.

His heart sinks. Way to ruin the moment, Sabrina. She's leaning against the open door, watching him closely. He's not surprised. He's been waiting for her to show up.

There's that signature sleek mane and pouty lips. A killer body that she shows off to advantage in a low-cut keyhole dress. High wedges with gold studs that Mac knows broadcast that they're a designer brand. He has no idea which one, but he knows it's not cheap. Nothing of hers is.

"Sabrina." His brief moment of victory is over. He eyes her warily. Is he going to get flirty Sabrina, or pissed off Sabrina? There's no way to tell.

She walks over to him slowly, her hips moving in that slow, sexy way she knows drives men crazy. "Congratulations. I knew you'd get it done."

Flirty Sabrina, it is. Mac raises an eyebrow.

"Even though you tried to stop it?" He's past trying to be nice to her. It doesn't work. He knows he sounds like an asshole, but it's pretty liberating. He should have tried this sooner.

Sabrina scoffs. "I don't know what you're talking about."

They're being watched intently by the designers and bartenders who are supposed to be setting up in the downstairs area. They're doing their best to overhear without being obvious about it.

Mac is sure that everyone there knows who Sabrina is. He's also confident that in a couple hours, their conversation will be all over town.

Take a deep breath, he tells himself. He doesn't need to make the situation worse, but he's damn sure not getting pulled back into the Elliot family drama. Sabrina has already shown him the psychopathic side of her personality.

You know what? No thanks.

"Let's just say our accounts of what happened might differ," he acknowledges. "Anyway, what do you think of the place?" Even she will have to admit it's stunning.

Sabrina *is* an interior designer, although the homes she decorates are usually her family's mansions. She does a lot of places around town. Whether that's as a favor for her father or as a result of her actual talent, he honestly doesn't know.

He's certain she feels slighted that the restaurant's owners hadn't gone with her.

"It's certainly…. colorful."

Yeah, she was annoyed. The backhanded compliment is actually more than he'd have given her credit for. It doesn't faze him.

"They definitely went bold," he replies agreeably. "It's almost done. I'm sure you'll be invited to the grand opening."

"Of course," she purrs. "That's another reason I stopped by. Are you planning on coming to our Memorial Day party?"

Shit, he'd forgotten about it. He'd been in attendance for the past few years, first as a resident developer and then as Sabrina's date.

"I was waiting to see what happened here," he hedges.

"It looks like it's all done. So, you'll be there."

Why not? "Yeah, I will." It's always been easier to agree with Sabrina.

"Fantastic." She moves closer, so quickly he doesn't have a chance to back up. Plants one right on his mouth without any notice. He pulls back, but she runs a long nail under his chin, tipping his head back. Making sure he's staring into her dark brown eyes.

"I know Daddy wants to see you."

Mac doesn't answer. Anyone who calls their father "Daddy" at this age needs to do some growing up. He has no interest in her childish games. Kissing him in front of everyone.

"I doubt he's thrilled with me after our last conversation." He has no intention of dating Sabrina again, but in this small of a town, he doesn't need to make any enemies either. He takes the easy way out by accepting the invitation. It's not like he has to stand next to her or her father. There will be plenty of people at the party to give him cover.

"He'll understand if I ask him to. He always does." Sabrina stares at him for a few seconds more, then turns on her heels and walks out the front entrance without looking back.

"Wow, that's some woman," his foreman Silas says from behind. Mac turns around.

Every person in the building is standing there watching him. It's obvious they've heard every word.

It had seemed a little *too* quiet. Oh, well. Now they know his social calendar. Everyone already knows he and Sabrina had dated. This was a quick kiss. One he didn't ask for. As long as Margo doesn't hear about it, he'll be fine.

No one in Stone Harbor really gossips anyway, right?

Chapter 20

May 26

Sabrina doesn't understand why Mac was so distant at the new restaurant. She'd been happy for his success. In every way. Playing the part of the supportive girlfriend.

Okay, maybe their relationship is currently on pause, but they still have history. Chemistry.

They're going to work it out. Of course, she'd been annoyed when he asked for a break. Wouldn't any girl be upset?

The key is making him realize that they belong together. That they make the perfect pair. 7 Mile Island's darlings. Just as soon as he realizes it.

Mac's such an idiot, she thinks affectionately.

She's sitting at the desk in her office at the Seven Mile Hotel. She's not usually there, and it's not hard to see why. One of her staff members keeps bothering her about a project she insists has a strict deadline. Another dumped a stack of paperwork that she said Sabrina needs to review.

Sabrina ignores it all. She can't be bothered with petty details.

She has too much to deal with on her own, doesn't she? No one else gets it. Everything has to be perfect.

Her father is giving her a hard time about making a few silly phone calls to some people about the MacIntyre Development Group. Mac's company.

Like it was a big deal. He had already tried punishing her for some things she did over the winter. She still couldn't figure out what had made him so angry this time when he's never gotten mad at her before.

If that wasn't enough, her daddy also said she wasn't coming into the office enough. Overseeing her team.

They were a bunch of uptight bitches, in her opinion. The men *and* women. Completely overpaid for what they did.

Still, there was someone who had been helpful. One of her best confidants had told her they'd heard Margo and Mac had been flirting at The Plank. On the regular. This was not something Sabrina had been expecting to hear.

Did Mac break up with her for Margo St. James?

She's always been the town darling. Everyone liked Margo. The kid would go around in her grandfather's truck, helping fix things, and people acted like she was the best thing since sliced bread.

It was insane. She had seen firsthand how store owners would give Margo extra fudge, free refills, and other kickbacks they never offered Sabrina.

It didn't make sense. The Elliot family was responsible for the town's economy, while the St. James family fixed pipes. In her opinion, there was no contest.

Despite that, the past grudges she experienced as a kid are stirred up once again. Why did Margo always come out on top?

Sabrina was the one who lost her mother. Margo didn't suffer anything. She'd been pampered by everyone on the island, including her parents and grandparents. They all adored her.

It was so unfair.

Years ago, she had dated Margo's older brother, Eddie. After a few weeks, he broke up with Sabrina because his family didn't think she was a nice person. That's what he told her.

Who did that? Fuck them.

She knows her father had commissioned a large piece from Margo. It was going to be proudly displayed in their hotel lobby. A hand-carved wooden chandelier that was supposed to somehow reflect the island's habitat.

It has already generated a lot of talk. The town darling, carving a grand work of art. It's sure to get attention from the local papers and press outlets.

Sabrina saw the design concept and receipt for the initial deposit. She was the designer, wasn't she?

They'd been willing to pay six grand for it. She's heard that Margo has been working on it for more than six or seven months. All winter, while the town slept, waiting for the summer season. Probably hoping it helps pay her rent. Based on her clothing choices, the girl is certainly not getting paid enough money.

Well, you know what? That project is about to be canceled.

Sabrina picks up her phone and makes a call to the hotel.

"Stan? This is Sabrina Elliot. Can you please advise Margo St. James that her commission for the Seven Mile lobby is null and void? We're no longer interested in featuring it," she tells the employee.

The poor employee doesn't understand at first. "The St. James art installation? But it's almost ready. We're expecting to hang it this month."

"We went in a new direction. The design team."

"It doesn't make sense," Stan responds. "There was already a good amount of press about unveiling the piece. We paid a substantial amount."

"Rescind it. And make sure you tell her we need the deposit back," she says. That will make it even harder to swallow.

Stan is too terrified of her to protest. "I'll make sure it's done," he responds.

Sabrina hangs up the phone. She doesn't necessarily feel any better. But she's still glad she was able to have one up on Margo. The girl is a menace.

It's time someone showed her she's not as great as everyone thinks she is.

Chapter 21

May 28

"Hello? Is this Margo St. James?"

"It is," Margo responds. "Who's calling?"

"This is Stan from The Seven Mile Hotel. I'm afraid we need to cancel your art installation."

At first, it doesn't even compute. "What do you mean?" Margo doesn't understand how it's possible, but Stan gently lets her know they have a clause in her contract that lets them get out of the agreement if they go in a different direction. "I'm afraid the management has decided to do exactly that," he says.

This was her big break. The largest commission she's ever had - and the reason she thought she would have enough money to finally buy into a Plank location. All the work she did, for nothing.

Margo is ready to curl up in her office and cry. Just stay there for days.

The loss of her inventory from The Gables had already put her in the hole. She didn't have the heart to charge Martha for the extra pieces of artwork after she suffered so much damage to her store. So now she's out thousands of dollars.

It's hard for her to wrap her mind around how quickly her situation has reversed in one single day. Instead of worrying about investing, she's now wondering how she's going to pay her bills. The deposit they'd given her is long gone, and she still has to find a way to pay it back.

It's almost as crazy as the news that Mac and Sabrina are back together. She'd heard they were over. But from what Chelsea told her, Mac is going to be Sabrina's date to the hotel's Memorial Day celebration. The fact that he's going with a member of the Elliot family, who canceled her commission without notice, only makes her more upset.

Whose side is he on?

Chelsea has been busy listening to and passing on her knowledge of their meeting to anyone who wants to listen. She still can't get over that they'd been making out! In front of the entire waitstaff! *And* the inspector!

Margo really needs to stop hanging out by the front desk. She is *definitely* not interested anymore. She'd been planning on going to the party with Tyson and Eddie anyway. The next time she sees Mac, she'll grant him a cool nod and continue whatever she's doing.

She's disappointed that Tyson is stuck helping with the event setup. She really needs someone to talk to, but there's no one more trusted to secure the boats and move others out of the spots than Tyson.

He knows the quirks of each one. He's won every race on the water that he ever entered, even when he was a young kid. It's a skill he takes for granted, but Margo knows most of the boat owners are in awe of his boating and sailing prowess.

Chelsea is oblivious to Margo's distress. She can't stop talking about the party. "It's going to be so fabulous. I heard they're going to have floating islands with fireworks. They're bringing in hawks just to keep the seagulls away. And they got that amazing band Mere. They were headliners at the Boardwalk Fest last summer."

"Yeah, it's going to be something, I'm sure." Margo doesn't want to hear all the details. But nothing can stop Chelsea from gabbing. She just keeps going, only pausing to scan gym tags and offer a cold towel to guests. Then she's right back to talking about the party.

"You know how Taylor Swift used to vacation here? I heard she might stop by."

Margo rubs her forehead with her fingers. "I haven't heard that." There's no chance in hell.

"Well, there's always a chance she could. If she's around." Chelsea shrugs. "Anything can happen. There's going to be a sick light show."

Since the Elliot family never did anything halfway, Margo has to agree with Chelsea on that. The Elliots have a history of bringing floating barges with live music, acrobats, and even their own fireworks show.

Last year, the entire parking lot of the yacht club was covered with see-through tents that were lit with votive lanterns. Boats and small buses ferried guests back and forth from the hotel or designated pickup spots. It was spectacular.

The Elliot party isn't her problem. She's more concerned about making sure they have enough staff at The Plank to cater to the sudden rush of clients who are showing up to lose that last bit of summer weight or get a glowing complexion. Tish and the other two part-time facialists are booked solid for the next few weeks.

Tony and Hank are in such demand that they're offering streaming classes to clients they can't train one-on-one. Margo is compiling a list of trainers to reach out to so she can offer additional yoga on the beach and circuit training classes at the Stone Harbor Recreation Center. Jax and Adrienne are fully booked.

The center is a complex on 82nd Street that houses a rec center, covered basketball court, pavilion, tennis, pickleball, soccer, and baseball fields. They even have a cute playground area for the younger kids to play in. It covers a few blocks of open space where summer camps and programs are held.

"I've got to reschedule Pinky Wilson for her session," she tells Chelsea. "Can you give her a call?"

"Sure," Chelsea answers amiably and picks up the phone. This is why even when Margo is frustrated with her, she still keeps her on staff. Nothing seems to bother the girl. She's willing to do or say anything.

Like clockwork, Tina and Rafael Martinez walk in for their morning elliptical session. Margo greets them as she checks them in.

"Morning. All set for the big wave?" She knows they're also anticipating the summer crush of visitors who will be coming onto the island via the 96th Street Bridge or Ocean Drive.

They come from the Garden State Parkway, the Cape May Ferry, and the back roads of Southern New Jersey. Some fly into the Atlantic City airport or catch a ride from friends on the way back from college. And all of a sudden, the sleepy town turns into a party. With loads of Swells.

"We're ready for it," Tina answers. "The sand backfill project is finished. I heard your next-door neighbor is all set to open, too."

"Hmmm," she responds non-committedly. Mac and his project have been a pain in the ass for her business ever since his construction crew started. She's not about to give him any credit for finishing two weeks late.

It's already been a busy summer, and it isn't even June yet. Margo is glad that Quinn is better and all the sailboats are back in the water. The drill holes have been filled and recoated. It had taken a lot of overtime to get them ready.

She still wonders who could have started the rumor that they'd been shot up. It was a lot easier to simply drill them full of holes and toss them over the dock. And a lot less noisy than shooting off a gun in a residential area.

The store break-in is another puzzle that hasn't been solved. Who would want to hurt Quinn and destroy a small storefront? It had been done so viciously, too. Like it was personal.

And then there was her office. Margo continues to feel like she missed something. Her desk didn't look the same way she'd left it. She's a creature of habit, and she closes down the same way every night. She thinks her laptop had been moved, but there's something else that wasn't right.

Or was she overreacting? It was so hard to tell.

Sara checks in at the front desk. She has definitely committed to Tony's diet and fitness plan. Margo makes sure to tell Sara that she looks fabulous.

Honestly, she'd thought there might have been something between Tony and his client, but he'd gone out with Tish the other night, so Margo must have been wrong. At least, she thought he had. Tish had come in all moody the next day.

Margo didn't ask. It's not her business. Chelsea will probably end up telling her about it anyway.

"Thanks, Margo. Are you going to the party at the Yacht Club?" Sara asks.

"I am," she answers cheerfully. "Can't wait to see you there. Is your husband back?"

"No, Charles is still working a lot. He'll be here the week after."

"Gotcha. Well, it's going to be a great time. Sorry he's missing it."

Sara smiles and walks to the back, where the free weights are stacked. She starts doing a set. Her eyes scan the gym, looking for someone.

Maybe there *is* something. Still, not her problem. Margo's staying out of it.

She's going through invoicing at the front desk when he's suddenly in front of her.

"Hey, Margo," a familiar voice greets her.

She tells herself not to be friendly. He's a nuisance. No matter how cute he looks in his gray and black workout gear.

"Morning." Margo barely makes eye contact as she scans his key card.

Mac doesn't budge, just stands there looking around. "Wow, it's crowded. I haven't been here in a few days. The number of people in here must have doubled."

That's right, he hasn't been there in a while. He's probably getting enough of a workout in the sheets.

"Mmm hmm." Margo isn't engaging with him. Maybe he could get moving now.

But no. Mac simply moves closer and leans in. "Did I do anything wrong? I thought you'd be thrilled we're finally done banging on the walls."

Oh God, he said banging. She flushes. "Yeah, no, I am. Happy for you." It's all she can do not to grit her teeth.

"Umm, okay. Well, hopefully I'll see you around. Are you going to the Memorial Day party? I ran into your brother, and he said you were."

"I'll be there."

"Great." He smiles. "Want to go together?"

What is he doing? She knows he is with Sabrina Elliot again. "I thought you had a date," she answers, eyeing him cautiously. Oh, she knew. He'd kissed Sabrina in the restaurant.

"No way," he replies firmly. "I'm not seeing anyone right now. At all. But I'd *like* to see someone." The intent is clear.

She can't help smiling. Well, this is some good news. "I'm already going with Tyson, but I'll see you there," she says in a much friendlier tone.

"Fair enough." He nods and strides off, clutching his gym bag.

She looks back. Now that was interesting. Chelsea could be counted on to get things wrong. Maybe Margo will consider giving Mac another chance.

Chapter 22

May 30

The weather is perfect for a Memorial Day Weekend bash. The Elliots wouldn't have accepted otherwise.

Stone Harbor's legendary "bubble," currents of air that break as they near the Point (the top of the island), had kept the rain away from the party. Because the peninsula was bordered by the Atlantic Ocean on the east and the Delaware Bay on the west, storms often split and dissipated around Cape May. It could be raining all day in Philly and still be sunny in Stone Harbor.

The ideal temperature of mid-70 degrees meant it was warm enough to wear summer dresses and sports coats, but just cool enough not to sweat in them. It was like the Elliots had specially ordered the perfect weather just for the night.

The marina has been completely transformed. Strategically-placed lighting accentuates the oversized portico with plush navy runners leading guests to the main entrance. Large tents have been set up in a perimeter surrounding the club, replacing the usual spots where members park. They've even laid down flooring so the interiors flow right into the outdoors, allowing guests to mingle back and forth.

On the waterfront side, the band is setting up on a huge stage overlooking the bay and Muddy Hole Island. A hand-painted dance floor is laid out before them.

The high open ceilings of the tents are filled with cascading chandeliers and foliage to mimic the feel of a forest. Centerpieces of tall, clear vases overflow with white roses, willow branches, and hydrangeas. On the opposite area, facing Margo's home and Snug Harbor, are catering tables and carving stations.

The Elliots somehow manage to top their parties year after year. They fly in event planners from the West Coast who are between jobs during award season parties. These professional planners have spectacular taste and a wide-open budget, making anything they dream of become reality.

Margo was thrilled to find the perfect dress at the People People boutique. A bright white strapless column with draping panels under her chest, it gives her more cleavage than she can cop to while simultaneously accentuating her lean frame.

She accessorized with large gold hoop earrings and stacks of her wooden bangle bracelets, along with chunky gold espadrilles. She's also carrying a classic gold purse of her mom's from the 80's that has finally come back into fashion.

Her hair is parted down the middle in soft waves that fall to the middle of her back. Minimal makeup highlights her eyes and cheekbones. The effect is bronzed and beachy.

Margo waits in the kitchen and nurses a glass of wine alone. Eddie is still changing in his room, and Tyson is due to arrive any minute. He'd been at the yacht club getting the marina and boats safely secured for the party.

She hears someone by her sliding back door. Tyson's been coming in off the deck that way for more than 20 years.

She turns to greet him and is taken aback. "Wow, Tyson." She doesn't know what to say. "You look so… different."

Surprisingly, she hasn't had to convince Ty to clean himself up. He's done it all on his own. His white linen shirt offsets the deep tan he's already picked up despite the fact it's just barely the beginning of summer. Slim navy pants and tan loafers complete his outfit.

He looks gorgeous, especially considering he'd been working all morning.

"I feel honored to show up with such a hunk," Margo teases. She slips her hand around Tyson's waist and squeezes him.

He flinches at her touch. What's this? She's taken aback and is quick to apologize. "Sorry, I didn't mean to tease you. I just like what you're wearing."

Ty shakes his head. "No, you just caught me off guard. You look so fancy."

"Gee, thanks," she answers. "I do get dressed up sometimes."

He starts to respond, then stops. Like, he doesn't know how to explain. "You're like gold. Gilt. Too glossy." He turns away from her abruptly.

How's that for a compliment? I look like an Oscar statue. Well, thanks, Tyson. Because he's managed to piss her off, she crosses her arms and decides to give him the silent treatment. They stand there in an awkward gap of silence, each not knowing what to say.

Eddie unknowingly breaks the tension, walking in to grab a beer from the fridge. He's completely oblivious. Go figure.

"Want one?" he offers to Tyson, who gratefully takes the beer from his hands.

She convinced her brother to forego his typical Hawaiian shirt for a clean button-down and tailored pants. It looks good on him. He'd even gone to the barber for a fresh haircut and shave.

Margo still can't believe he's agreed to come along. These kinds of scenes aren't usually Eddie's style.

"Who are you guys and what did you do with my brother and best friend?"

"Look who's talking, sis. You look pretty."

It's one of the nicest compliments she's ever had from her big brother. Eddie isn't known for flattery, so when he says something, he means it. She leans over and kisses him on the cheek, then gives a wink to Tyson, who's watching her warily.

All is forgiven. She's not one to carry a grudge, anyway.

"I'll have another drink too. Give us some time to avoid the chaos." They walk out back to the patio so they can see the massive tents and staging across from the dock of their house. It's one of the perks of living on Snug Harbor Bay.

It looks like a movie set. Large vans are coming and going, dropping off and picking up supplies. Circular ground spotlights light up the sky.

Tyson counts at least thirty people walking the perimeter of the parking lot and dock. "They better not touch any of our gear," he says as he pulls from his beer. "Drunk guests are the worst. We've had to clean up after too many weddings and parties at the club where someone got out of hand."

"Quinn told me they caught a bunch of skinny dippers in Avalon that wouldn't get out of the water," Eddie laughs. "The firefighters made them stand on the beach without their clothes while they read them the riot act about riptides."

"I bet you've done that before," Margo says.

"Of course," Ty shrugs, "but I never got caught."

They sit on the dock watching the free entertainment for a good half hour before deciding to head over to the club.

"I wonder who we'll know at the party?" Margo asks. *And if I'm being honest, what Mac will think of my glammed-up look.* It's much better than the yoga pants he usually sees her in.

"Oh yeah," Eddie says as casually as he can. "Are any of the people from the Plank coming? I met your girl Tish. Did she say anything?"

She arches an eyebrow. "When did you meet Tish?" This is a new development. Have they gone out? Funny, she wouldn't have put them together.

Eddie flushes. "I met her at the Watering Hull one night. She's nice."

"Yeah, she is. And naive." She gives him a look, then turns to stare at the club. "I'm sure there will be a lot of people you know."

"I don't need to give advice to some rich dude about his new Class 3 high-powered motorboat," Tyson interrupts.

Eddie's happy to take the attention off what he just said. "Happens every time. They have no idea how to handle their toys."

"They're clueless. Also, can't wait to see Margo getting checked out by every guy at the party."

There's an awkward pause while Margo and Eddie stare at Tyson.

He swallows the rest of his beer and stands up. "Let's head over." Back to gruff Tyson.

They make their way to the club.

The Stone Harbor Yacht Club is set at the end of a cul-de-sac of houses right on the bay, with views of the water in three directions. It's still early, just a little after 7 pm. The majority of the guests are still arriving.

In the past, there has also been plenty of drama as the night went on, which always proved to be entertaining. Fights! Ex-partners glaring at each other! Passive-aggressive behavior! This year shouldn't be an exception. The influx of new homeowners and club members who bring their own complications - hookups and breakups, secrets and affairs.

There's still the mystery of the Sunfish and the store break-in. The opening of the town's trendiest new restaurant. Old and new friendships and relationships.

It's going to be a great night.

Chapter 23

May 30

The party is in full swing. The headliner Mere, a band from Hoboken, has already finished their first set. Right now, a trio of vocalists is leading the crowd in classic R&B. They're getting down to tried and true hits from Marvin Gaye and the Temptations. Thankfully, no one has played *Staying Alive* or the *Macarena*. Although there's still time.

Margo leans against one of the columns, casually sipping from a glass of wine. She's already been talked to, offered advice by, and given updates from almost everyone she knows at the party. A few potential clients have approached her for larger commissions. Her custom-carved replica sailboats are really taking off. It will help offset her loss in income from the hotel's cancellations.

Even though she's excited by the new projects, she's still feeling some tension behind her eyes. She's enjoying having a quiet moment to herself.

It's all part of growing up in a smaller community, especially being a member of a family that has lived there for generations. She knows they all want the best for her. They just each have a different idea of what that is.

Funny, no one ever gives Eddie advice. They just allow him to do whatever he desires, even if that means putting whatever he wants before anything else. Everyone knows her brother hasn't filed his taxes in at least ten years. But they all just pat him on the shoulder and continue letting him fulfill their low expectations.

She tucks her hair behind her ear, scanning the crowd for Tyson and Eddie. Tyson is easy to pick out. He surprised her tonight, all dressed up. She's so used to seeing him one way that it's hard to adjust her point of view to look at him differently.

She spots Mac. He's engaged in a very enthusiastic conversation with an older gentleman who is wearing a three-piece suit and a bow tie. She smiles as she recognizes Jim Trainor, one of the island's most prominent architects and an amateur historian. When he isn't working at the B.L. Wiley firm, he helps run the Stone Harbor Museum and serves as the museum committee representative on the borough council.

It doesn't surprise her that Mac and Jim know each other. They're in the same profession. Mac works to preserve historic homes, and Jim comes up with plans to update them. She's sure they've worked on the same project at some point, or at the very least, shared the same clients. They're both in the high-end residential renovation market.

Mac looks good. He wears his light tan suit casually, as if he's used to dressing formally. He's even in dark brown loafers. She pegs him as a prep school graduate. He probably wore a jacket to class every day in high school.

Why won't he tell her his first name? His paperwork at the gym says Mac Jr. The fact he won't give it up presents her with a challenge. She's going to find out one way or another.

The trio starts on a round of *Louie, Louie*. It's time to say hello. Margo heads casually in his direction, careful not to knock into any of the dancers energetically jiggling and bouncing around.

Mac turns his head as she strides over. It's like he's been waiting for her. But he hasn't approached her once in the two hours she's been at the gala. And she knows he's seen her there. It's not *that* crowded.

He gives her a wide and generous smile, and she gets it. He was letting her make the decision. To come to him, instead of him always coming after her. It makes her like him more. Damn it.

"You look dazzling." At Mac's compliment, she feels a lump in her throat. This night has all the romance of a Gatsby party. The night has mellowed her. And the scene is romantic – the elegant forest of flowers, the overhead chandeliers, the shimmer of the bay.

You'd have to be heartless not to get a little carried away, she thinks. "Thanks. You're not so bad yourself."

So, they're back to being nice to each other.

Mac offers an introduction to Jim, who shakes his head. "I've known Margo St. James since she was three years old. Her grandfather taught me how to repair drywall when I was just starting out."

Margo gives him a quick, warm hug. "Nice to see you, Jim. How's the museum doing? It opens this weekend, right?"

"Yes, we're open all weekend. A lot of big things. We're launching a capital campaign for the summer, and of course, there's the gala in August."

"I'll make sure I'm there," she promises.

"We have some new ideas this year," he says with pride. "And a few big guest speaker lectures that I'd be happy to send you details about."

"That would be great." The museum isn't very big, and is run by a crew of volunteers who donate their time and resources to make people aware of the history of their town. She's always happy to support them. "I can post flyers of the talks and gala at The Plank. Just drop them off when you get a chance."

"I will, thank you." Jim has always had the best manners of anyone she knows. He and his wife Gail, had been close friends with her grandparents. They'd taught her more about the town's history than any of her former teachers combined.

"As I was telling Mac, hopefully we'll have the exhibit back before our first speaker. We're still looking for the piece. Someone must have misplaced it."

Mac cocks his head. "You lost pieces of an exhibit? What was it about?"

"Our newest," Jim says with a shrug. "The one about the Stone Harbor Boardwalk, before it washed away in the Great Atlantic Hurricane of '44. There was a time capsule in there, too. We think it's quite valuable."

"A time capsule?" Margo asks. "I didn't even know we had one." She'd forgotten all about the tradition of storing time capsules in monuments or buildings.

Jim laughs. "We didn't either! We actually just discovered it. It was placed in a section of the original boardwalk, but when the hurricane hit in September of 1944, they decided not to rebuild that mile and a half of wooden planking."

That was right, Margo realizes. Her grandfather had always talked about the boardwalk. "I've seen photos of the boardwalk, but I didn't know they'd put a time capsule inside."

"No one knew. Someone from our town must have decided to store it, but then it was forgotten about."

"A new homeowner on 80th Street gave us a call about it. The contractor discovered it in a crawl space right before they were about to demo the house." She hasn't seen Jim this excited in years.

"That's fascinating. Did you open it?" Mac asks.

"No." Jim shakes his head, pushing his glasses back up his nose. "We were waiting to announce it to the council members first. Then host a grand opening ceremony. We just have to find out who has it now."

It seems like Jim should be a little more concerned about the whereabouts of the capsule. It could be extremely valuable, if not monetarily at least historically.

"Are you sure it's gone? Do you think there's a chance someone stole it?"

Jim gives a short, barking laugh. "Stole it? Who would ever *do* that?"

"Well, there's been a lot of activity lately," Mac offers. "You heard about the boats that were damaged, right? And the break-in at the Gables store?"

"I've been out of town," Jim answers. "I had an archaeology conference in Phoenix, and then I went to see my grandchildren for a week. I only just got back. I'm pretty sure someone from the museum just moved it and forgot to tell us where they put it."

"When did you realize it was gone?" Margo is almost certain the time capsule hasn't been misplaced.

"I looked for it when I stopped over yesterday. No one had seen it." He chuckles. "They thought I'd had it at my house. As if I would leave something that's 80 years old lying around like that."

"Jim, I hate to tell you this, but I'm pretty sure it's gone. Do you have any cameras at the museum?" Mac asks.

Margo and Mac share a look. Margo has a feeling they know what the answer is going to be even before Jim answers.

"No, of course not." Jim shakes his head. "We don't have the budget for that kind of security. It's such a small area. Nothing that's of value, money-wise. Just valuable to us history buffs."

"I think you should report this to the police," Mac tells Jim. "They need to hear what happened. File a report and go from there."

Jim rubs his eyes. "You'd never suspect we'd have something important enough to get robbed. It's mostly old memorabilia, from Henny's or Springer's. An old lifeguard stand. Nothing anyone would want to break in and steal."

"I hate to ruin your night, but you probably need to report this as soon as possible. Do you know who else knew about the time capsule?" Margo feels sorry for Jim. He's a generous man, always giving his time and experience to the town.

"It wasn't a secret," Jim replies. "We hadn't made any sort of official announcement, but everyone at the museum and on the town council knew about it." He's starting to look worried. "I'd better notify the police department. The sooner they know, the better."

Margo gives him another hug, this time in sympathy. "I'm so sorry."

"It would just be a shame if we never found out what they put in it so long ago. Damn shame," he repeats as he heads out, pausing to say goodbye to fellow guests.

Margo looks after him. "Another one," she says to Mac.

He nods. "Someone has a big ax to grind. This seems petty." He pauses. "And personal. They're messing with the town."

"I agree. It's definitely someone holding a grudge. This isn't about money."

"We need to figure out who could possibly be behind this." Mac reaches out for Margo's hand. "We never seem to catch a break, huh?"

She knows what he's saying. Every time they've run into each other, there's been some kind of conflict. "There's nothing we can do now. How about a dance?"

Mac smiles. "I thought you'd never ask."

They make their way to the dance floor. It's already ten, and the band Mere is back on stage for their second set. They're playing one of their slower songs, *Sullen Girl.*

Mac pulls her into his arms. "Never a dull moment around you."

He smells as good as he looks. Figures. She rests her head against his shoulder and sighs. "I know."

"Do you think you'd be up for dinner one night? Sunset sail?"

"I can make that happen. I'm usually done by six."

"Yeah, I know. I checked up on you. Quinn told me everything."

Is he teasing? He keeps throwing her off. "Oh yeah? Was it good?" She hopes Mac didn't ask Quinn for a background check. He'd absolutely say the wrong thing. And she *really* hopes he hasn't met Eddie. The stories her brother could tell about her awkward years.

"I'll keep you posted." He pulls her closer, guiding his hand along her back. "This turned out to be a good night after all."

She smiles. "Yeah, it did." She turns her face up to him. Another inch and they'll be kissing. His eyes darken as he leans down to meet her mouth.

This is going to be good.

"Mac! Margo!" someone shouts, then bumps her hip against Margo's. It jolts her just enough to break off contact with Mac, sending her back a step.

Sabrina is holding two glasses of champagne. She hands one to Margo. Flustered, all Margo can do is take it from her hands.

She feels the chill of the glass as she loses the heat of Mac's grip.

"I didn't realize you two knew each other," Sabrina says, narrowing her eyes. She stands there, one hand under her elbow, the other hand clutching her glass. It's clear she isn't going anywhere.

This is an awkward standoff. They move off the floor so they don't disturb the other dancers.

Mac looks annoyed. "We've met," he responds. "And we were right in the middle of a dance."

"Silly me!" Sabrina giggles. Her voice has gone high-pitched again. "I just wanted to stop by and say hello." She takes a hold of Margo's arm. "Be a dear. I need your help in the ladies' room."

Now that Sabrina's there in person, it's not easy for Margo to hold a grudge against her. It couldn't have been Sabrina's fault that they cancelled her artwork. It must have been an administrative decision by the hotel to terminate its agreement.

Margo's also not great at confrontation. She lets Sabrina guide her away, throwing Mac an apologetic face as she leaves.

It takes fifteen minutes to help Sabrina with her zipper and wait for her to reapply all her makeup. By the time they leave the restroom area, Mac is in discussion with a group of local business people.

Another moment lost. Margo's romantic moment with Mac is gone, unintentionally ruined by Sabrina.

Or was it deliberate? It's very possible Sabrina doesn't want them together. And as she's well aware, what Sabrina wants, Sabrina finds a way to get.

Chapter 24

June 2

It's been three days since the Elliot gala. Enough time for *plenty* of things to happen.

The time capsule is nowhere to be found. By now, it's universally acknowledged that it was stolen. Nearly everyone agrees on that.

But who took it?

The Seven Mile Times is all over the story. There are quotes from Jim, town council members, and locals expressing their shock and disappointment at the theft of the capsule. It had been meant as a gift for the town, something to open decades later to show how things had been "back in the day."

"It was a special discovery. A gift for future generations to uncover," according to the mayor.

"A tragic loss," declared the Stone Harbor History Museum.

"We're closely monitoring the situation," says the Stone Harbor Police Department. They even have a detective assigned to the case: Nate Shroud.

One of the problems is that the detective has little real-world experience investigating major property thefts. How could he when there's so little crime on the island? The police are usually called to handle bike thefts, missing kayaks, and maybe a few loud parties after the noise curfew. Nothing like this.

The other concern is that Detective Shroud just started working there. He graduated from the academy less than a year ago.

And the third issue? He has absolutely no leads. Zero. Zilch.

It's a shame because no one has any clue what could have been in the capsule. They weren't even aware there was one. There's no mention of it in any archives.

This is known:

1. The capsule had been found by the new owners of a recently purchased beach house.
2. The original homeowners had passed away years ago and their children had never seen or heard of it before.
3. The contractor had come across it while cleaning the home out before demolition.
4. The only reason they know it had been placed under the board-walk was a handwritten note that had been packed with the capsule.
5. The museum is checking, but they can't find any stories about the town sealing the capsule in any sections of the boardwalk.

The mile and a half of wood planks originally stretched from 83rd to 106th Street. Originally built in 1916 in a style similar to nearby shore towns, it was destroyed by the devastating storm in 1944. Stone Harbor decided not to rebuild the boardwalk, unlike the nearby towns of Atlantic City, Belmar, and Ocean City.

After the hurricane, they must have needed a place to store the capsule, and a resident stepped in and offered to hold onto it for a while. And they did such a good job that it sat there for decades, just waiting to be discovered. Until it was forgotten about completely.

A group of Stone Harbor residents who lived decades before had gathered together what they thought would be useful for future generations. The question was, what did they consider valuable?

The possibilities are nearly endless. Except now, there was no way of knowing.

Sabrina couldn't care less about the damn thing. She was done hearing about it. She had other things that were much more important to worry about.

The other night, towards the end of the Memorial Day opening party, the precious Margo St. James had asked her father about the termination of her art installation. Naturally, Roger didn't know anything about it, since he wasn't the one who had canceled it.

He had called Sabrina over to ask if she knew anything about the situation. She'd acted shocked, but he hadn't bought it. So she had to fess up.

"Maybe," she cautiously answered her father. And then all hell broke loose.

There were two things Roger Elliot did not like: being in the dark about a situation that involved him and being made to look bad in public.

Sabrina had accomplished both. And that was on top of the trouble she'd gotten into this past March over a little DUI. He still hadn't gotten over that. He even took away her Porsche for a few weeks.

This ... developing situation made him livid. Absolutely furious.

Of course, her father didn't shout at her in the middle of their gala event. He waited until he got her in private and gave it to her. Accused his daughter of being a spoiled brat. A petty child. He couldn't believe she'd tried to sabotage two local business owners, Mac and Margo. People he admired.

Sabrina rolls her eyes. He'd been so angry that she called the building inspector on the MacIntyre Group.

"What's the big deal?" she'd asked. "All they did was double-check his work. I was trying to make sure everything was done to code."

"You have absolutely no idea what it's like to feel the pressure of a looming deadline or a tight budget," Roger had said. His voice was so *cold*. He never used that tone with her.

"Daddy, trust me. It's not that serious."

"It is to Mac and to Margo. She thought we weren't going to pay her! She needed that commission. Did you know she's planning to use the money to open a second location for the Plank?"

"Please. It's not even that nice," Sabrina had said with a roll of her eyes. "Our home gym is better."

"At least she has motivation. She's working non-stop to make her dreams a reality. While you coast by."

Sabrina scoffed. "You want me to be a sweaty gym owner? C'mon, Daddy."

"That you would even respond that way makes me realize I've let your mother down. I promised her I'd take care of you when she was sick, but I failed," he said. "I gave you too much. I won't make that mistake again."

Sabrina didn't know what he meant. Until he took away her credit cards. Canceled her driver. And made her *call Margo and reinstate the agreement!*

She wasn't even sure what to do with herself. Margo had been so damn nice about it, too.

"Don't worry about it. I'm sure it was all a miscommunication," Margo said. Like the freaking angel she was.

"It won't happen again," Sabrina promised as she gritted her teeth over the phone. "My dad also wanted to increase the amount he promised. An apology for the trouble." She could positively feel her veneers grinding.

Of course, Margo had accepted. Greedy bitch.

Sabrina seriously contemplated driving over there and smashing the chandelier to pieces. She didn't know how she was going to handle seeing Margo get all the accolades when they finally hung it. Hear their guests commenting on it when they walk into the lobby. Watch the press give her piece rave reviews. Even though, in her opinion, it was basic as hell.

It was galling. She had flat-out refused to call Mac, telling her father the break-up was still too raw. He'd reluctantly let that apology drop, although he told her he was planning to call Mac himself to apologize.

He did make her contact the building inspector and let her know there wasn't any credibility to her report. The inspector tried lecturing her on making false reports. She hung up on her mid-sentence.

That wasn't all. Going forward, her father said she had to report to work EVERY SINGLE DAY by 9 in the morning. Five days a week. Monday to Friday. And she couldn't punch out until 5 at night!

That was eight hours a day. Who worked those kinds of hours? A masochist?

It was absolutely ludicrous. And it was all Margo's fault. She was the one who'd gone after Mac, making him break up with Sabrina. Flirting with her boyfriend and then turning around and getting Sabrina into trouble with her dad.

He was never mad at her. Her daddy always felt bad for her, his motherless only daughter.

Sabrina sniffs. It's a freaking tragedy. Her life had been going so well this spring. And now her entire summer is ruined. All because of that girl who kept showing up and ruining her life. Why did everyone like her so much? It was maddening.

Let's see how happy Margo is once Sabrina's done with her, she thinks. Because this isn't over. Far from it.

Chapter 25

June 4

It's finally the weekend! Margo and Tish take the Jitney down to Avalon. The small van makes runs up and down the island from 6 at night until 2 in the morning every weekend. For a few dollars, it's a bargain.

The Princeton is going to be packed tonight. It nearly always is. The huge building takes up almost an entire block and corrals three nightclubs under one roof. Centrally located in the prime center of town between 20th and 21st Street, it's been a destination for partiers since the 1970's. It's also one of the best spots in Avalon to listen to live music.

One of the reasons Margo loves going to The Princeton is that you are likely to spot a Philly news anchor eating at the Circle Tavern, a local celebrity hitting the dance floor, or an Eagles player catching a live show at the Rock Room. *Everyone* has a good time at The Princeton.

They're dressed up and ready to party. Tish has a strappy sundress highlighting the tan she's picked up on her days off. Margo is wearing a navy jumpsuit that shows her long, lean frame to advantage.

"I heard L. Boogie is playing tonight. She's incredible," Tish says, reapplying her lip gloss.

"I've seen her play at the Icona before." Margo's fiddling with her phone, debating if she should text Mac to meet up for a drink. They've talked a few times this week, but nothing serious. She had such a good time with him at the party that she couldn't let it go. It feels so unfinished. Not being able to follow through on that kiss? Deadly.

He's probably already back home in Cape May, fried after a long day of work. She knows now that the restaurant is completed, that he has some other projects he will be working on, and even more that he's just beginning to design.

Obviously, it's never a good idea to text a potential date while out drinking. The drunk romantic text never goes as well as intended.

She knows she shouldn't, but she has a feeling her resolve will disappear after a few more vodka tonics.

There's more to Mac than she initially thought. Depths that she glossed over the first time that she'd begun to recognize after a few conversations. She didn't notice them when she marched over next door, yelling at him for the construction noise. She certainly didn't see them later, when she'd thought he was flirting with her and dating Sabrina at the same time.

So yeah, they haven't gotten off to a great start.

She asked around and learned some interesting – and revealing – things about him. Like the fact that he has his degree in architectural history. From Yale. And that he specializes in saving historic homes, something that appeals to her after watching so many properties get razed by bulldozers.

Also, he plays the ukulele. Who knew? It's totally unexpected but seriously cute.

Mac has quickly become a recurring thread in her line of thought. And the worst part is, she doesn't mind it at all.

Tish looks at Margo toying with her phone. "Is something bothering you? You look tense."

Margo shakes her head. "No, it's nothing. Just wondering who will be there."

"It's a Friday night in the summer at the shore. I'd say just about everyone."

Margo can't argue with that. Tish has handily picked up the rhythm of Stone Harbor. She's gotten to know so much in just one season, recognizing the quirks of the residents and visitors. By the end of the summer, she'll be a local.

It's pretty impressive. Not everyone can assimilate as well as she has.

They pull up to The Princeton's brick facade and wrought iron patio and make their way across the outdoor seating area spanning the building. Doors are flung open to the outside as guests eat al fresco.

"Hi! Nice to see you." Margo greets a few diners as they weave their way between the tables. There are a bunch of people she knows, including Tina and Rafael Martinez, who seem to turn up everywhere. They look like they're deep in conversation, so she gives them a friendly wave and moves on. She knows she'll see them at one of their morning workout sessions.

"Want to get a few apps at the bar before we see the band?" Tish suggests. They make their way to the bar, a wide square spanning the first floor of the restaurant. Margo nabs two spots, and they settle on bar stools.

Something about seeing the Martinezes sparks a memory. Today in her office, she'd found a piece of one of the Plank's scan tags under her desk. It must have fallen off someone's key chain – the round hole had been torn, and a piece was missing. She discovered it the day after Chelsea had told her about the lost keys.

There weren't enough numbers to see whose it could have been, and since the tags were eight numbers long, it would have been impossible to narrow down whose it could be.

Although the tags are always turning up somewhere, the only person who'd come to her asking for a replacement was Tina Martinez.

Could Tina Martinez have possibly been in Margo's office? What reason could Tina have had to search through Margo's things?

Or could it have been Rafael? They share a family account. Margo thinks their kids might be on the same member number, even though they're fully grown and married.

She'll have to look their number up tomorrow. The only thing she could make out on the piece was the beginning numbers – 002 – which were nearly the same for 75% of their members. The last two or three numbers were the ones that changed the most frequently as they added new clients. So, that doesn't help much.

Margo's deep in thought when someone puts a hand on her shoulder. She nearly jumps off her stool.

"Hey sis!" Eddie shouts as he leans in for a kiss on her cheek.

"Geez, Eddie, you scared the hell out of me," she complains.

He's with Tyson, Quinn, and Banksy. Tish is talking to all three of them.

Funny, Margo had no idea that Tish knew her best friend. Or Quinn. Obviously, Tish knows Banksy because he also works at The Plank. They both see him often enough. But she's surprised to know she's hung out with the other guys.

Eddie had briefly mentioned meeting her at the Watering Hull, but Margo didn't realize they knew each other that well.

It makes her feel weird. And oddly possessive because they were her friends first. Which is an incredibly immature emotion. It's not really that surprising they ran into each other. They're all the same age, and this IS a small island.

The guys hang over their stools, reaching over to help themselves to their food. Margo swats Eddie's hand away. "Those are my fries."

"Yeah, but you never finish them."

He knows her too well. Margo shoots him a fierce glare that does little to keep him from leaning over for another handful.

"Are you here for the band?"

"Of course," Tyson answers. "We still have an hour to kill before they come on."

She hasn't seen him since the Memorial Day party, when he abandoned her side after she slow danced with Mac. It was odd. Something has shifted in their easy friendship, and she still isn't sure what happened.

She decides to take the coward's way out and try to act easy and approachable. Which is a shame, because she usually *feels* easy and approachable with Tyson.

Banksy is his usual good-natured self. He helps fill any uncomfortable pauses in conversation.

Like Tish, he's already beginning to fit in like a town local. He knows a ton of people due to working at the yacht club and the gym, two places with a lot of traffic.

"Thanks for everything you did this week," Margo tells Banksy. His mechanical knowledge has been invaluable in dealing with all the damaged machines and pieces of equipment. "I know we've been packed and things are breaking down much sooner than they usually do."

"No problem. Everyone there is a good egg," Banksy responds. He tips his beer bottle back for a drink. "And I'm taking one of your members out for dinner later this week."

Good for Banksy. At least *someone* is finding dates.

She hasn't seen Quinn since she went to visit him at home after he was ambushed at the store. He tells her the police are running background checks on new employees at the marina and sailing clubs. They're also reviewing footage from home security cameras and doorbell cameras to see if anyone was close to the yacht club, museum, or storefront. Nothing so far.

He seems confident something will turn up. There's a new piece of gossip Quinn is happy to share. "The house where the time capsule was found was originally owned by Kirby Bennett's grandparents," he says. "Were you aware of that? Because I sure as hell wasn't."

Kirby, Margo remembers, is unhappily married to Jacob Martinez, Tina and Rafael's son. "No clue," she says. "I'll ask Kirby about the connection the next time she's in the Plank for a treatment." She's there often enough for Tish.

Margo realizes that Tish didn't look very surprised to see the boys there. Was she given advance warning?

Eddie is speaking softly to Tish from her bar stool. From the look on his face, he's actively flirting.

Tish? And Eddie?

The thought has never crossed Margo's mind. But Tish is smiling right back at him, nodding as she stirs her peach paloma. She has a pleased look on her face.

Maybe. They do look cute together, Margo has to admit. Tish's long dark, curly hair and Eddie's shaggy mop. The aesthetician and the surfer. Margo thinks that as long as Tish understands that Eddie will be gone by fall, they could have an enjoyable summer together. Good for them.

It figures. Everyone is getting lucky but her. At least she has some money coming back from the reinstated commission. Even though she'd taken a dive on the damaged pieces at The Gables.

It's disappointing but not surprising. She's too busy managing the gym, figuring out the mystery, and finding a way to keep her artwork profitable so she can save enough money. Her brother and friends are actually enjoying their summer. They don't have any worries. Just dating and drinking, enjoying the beach.

It isn't fair.

It's time to do something about her sad situation. Margo decides to send that text to Mac after all. It's time to make a move.

Chapter 26

June 5

Mac can't believe he missed a message from Margo. He'd been out on his buddy's boat, so he didn't have great cell reception on the water. He never even saw the missed call.

When they got back to the dock, Mac tried calling Margo back, but she didn't answer. Then, he'd done the remarkably clever and original move of calling her again. Really. So, he'd actually called her twice, like a lovesick puppy, and was now wishing he hadn't.

He'd had a few too many drinks on his friend's boat and was regretting it today. There's nothing like waking up the next day regretting what you'd done the night before.

Even though it's early Saturday morning, Mac takes a shower and gets dressed before driving up to 7 Mile Island.

His team is still working on adding a two-story addition to the $21 million beachfront property in Avalon. The restaurant has taken so much of his time that he needs to give this addition more of his attention, even though it's a Saturday. When you own your own business, there isn't ever a true day off.

Everything is super luxe, so it requires custom installation and intricate work. He's lucky that the crew he's been working with on the home with are second and third generation masons.

He can't *say* who they're working for, but the name is recognizable to anyone who reads celebrity magazines. She grew up summering in Stone Harbor and just finished a record-breaking tour. But he can't say her name.

Honestly, he can't. Even though he might continue dropping hints. Especially to her teenage fans.

He's just pulling up to the three-lot-wide property when his phone rings. Hoping it's Margo, he automatically picks up the call.

It's only Quinn. Mac answers anyway.

"What's up?" he asks.

"I need to talk to you about something, but it HAS to be kept on the down low," Quinn stresses.

"Is this something I'm going to regret knowing about?"

"Probably."

Mac sighs. "Give it to me."

"I got a call from a friend at the police department." Mac figures he knows who it is. Quinn doesn't have that many friends.

"And?"

"They got a hit off Banksy. He did some time for mechanical theft in New York. Has he ever mentioned anything to you?"

Mac really wishes he hadn't taken this call. "No, nothing. From what Tyson has told me, he's an ace mechanic. And a good employee."

"Ty is next on my list to call. They're just wondering what made him decide to leave Queens for Stone Harbor."

"That sounds a little elitist," Mac replies. "Why can't someone from Queens end up here? They're both on the water."

"I'm not going there." Quinn was nothing if not diplomatic. "And don't repeat this to anyone. I just wanted to ask if you noticed any red flags."

"Zero. He's a good guy. Anything he did in the past doesn't mean he'd do the same in the future." He pauses as he takes in the situation at the estate on 53rd Street. "Let me call you back."

He pulls up the winding drive discreetly camouflaged with verdant landscaping. The curve of the drive and its hedge of tall trees and plants help shield the home from the main road of Dune Drive. Privacy is extremely important to these types of homeowners. These secluded oceanfront homes are some of the biggest on the island.

Mac has never met his client in person. Everything is done through her assistants and design team. He figures that when you get that famous, you don't need to talk to as many people to get the job done. They do it for you.

As soon as he pulls up the circular drive, he sees Sabrina. Great. The day keeps getting worse.

What the hell is she doing here? He doesn't trust her next to his crew, considering everything she's done in the past. He knows how angry she can get when she feels like she's been wronged.

He hasn't spoken to her since she kissed him on the mouth at the restaurant and then pitched a fit at the party. Now here she is at his job site, tottering around in ridiculously inappropriate heels.

Sabrina is standing next to Silas, one of the project managers Mac subcontracted for this project. It's such a large job that he needs additional crew members to finish it. Mac doesn't know Silas well, but he watches as he nods at whatever Sabrina is telling him. Silas looks either smitten, intimidated, or confused. Take your pick.

Mac gets it. Sabrina's wearing a hot pink tweed suit with gold buttons, holding a pink clipboard and a pen with a pom pom attached. On a job site. She's absolutely ridiculous.

Mac gets out of his truck and heads over to where she's standing. "What are you doing here, Sabrina?"

"Mac. Good to see you." As if the last time they'd talked, everything had been peachy.

"I told you before I'm not interested."

Sabrina flicks a piece of her hair behind her shoulders. "Get over yourself. I already apologized. And I'm not here for you, Mac." She marks a check on her bedazzled clipboard. "I'm here for my client."

Mac doesn't trust her. Why should he? She's screwed him over so many times and then lied about it. "How did you even get on the property?" He looks around in disbelief, then turns and stares her in the eyes. "Sabrina, if you mess with one of my projects one more time, I'm getting a restraining order."

It's way too early in the morning for this. The caffeine hasn't even kicked in, and he's still feeling the effects of too many drinks the night before. Not like there's an ideal time to get blindsided by Sabrina.

"Didn't you hear? I'm one of the newest designers on the project. *Our* client thinks I've got exquisite taste." Sabrina delivers the news with a smile as she hands over paperwork showing a signed contract with her design firm. She knows she's got him.

Mac can't waste any more time on her. She's not worth the effort. "Whatever. I've got work to do," he says as he walks away.

"So do I," Sabrina practically purrs. "I'm looking forward to working together. You know we've always collaborated so well in the past."

Mac doesn't give her the satisfaction of turning around. He just keeps putting more distance between them. He wishes she'd just leave him alone.

Chapter 27

June 7

Tish hasn't felt this happy in years. She loves her job, adores where she lives, and is crazy about a fantastic guy. She's pretty sure Eddie feels the same way.

They closed down the dance floor at the Rock Room over the weekend. She'd had so much fun jumping up and down, sweaty and flushed, only stopping to grab a hard seltzer before rejoining the crowd to sing along in front of the band.

She and Eddie had bumped and grinded, doing the makeout dance. The one where they knew they'd be doing more eventually. Singing and sliding as they sweated in the packed space. It had been the ultimate turn-on.

Although Tish had a major buzz, she'd turned down his offer to spend the night – it would have been awkward waking up at the same house as Margo (she was still Tish's boss, after all) – but the chemistry had been off the charts.

Tish had woken up to a sweet text the next day from Eddie checking in on her.

Even spotting Tony and Sara necking in a corner of the bar hadn't bothered her. They'd been running their hands over each other like a couple of horny teenagers. Tony was all over Sara's ass. It didn't seem like they cared if anyone saw them out in the open, Sara brazenly cheating on her husband.

Tish shrugs. It isn't her problem to worry over.

Sara's husband, Charles, on the other hand, *might* have something to say about it. Tish has a pretty good hunch that he has no clue that his wife is having an affair with her trainer. The way Tony and Sara carry on in public makes Tish feel that Charles is going to find out any day now.

Hank had warned her about Tony from the beginning. She's grateful for his early advice. He had probably seen the same pattern take place over and over during his years of working at The Plank.

Sweet Hank. He's her favorite of all the people at the gym.

Tish floats into work, granting Chelsea a serene smile at the main desk as she makes her way to the spa area. A couple of regulars are working out, but the place is still pretty empty this early in the morning.

"Morning, Chelsea!" She waves but doesn't stop. Tish has an hour to take inventory and restock the towels and products. Humming happily, she sorts out her schedule and checks to see if she has the right supplies for each facial and waxing appointment.

She's going to talk to Margo about buying a new machine for fine lines. They are going to need to find a nurse or a physician's assistant to come in for injections. Tish doesn't have the medical qualifications to inject people.

Besides, she hates needles.

Margo walks in as Tish is still deep in thought. "Do you have a minute?" Margo asks.

"Hey, Margo! What a fun weekend!" She wonders what her boss wants to talk to her about. Her relationship with her brother?

"Are you interested in adding some more hours?" Margo asks. "You've become our most popular team member. Everyone wants one of your hydrafacials."

Phew. She's there to talk business. Tish is working 30 hours a week right now. If she goes up to 40 hours a week, she'll get benefits.

It was as if Margo read her mind. "You'd be a full-time employee. Health care plan, 401k, two paid weeks of vacation."

It sounds fantastic. And will help fill in the gaps for her expenses. Still, she doesn't want to seem too eager.

"Can you give me a day to think it over? It sounds great, but I just want to make sure I can juggle it all."

"Oh. Yeah, sure." She can tell Margo is taken aback that she isn't leaping at the opportunity. But she's a new Tish, isn't she? She isn't going to jump at everyone's offer or be the answer for someone else's needs over hers.

"Thanks, Margo." Tish shoots her a wide smile. "I really enjoy working here."

Margo smiles back. "Tish, about that elephant in the room. I think you and Eddie look good together."

They do, don't they? Tish wonders if her day could get any better.

An hour later, it did. Eddie sends a message asking her to meet him for a game of miniature golf. Why bother playing games? She responds with a yes right away.

Over the course of the rest of the day, every single one of Tish's clients comments on the grin that won't stop spreading across her face.

Chapter 28

June 17

Fourth & Bay is finally ready for its big debut. Only a few weeks past the original opening date, the two-story bar and restaurant is all glossed up and ready to go.

To celebrate, the owners are hosting an opening night party. They'll have a soft opening with 50% seating capacity over the weekend.

This gives the staff more time to get used to running plates, food and drink menus, and table seating numbers. It also helps the crew with a slower pace over the next few days while they work out the initial kinks that come from opening a new business.

Mac is as surprised as anyone with how well it all turned out. When his old college friend Kyle had initially approached him about rehabbing a vintage restaurant and bar, Mac had explained that it wasn't his line of work. He specialized in renovating historic residential homes. He didn't dabble in the commercial space. And especially not a two-story restaurant with more glitter than an Elton John concert.

But Kyle wouldn't stop asking. He'd bring it up every time they talked, pushing and prodding him. He kept saying Mac was the only one he trusted to do it right.

He'd been relentless, not taking no for an answer. Kyle has always been one of the most persistent of Mac's friends. And the savviest.

He told Mac he wanted a place with plenty of areas for Instagrammable pics. When Mac told him he wasn't even on Instagram, Kyle insisted on creating one for the firm, along with a TikTok and YouTube channel.

Now, Mac is on Instagram, and the MacIntyre Development Group even has a few thousand followers. His admin had a lot of fun posting pics of him and his crew hauling and nailing while rehabbing homes. He just lets her do her thing and ignores the comments.

Although his true love is and always will be preserving and restoring the grand old homes along the East Coast, he has to admit the project had been fun… even when they'd been working around the clock to get everything finished up. Not to mention that it was how he met Margo.

Kyle had been right, like usual. He and his husband and business partner, Ryan, owned a few other places in the nearby shore towns of Sea Isle and North Wildwood, as well as a breakfast spot in the charming historic town of New Hope, PA. But this was their most daring venture yet.

A huge backdrop of mirrors in all shapes and sizes glitters at the insanely large front door entrance. The super-sized doors had taken Mac twice as much time to install as regular ones. But what Kyle wanted, Kyle got. And even Mac has to admit it makes a statement.

Fourth & Bay is spelled out in pink neon across the top, giving guests a photo opp before they even set foot inside. A red carpet with stanchion rails was laid for tonight's opening. It gives off a movie premiere vibe.

He has to concede that Kyle and Ryan had been right about a lot of things. Right now, though, he's too busy installing hundreds of disco balls on the ceiling. It was Kyle's last-minute idea to make the opening party shine. Literally.

The place will soon be packed with people Mac knows. He invited Quinn as his plus one. That way, if he wants to bail, he can exit without feeling bad for leaving his date in the lurch.

Quinn can fend for himself. He's just as much a part of Stone Harbor as anyone. He went from working at the local fishing stores to joining the Fire Department as a full-time employee. And on his off days, he does odd jobs. He can't walk into a store or restaurant without striking up a conversation with someone he knows.

Since Mac is still trying to avoid the entire Elliot clan as much as humanly possible, he's not going to worry for one second about making sure Quinn is entertained.

There's no doubt the Elliots will be there to give their blessing to the new venture. Sabrina never misses a chance to be in the spotlight, in spite of the fact that she's still pissed Kyle and Ryan didn't use her as their interior designer. They knew better.

Working with her on the beachfront mansion is getting harder and harder. If she had taken the job to make Mac change his mind about their relationship, she definitely wasn't acting like it.

Sabrina made him completely redo an entire wall of cabinets in the butler's pantry because she didn't like the way they opened. *They were so cringe*, she told them.

So now they had to wait another six weeks for a new set. It was silly, petty shit that was a waste both economically and environmentally.

It doesn't make sense to him why some people seem to enjoy being difficult. Does it make them feel more important? Because it just made him want to avoid them. There are enough problems in the world; he doesn't want to worry about cabinet choices.

Shaking his head, Mac affixes the last ball to the ceiling. There have to be 300 of them. Ryan's nickname for Kyle is pigeon, since he always says that Kyle loves anything that glitters.

Mac bends down to put away his nail gun and other equipment. He's almost done and then he plans to hit The Plank for a quick workout. With any luck, he'll run into Margo and casually ask if she's going tonight.

They've completely stalled on whatever it was they were doing. He can't tell if she is interested or just doesn't want to let him down. He's known her for a month and still hasn't even kissed her.

The sexual suspense is frustrating, but also sexy. Like they're in high school again. The nervousness, excitement, and second-guessing what they think of you.

It's so different from any other person he's been interested in. Usually, Mac meets someone, and if it clicks, he asks them out. And then if it keeps clicking, they'd keep going out until they sleep together. And then they meet each other's friends and later their family.

But with Margo, to say they are taking it slow is an understatement. And he's already met her friends and family. Before he even kissed her.

Maybe Mac hasn't been giving her his full attention. He's been so wrapped up in these all-consuming construction projects. She deserves the same time and consideration that he gives to the historic homes he rehabs. What was built with care and concern needs the same amount of understanding.

It's a revelation, but his family would have probably knocked him over the head for taking so long. *What an idiot I am*, he thinks.

Mac opens the door of the equipment room to store the rest of the disco balls. Kyle ordered enough to reflect back against the Atlantic City boardwalk, and Mac can't possibly hang them all. Whenever he drops one, they keep rolling away. They're surprisingly fast.

And there goes another one. Mac squats and bends down to pick it a disco ball that has rolled under a tall gurney. He puts his hand underneath the equipment to grab the mirrored ball. Something stopped the disco ball from rolling all the way to the back wall. Something solid. And cold.

Well, this is weird. Mac has just barely wrapped up this project, so he's still intimately aware of where everything is stored. Despite people coming and going with food deliveries and staff training sessions, he's done his best to keep everything organized the way it was intended.

It feels like metal. There's no reason for whatever it is to be crammed under the cabinet.

Mac pulls it out from underneath and closely examines it. He has no idea what the hell he's looking at.

At least two feet long, maybe eight or nine inches wide. It's made out of aluminum. That much he can tell. Probably weighs 20 pounds, give or take.

The tank is scuffed and dull, like it's been around for a while. There's a cap on top that's sealed tight.

A scuba diving tank? Nitrous chamber? Old WWII rocket? Not a chance. It has to be the missing time capsule.

Whatever it is, there's no way Mac is opening this thing without someone else looking at it first. He pulls out his phone and calls Kyle, who confirms he has no idea what it is.

"Take it with you. If it's oxygen, I don't need it blowing up my disco party," Kyle tells him over the phone without breaking stride. "I'm in the middle of an acupuncture appointment. I don't have the bandwidth to deal with any distractions right now."

"I'll take care of it." Mac replies and hangs up. Now what's he going to do with it?

The obvious age of the metal makes Mac think of Jim Trainor. This could definitely be his missing time capsule, or something else he'd recognize. Mac decides to walk over to the museum and ask him about it. Jim is usually there, killing time waiting for someone to stop by.

He's pretty sure, but if it's not the capsule, there's no way for Mac to tell if it's explosive. Or toxic. Better to have it looked at by a professional. Now. He doesn't want to risk it rolling around and blowing the place up.

It looks like he's going to miss his workout. Yet another delay, another hurdle to clear before he can ask Margo out.

Mac sighs. He's going to be late for the party, too. He'd better let his date know. Quinn gets angry when he's stood up.

Chapter 29

June 17

"Fourth & Bay is officially a success," Margo tells the owners, Kyle and Ryan.

"You like it?" Ryan asks. The pair are radiant as they greet guests in the wide-open arches, their disco sunglasses and wide-neck silk shirts showing off enviable tans and well-oiled skin.

They've been together since meeting at a house party. After more than ten years, they've established themselves as one of the area's power broker couples. This is their most ambitious bar and restaurant to date.

The disco ball wall has a line twenty deep of teens and tweens waiting to take their photo opps. The hashtag #bythebaybay is trending, rolling with the excitement of all the wannabe Instagram influencers posting their selfies. They're unreasonably excited to be attending the opening of anything new and fresh.

Fourth & Bay's owners recognized this and capitalized on it with captivating backdrops and fantastic drinks.

Margo can't help being happy for the pair, in spite of the headaches the pounding next door has caused her over the past few months.

She doesn't hold it against them. Any new business is good for Stone Harbor. So many new, smaller companies go under from the pressure of only making money three months out of the year.

Kyle and Ryan were thoughtful enough to send an invite to the entire staff of The Plank, in appreciation of their patience during construction. Most of the crew members accepted and are planning to attend tonight.

In keeping with the 70's disco theme, she's wearing a white halter jumpsuit and stacked golden heels. Glitter hoops and fringe bangs give her a Studio 54 vibe. She's promoting a set of wooden bangle bracelets she designed on her wrist. Carved to fit as one unit or worn alone, they're one of her best-selling items.

Even Tyson was persuaded to come to the soft opening. He's still being a bit standoffish, but after their night partying at the Princeton, they seem like they're on more even ground.

Tyson is wearing a pair of light blue shorts and a striped navy blue polo shirt. She hadn't been able to persuade him to wear anything else.

"I'm not wearing polyester. I don't care what the theme is." So that was the end of *that* discussion.

Eddie left an hour ago. He's picking up Tish and meeting them at Fourth & Bay. At least he committed to the party, wearing 70's-style striped trousers and an open-neck shirt. He actually seems excited to attend an opening night party. With people. And crowds.

She's never seen her older brother like this. It's exciting and alarming at the same time. Eddie has a history of never committing to anything or anyone. She wonders if that's about to change.

Margo really likes Tish. She's a hard worker, a good listener, and a talented aesthetician. This season, she brought the Plank into the rarefied world of a high-end spa. Their retail volume had more than doubled with the product line they now stocked, courtesy of Tish's recommendations.

Tish is thoughtful. She never makes a guest of the Plank feel bad about unhealthy habits – such as not washing their face – or feel like they'd gotten older and wrinkly. She always boosts the self-esteem of her clients. When someone else would be catty, Tish chooses to be kind.

She's fantastic. But is Eddie going to be a good match for Tish? Margo worries he'll grow bored with her, as he always does with the women he dates, and move on to a new town and another lover. Leaving her broken-hearted without any explanation.

It was a pattern he's had for more than a decade. Margo doesn't see it changing anytime soon. Which is a shame, really. But you can't change other people, she knows. You can only change your own reaction to them.

"Thank you, darling!" Kyle exclaims as he scoops Margo up for a warm hug. "You look like a young Bianca Jagger."

Ryan nods in agreement. "Sexy beast." He's not looking at her, though. He's staring at Tyson. She doesn't take offense. Tyson *is* hot.

Margo grins. "This place is simply amazing. I can't believe how different it looks." Especially since the last time she'd been in there when the framing wasn't even finished. And now there are pools of water. And fire. Who would have thought?

"You know we'll send all our overindulged clients over for an IV replenishment tomorrow morning," Kyle tells her. She doesn't say this isn't something the spa offers. They're all the rage at ski resorts and bachelorette parties for helping clients recover from heavy drinking the night before.

Kyle's too distracted to listen anyway. The line behind Margo is quickly growing, so she steps aside to allow the beaming owners to continue accepting congratulations from their newest fans.

Inside, the ceiling is a simulation of the night sky, juxtaposed with a bevy of hanging disco balls, a raving dance floor of dancers in 70's outfits, and an energetic DJ who looks like he's taken too big a dose of LSD. Margo's never seen anything like it.

The two-story foyer with glittering disco balls? A wall of fire blazing around the banquet tables? A cascading waterfall with fish and baby seahorses bobbing around in the pool below?

Incredible.

"Five minutes," Tyson's mouth is near her ear. "Then I'm out of here."

"Oh, give me a break. It will be fun. You can take a breather from the Salt Life," Margo teases. "It will be there when you get back."

Tyson shakes his head. "You know this isn't my scene. I'll get us drinks. Potentially doubles." He heads over to the bar, bobbing and weaving his tall frame through the crowd of excited partiers.

One couple is having a fabulous time. Margo spots Eddie and Tish doing the hustle on the dance floor. They're laughing as they point their fingers up and down, wiggling and dancing as they move with the crowd.

Eddie has a wide grin on his face, his eyes locked on Tish. He doesn't look anywhere else. He's completely focused on his dance partner.

Margo likes seeing him happy. Really happy. She can tell he is. She might have to revise her opinion about the future of these two lovebirds. This relationship could have some legs after all.

Tyson is waiting impatiently at the packed bar as oblivious guests order time-consuming cocktails. Margo knows it's one of his biggest pet peeves. He hates long lines, obnoxious people, and trendy drinks. So basically, he hates absolutely everything about this party.

Margo is not about to put down a sucker bet over how long he'll stick around. The only thing she has working for her is the fact that Tyson is loyal to the core. He won't leave her here alone unless she finds someone else to hang with… and then he'd be out the door as quickly as possible.

Speaking of other guests – where is Mac? This project was his baby. The reason she'd gotten off on the wrong foot with him in the first place. And he isn't anywhere to be found.

Margo recognizes a few people and gives friendly nods or brief hugs as she moves through the crowd. The majority of people there are strangers, guests of the owners who had come in for the opening night. Shoobies in their town, if just for the night. That's what they do.

The DJ starts spinning a remake of Blondie's *Heart of Glass*. He hasn't calmed down one bit, flailing around like a used car inflatable as he boogies to the beat.

More and more people are flooding the front entrance. Margo is bumped and jostled a few times.

Where have they all come from? It's still early. She wouldn't normally expect such a crowd.

Tyson is STILL waiting for a drink. She knows he's just about reaching his limit. It's already been at least 15 minutes.

Time to cut and run, as her grandfather taught her. She squeezes through a pack of young girls and slides her arm through her friend's.

"Let's do an Irish exit."

The look he gives her could melt butter. "Really? You're not fucking with me?"

"Yeah, let's go. This place is chaotic."

Tyson looks at Margo like she's his savior. "You don't have to tell me twice." He grabs her hand and pulls her out the back entrance, facing the backs of the stores on 96th Street. It's not even that dark out, and the line to get into Fourth & Bay is already extending around the block.

"Ugh, what a scene. Another ten minutes and I would have been trampled by a teenager asking for an Aperol Spritz." Tyson pauses and gives her a look. "What the hell's an Aperol Spritz?"

"Nothing you'd ever drink," Margo assures him.

"Yeah, figured that much. Want to grab a drink?"

"Since I'm wearing a disco jumpsuit, how about we go back to my place? I can change out of this thing. And I have cold beer."

"Now that I'd drink."

She rolls her eyes. As if she doesn't know. They'd been sneaking alcohol since they were going to high school parties on the beach back in the day. He had never and was never going to try a canned cocktail.

They casually walk back to the St. James house, ducking parents pushing strollers and groups of teens prowling the sidewalks. They're in no rush. Margo knows Tyson is just happy to be out of the crowded scene.

Eddie outfitted the dock with a new set of outdoor furniture. A low-slung chaise, a few comfy wicker chairs, and a wide coffee table offer a cozy setup. He bought the new outdoor set as soon as he cashed his first paycheck, in true Eddie style. Generous to a fault. Margo knows he can't keep a dollar in his pocket.

Nearly all the homes around the bay are occupied. They've sat unused all winter, waiting for their seasonal owners or weekly renters to return. Now they're lit up as hives of activity.

Lights on the nearby dock railings gently illuminate the water underneath, casting a soft glow in the night. Boats and kayaks are tied to the dock poles, bobbing gently with the calmer wake in the Snug Harbor Bay.

This is why Margo loves Stone Harbor. And will argue with anyone who doesn't believe it's not the most stunning spot in the world.

Margo hands Tyson an IPA and pours herself a glass of white wine. He settles down in one of the wide chairs. They sit for a bit in easy silence, each of them comfortable in the predictability of their friendship. She sprawls on the chaise.

Tyson shakes his head. "Oh my God, I couldn't wait to get out of there. The champagne wall. The disco balls. Those people."

"It was pretty over the top," Margo agrees as she sips her drink. "Eddie and Tish didn't seem to mind."

Tyson snorts. "Eddie would have fun in a fish tank."

"Pretty much. I think he and Tish might be getting serious."

"Eddie is never serious. He won't be here in October."

She begs to differ. "I don't know. This year, something's different. I think he's growing up."

"Our little boy." He smiles as he pulls from the can, his long legs sprawled out on the dock.

When had Tyson last gone out with anyone? She tries to think of his most recent girlfriend. He'd been with Ria for a while, but that ended a couple years ago. Margo never asked why. Their friendship didn't normally extend to deep confidences.

It isn't that Tyson is a bad listener. He's a great one. But he doesn't offer much in the way of advice, tending to pat her shoulder and tell her it will all work out. Or some other cliche that wasn't helpful at all.

Come to think of it, he never unburdens himself to Margo. She doesn't even know why he broke up with Ria in the first place.

"Whatever happened with Ria?" she asks innocently.

Tyson swivels towards Margo, his eyebrow raised. "What made you think of her?"

"I just realized you never tell me anything. Like who you're dating. Or *not* dating." She's suddenly beginning to notice their relationship is lopsided. "I have no idea what you even do on your days off."

Tyson nods to the marina. "I've got a regatta to get ready for. Couple of charters. I don't know." He shrugs his shoulders. "Stuff. Hell, why are you even asking?"

"I just feel like I don't know what you're dealing with. You never confide in me." She gets up and moves closer to his chair, touching his shoulder.

"What do you want me to say?"

"I don't know," she shrugs. "I heard you paid for the dinghy cover yourself. But you didn't tell me that. You never tell me things like that."

He's gone still. She doesn't know if she's offended him. "I'm sorry, I didn't mean…" She doesn't get to finish.

Tyson grabs her hand and pulls her down into his lap so quickly that she barely has time to react. They're suddenly at eye level. His dark brown eyes, those familiar eyes, focus on her face.

Margo flushes under his scrutiny. Is this happening? She knows that look. Can read his intent. And she's into it.

Kissing Tyson? It's worth finding out. She gives him an encouraging smile and he swoops in, finding her mouth and taking possession, his hands spanning her jawline. He opens his mouth and she joins him for a deeper kiss.

She had no idea he'd be such a good kisser. She shifts to give him better access and he wraps his arms around her waist.

Margo feels a sharp tug of desire as Tyson pulls her deeper onto his lap, his hands moving up and down her back in the thin polyester jumpsuit she hadn't had time to take off. *Oh God.* What's happening?

The thought of him unpeeling it on the dock is hot. He's already dipping those clever fingers in the deep V of her front.

Whoa. Margo can't catch her breath.

"Ty? Hey." Tyson is nuzzling her neck, nipping at the spot under her ear. "We need to slow down."

He shudders, then stops moving. His hands. Those glorious hands.

Tyson closes his eyes and rests his forehead on hers. Margo is still stretched across his lap. He's so suddenly sexy she doesn't want to take a break. But he does, pulling back to stop what's happening.

Confused, Margo pulls her halter top back into place and stands up, feeling the chill from the night wind whipping the water. What should she say? For once, she's at a loss for words.

The silence is deafening.

Tyson pushes up from his chair and looks at her, his familiar face looking foreign. She can't read his expression.

"I gotta go," Tyson tells her as he adjusts his navy polo shirt. It's one she's seen him wear a million times. It suddenly looks different. He suddenly looks different. Everything about him that was so familiar is now completely unknown to her.

"Wait. What happened? You can't just walk away after this. We need to talk about it." Margo wants to ask him if it was a one-off or if he has feelings for her, but she's afraid of the answer. She's on unsteady ground.

"I don't want to talk about it right now. Just give me some space." Tyson takes off down the dock without looking back.

Margo is left standing there watching him go. She wonders if everything between them has just changed forever.

Chapter 30

June 22

The Tuesday night Borough of Stone Harbor council meeting lasts as long as you would expect it would. They take more than 20 minutes to actually get started with the main agenda. After a call to order, the council's roll call, and a statement of notice, they salute the flag and approve the minutes from last month's meeting.

Mac is ready to topple over from exhaustion. He's been on job sites since 6 AM, checking the progress of the 53rd Street house project and reviewing design plans for two new restoration plans with Silas, his project manager. Then, he had two video calls with an architectural firm in Boston. After that, he spent a couple of hours paying invoices before another few hours returning emails he missed while he was on the road.

Now, he's sitting with Jim through a town council meeting to introduce the metal canister as "new business" to the council's monthly agenda. And trying desperately not to fall asleep while sitting up.

He'd gone straight from the museum to Jim's house with the metal canister from Fourth & Bay. It was worth it. Jim examined the metal object and immediately identified it as the missing time capsule.

How it had been taken from the building and ended up at the restaurant is still a mystery. One he and Jim are doing their best to solve.

Jim had been so excited about Mac's find that Mac hadn't been able to get back in time for the opening night party. After they talked about what could be in it for a good amount of time, the pair decided to store the capsule in a locked closet at one of Jim's friends' homes.

Mac ended up waiting at Jim's house while the amateur historian made calls to other museum volunteers and local history buffs.

Right now, Mac is propped up on a government chair listening to the monotonous list of proposed ordinances.

"Ordinance 1675…. The authorization of a new handicapped parking spot at…" a council member intones.

"Everyone in favor?"

"Aye."

"Aye."

"Motion passed."

How do people sign up for this? Why wasn't there any way to make it run quicker? More efficiently? Mac was going to fall out of his chair. Just curl up and die from sheer boredom and sleep deprivation.

He gives major credit to all the local government officials who have to go through this protocol for each proposal. He wouldn't be able to do it.

After what feels like hours and very well might be, it's *finally* time for new business. Mac and Jim approach the podium.

Jim is the museum liaison with the council, so he knows town protocol. Mac lets him take charge.

"Hi, everyone. Most of you know me. For those who don't, my name is Jim Trainor. I'm a volunteer at the Stone Harbor Museum and an architect at B.L. Wiley." He pauses. "I'm here with Lloyd MacIntyre, owner of the MacIntyre Development Group."

Mac sits up. Did Jim just say his first name? The one he's hid for decades?

He *despises* his name. Always has. Since first grade, he's insisted every teacher call him Mac instead. Even his parents agree it had been an awful decision to name him Lloyd.

How had Jim even found out? Research, most likely. It's what the man is good at. And he didn't even realize Mac never uses it.

Jim continues, oblivious to Mac's inner torture. "We're excited to announce we've found the recently missing time capsule from our town's past boardwalk-"

Someone interrupts. "Didn't we just find it? How did we lose it again?" asks one of the town council members. Burt Feldman. He looks confused.

"We did, yes. It was discovered in the attic of a recently sold home. But then we lost it."

"What home?" Burt asks.

"The former residence of the Bennett family. Mr. Bennett passed away a year ago, and his grandchildren put the home up for sale," Jim says patiently. "The new owners are demolishing it. When one of the contractors was getting rid of things before the teardown, they found the capsule."

"So, the Bennett family had it, but now they're gone. Then who keeps moving it?"

"We don't know," Jim answers.

"Odd thing to keep popping up," Burt mutters. "Someone should be more careful."

Mac interjects. "I'm pretty sure someone stole it. But it was located, and it hasn't been opened."

Tina Martinez leans forward into the mic on her desk. "It does seem strange," she agrees diplomatically. "But we're glad it was found. Now the question is, what are we going to do with it?"

Jim's been waiting for his turn to answer. "I think we should make it part of our 4th of July celebration. We'll open it right before the parade."

Mac can tell Burt doesn't like this suggestion. "How do we know what's in it? Could be dangerous. Could even blow up. The thing can't even stay in one place."

It's all Mac can do to keep a straight face. "It's a time capsule. Our forefathers put it together. I highly doubt it's a bomb."

Tina steps in again, thankfully, to smooth it over. "I think that's a fabulous idea. We discussed doing this before, and then it was taken. Now that it's turned up, let's go ahead with our original plan to open it up during the Fourth of July parade."

Jim nods. "I think that's a great idea."

"What if there's something in there that's dangerous, though?" Burt isn't backing off his concern about the canister's potential to explode.

"I don't think the former council members would decide to put together a time capsule that would injure our residents," Mac replies calmly.

Burt gives a humph. "Just saying."

Tina rescues them again. "I agree with Mac. Our history museum members confirmed this capsule. That's good enough for me."

"Where is it right now?" Burt asks. He's not letting this one go. "I just want to make sure I avoid that street for now."

"It's being held for safekeeping at a friend's house," Jim tells the council. "It's locked away and the only people who have access to it are Mac, me, and my friend who owns the home."

"That's good enough for me." Mayor Chloe looks around. "So, do we have a vote?

The other four council members nod their heads in agreement.

Mac is impressed by Mayor Chloe Shivo. She's guided the town council for the past few years, but he's never interacted with her much before. She gets five yeses and one no (if you guessed the no was from Burt, you were right).

"All right, it's been decided," the mayor says. "We'll have the time capsule opened in front of the town during the Fourth of July celebration. I think it's best to do it at the beginning of the parade."

Jim sighs in relief. "I'm just glad it's back in our hands. I'll make sure to keep a better eye on it in the future."

They sit back down in the general seating area. The council has several other new business ordinances to review and vote on. Mac figures they'll probably be at it for hours.

Mac has a new appreciation of the amount of time the council members devote to their town. He also has absolutely no interest in running for local government.

He leans to Jim and whispers, "So are we good?" He needs to get back to work. Or take a nap.

Jim nods. "We have the go-ahead. I'll run over to my friend's house now so he knows we're going to keep it locked up until the parade. We don't need to lose it again."

Mac laughs inaudibly. "Burt would have our heads."

They get up quietly and walk out of the Borough Hall on Second Avenue. "Thanks for all your help, Jim."

"Anytime."

Shaking hands, they say their goodbyes.

Mac has a feeling Jim won't be straying far from his friend's home until the July 4th celebration. Losing it one time is forgivable, but twice? Not as much.

He wonders if he should try calling Margo. Probably too late. He'll try to catch her at The Plank tomorrow.

She's already agreed to a date. He knows he missed her at the Fourth & Bay opening party, but he heard it had been really loud and crowded. Not the right place to get to know each other.

As soon as Mac gets back from the business conference next week, he's going to do something about it. Ask her out on a date. A real one. He can be romantic when he tries.

Chapter 31

June 25

If there was a hole big enough to climb in, Margo would have dug it. She does not want to go to work today. In fact, there's literally *nothing* she wants to do less.

For the past week, she's done her best to avoid both Tyson and Mac. It's been pretty successful. To be honest, it hasn't been that hard.

Tyson hasn't seemed interested in having any kind of conversation about what happened on the dock. Mac has been off-island at a meeting in the Chesapeake. He texted her and called once, but she hasn't seen him in person. Which has been a huge relief.

But now he's due back in town, which she knows means he'll be stopping by The Plank at some point in the next day or two. Her temporary reprieve will be over.

She rolls over in her bed, dragging a pillow across her face. Ugh. Anything to block the sun horribly shining through her curtains.

There's no one to confide in. Eddie is sleeping peacefully in the room next door. Then again, what's new? He always sleeps in.

She can't talk to her brother about it. He's known Tyson as long as she has. He won't want anything to do with being involved in the messiness of another person's relationship drama, especially one with his little sister and oldest friends.

Margo isn't even sure there's anything to talk about. Maybe Tyson had too many drinks. Or he hadn't gotten lucky in a while. Why else would he grab her and pull her down onto his lap? Kiss her like he couldn't do anything to stop it?

The look on his face had been needy. Longing. Sexy as hell. And then just like that, he shut her out.

The memory makes Margo's lips tingle. She'd had no idea he was such a good kisser. Five stars. Would highly recommend.

She hadn't seen it coming. Tyson has never been one to talk about what he's feeling. He's never given her solid advice when she's gone to him with problems. He never tells her what to do. He just listens.

Ty *is* great at sitting there and hearing her out. He's never turned her away or told her she was being melodramatic. He doesn't interrupt. He never dismisses her feelings.

The problem is, he doesn't share his own. Margo never has any idea what he's feeling. What Tyson meant. If he ever thought of her as anything but a little sister. Or that he was going to go in for the kiss.

She'd been completely taken by surprise. Honestly, Margo hadn't thought any chemistry existed between them until that night. But it did. Man, it did. There was a good chance she would have straddled him and let him have his way if she hadn't come to her senses and made them slow down.

What is she going to do now? Stone Harbor is too small a town to date two guys at the same time. It isn't her style anyway. She doesn't like seeing people get hurt. And she really isn't interested in being involved in situations that make her feel uneasy. Awkward. Guilt-ridden.

Not that Tyson even seems interested now.

The whole thing is a mess.

Her alarm clock goes off again. She's already hit snooze twice. Time to get up.

Slowly, agonizingly, Margo crawls out from under the covers. Her hair is a wreck from tossing and turning all night. She's barely gotten more than a few hours of sleep.

But who's going to open The Plank if she's not there? Liz will lose her mind. The Martinezes won't know what to do if their morning routine is thrown off. She has to go.

Defeated, Margo takes a quick shower and pulls on a semi-professional gym look of leggings and a tank with the Plank logo. She tosses a cropped zip-up over the outfit. Light blush, eyebrow tint, black mascara, and she's good to go.

Nope. She dashes back for undereye concealer. She doesn't need people commenting on how tired she looks.

The Plank is empty when she opens it up. At least no one's anxiously waiting for her to let them in.

Thursdays aren't big workout days. Margo has a little time to make an espresso at the café and log in to the system without being interrupted. She sits at the reception desk, checking messages and paperwork left behind by Chelsea the night before.

The caffeine kicks in. Okay, you can do this, she tells herself, rubbing her temples. You've done way worse.

Banksy strolls in a few minutes later, his dreadlocks swinging as he whistles happily. "Margo! I'm here to rotate a few machines out on the floor."

He's new, but he's one of her favorites. He's her most reliable and attentive employee, maintaining the fleet of workout machines and equipment in addition to repairing any mechanical issues that come up. He even notices and fixes small issues around The Plank before anyone else. What did she do before him?

"I didn't even realize that was something that needed to be done," she confesses. "You're amazing, Banksy."

"Happy to help. I was the co-owner of a gym back in Queens, so I have a general idea of what needs rotating out. You don't want your equipment to get too much wear and tear."

"Well, I'm glad you did. You're the best."

He smiles shyly. "It's been great working with you and with Tyson. And I've never seen such a beautiful shoreline before coming here."

The mention of Tyson's name makes her pause. "That's right, both of us." She almost asks if he's seen Tyson lately, but stops herself. That would sound strange. He'd wonder why she would be asking him about her childhood friend.

Liz the realtor strolls in, distracting her. Margo reaches out to scan Liz's key card and Banksy heads to the back of the gym.

"Morning, Liz!" Margo greets her brightly. Probably too eager for 7 am, but she's grateful for the rescue.

The rest of the morning is typical Plank. There's Kirby Martinez, here for another facial with Tish. Chris from the township, who will huff and puff on the treadmill for half an hour. A few guests on temporary day passes from the nearby hotels.

It keeps her busy and distracted from thinking too hard about what is happening in her life. Except for one thing.

Mac.

He's leaning across the desk, and she can't help noticing how buff his arms are looking. The regular workouts are certainly helping.

"I've been trying to ask you to dinner for weeks, and for some reason, it never pans out."

Margo's stomach drops. What should she say? "I know. There's always something standing in the way."

"Can we change that? How about next week? I'm open next weekend. Really, any day."

She doesn't know what to answer. It seems silly to say no based on something so fleeting. Tyson hasn't even tried to talk to her. Mac is the complete opposite – open and friendly, charming and talkative. He asks for what he wants instead of clamming up and freezing her out.

She says yes. It's a date.

She wonders why her stomach is still a mess after he leaves. But then she doesn't have to think about it anymore. A few more regulars walk in with special requests: bringing an extra guest to morning yoga, fixing a locker combination, or changing their training package to another kind.

By the time she's done, Margo's been so distracted she forgets to be nervous anymore.

Chapter 32

July 4

The official Fourth of July celebration and town parade is here! Jim has been anxiously waiting for this day to arrive.

They still have no idea who took the time capsule. He had to sit through repetitive interviews with Police Department Detective Nate Shroud, who was skeptical about the timeline of the missing time capsule. But he didn't have anything else to tell him. Jim has no clue who could have stolen it. Or why it had ended up in the restaurant.

Nate is barely a year out of the academy and actively trying to create more out of the timeline that Jim provided. The detective is young and eager. Jim wishes he could offer him some more to go on. They both know if Nate caught a break in the case, he'd become instantly and utterly famous.

Unfortunately, there isn't so much as a drop of evidence. The only fingerprints on the capsule were Mac's (which were on file due to an underage drinking incident in college). There's no security footage.

The previous owners of the home where the capsule had originally been found had passed away, and the new owners of the home have no clue how it came to be in their storage space.

The entire town is talking about it. Everyone wants to know if Quinn's accident, the sinking boats, and the damage to The Gables is related to the time capsule.

The Stone Harbor Museum hasn't seen this much foot traffic since opening day. Even though the capsule has been under secure lockdown at an undisclosed location, the museum volunteers created a pop-up exhibit about its discovery.

It's turned out to be extremely popular. Visitors stop by to take selfies in front of the model capsule. They also stop by a cardboard cutout of Taylor Swift, who got her start playing guitar at the since-closed *Henny's*. Who knew?

The Stone Harbor Museum Board of Directors couldn't be happier. They've never had so many visitors. There's talk of adding more activities for young kids, hosting cocktail and book club receptions, and even getting a blog post going. The opening of the time capsule is one of the most hotly anticipated dates of the season.

Mac leaves to retrieve the time capsule from Jim's friend, who kept it at his house after Mac found it at the restaurant. He checks it. Phew. All safe.

"I can't thank you enough," he tells the fellow history fan. They load the capsule in the car and drive down to the 82nd Street Pavilion.

Jim is coming from a different location, so he drove separately and is planning on meeting Mac there before the parade.

For the patriotic holiday, the town is hosting a sand sculpture contest, a home run derby, a candy scramble, and a bike parade. And then tonight, of course, the main event: fireworks. 7 Mile Island puts on a major fireworks display over the Atlantic Ocean.

All the borough council members are there. There will be plenty of photo opportunities for the big event. For once, it's not only the *Cape May Herald* and *Seven Mile Times* there. Philadelphia's NBC 10, 6 ABC, and Fox 29 news trucks are parked and ready for the opening ceremonies.

Mayor Shivo wraps up an interview with one of the reporters. Spotting Jim, she heads over to greet him. She looks sharp in a light pink blazer.

"I'm glad to see the time capsule is safe and sound. Thanks for taking such good care of it."

Jim smiles in response. "I don't know what I would have done with myself if we lost it again."

"I'd like you and Mac to say something before we have the opening ceremony." She looks around the crowd as it continues to grow. The turnout is impressive. Jim knows that as a politician, Mayor Shivo is happy to see it. It can only help with her reelection campaign.

"Have you seen Mac?" she asks.

"He's on his way with the time capsule. He said it's safe and sound."

"If he's not here in ten minutes, let's give him a call." The mayor isn't about to let anything go to chance. She strides off to make things happen.

Jim admires her competency; at the same time, he's completely intimidated by it. He makes sure to stay out of her path.

Mac arrives and delivers the capsule. Burt is standing at the very edge of the pavilion, eyeing the metal canister with suspicion. Jim has a feeling Burt won't be on the stage when they actually open it up.

Jim doesn't care. As an amateur historian, he almost can't believe that he's getting the opportunity to open something that's been hidden away for decades.

Tina and Rafael Martinez are there. Jim's never been a fan of Rafael. There's something bogus about him. Rafael is always agreeing with what someone says, not matter what they say. He takes both sides. And he repeats stories *over* and *over*, something Jim absolutely hates. Then there's the shady business of how he was forced to retire from the borough.

Still, Tina did get the council to vote in favor of today's event. *Have to give her that,* he thinks. He walks over to greet them politely. "Thanks again for supporting this," Jim tells Tina.

"We're excited to see what's inside. What house was it found in again? The Bennett family on 2nd Avenue. Do I remember that right?" From the look on her face, something is bothering her.

"Yes, if you mean the one on 2nd and 80th Street? They owned it for a few decades."

"Interesting." Tina's eyes narrow. She's definitely annoyed. "That house was owned by our daughter-in-law's family. Kirby grew up coming for the summers to visit her grandparents there. That's how she met our son, Jacob."

"What a coincidence!" Jim doesn't understand why the news is upsetting her. It seems like a good thing.

Tina nods. "They passed away recently. That's why the house was sold. Their kids couldn't agree on how to buy out each other's shares."

It's a common problem in this area. The houses grow in value so much that they become simply unaffordable when split between family members. Whoever wants to keep it can't afford to purchase shares from others. So, they either retain the home for summer rentals or put the house on the market so everyone gets an equal payout once it sells.

"Funny, she never mentioned it to us, though," Rafael tells them. "Finding the capsule."

Tina shakes her head. "Our son and daughter-in-law aren't on the best of terms right now. They're separated."

"But working on it," Rafael adds cheerfully.

Tina flicks her gaze to her husband. "Rafael, he won't even tell her where he's living now. And he's threatening her with full custody. I wouldn't say that's positive."

Jim doesn't know how to respond to this, so he smiles weakly. Family drama is out of his depth. "I'm sure it will work out," he says lamely. He's saved by spotting Mac arriving with the capsule. The man is his new hero.

Mayor Shivo must also think so, as she's hustling Mac up to the podium, which has been decorated with banners and flags.

It's getting more and more crowded. The entire Stone Harbor Borough Council, Police Chief, Stone Harbor Museum ancillaries, Fire Department, and VFW members are all assembled on the pavilion. Camera crews are filming while crowds of kids stand next to their parents.

There's even a clown. *A clown?* Jim's not going to ask.

The mayor motions for Jim to walk over to the mic. She already has a good grip on Mac. He's not going anywhere.

Mayor Shivo leans in and says, "Good afternoon, everyone. And happy Fourth of July! We're excited to welcome everyone to our town, especially this year as we celebrate more than 110 years of the seashore at its best."

Applause. A seasoned pro, she waits for it to die down before continuing.

"As many of you know, one of our generational families discovered a time capsule that was gathered together by Stone Harbor's town council many years ago. We decided to open it today, as we celebrate the birth of our nation."

More applause. She turns her head to Mac and Jim. "I'd like to introduce Jim Trainor from the Stone Harbor Museum and Lloyd MacIntyre of the MacIntyre Development Group."

Mac groans. Two decades of hiding his name for nothing. Thanks to this damn time capsule, which he hadn't ever wanted to be a part of, his secret is out. Thanks *Jim.*

Mac's done for. Now, everyone who's ever asked for his real name knows. And will never let him live it down. Not only was it said in front of a large audience, but it was also broadcast on the news.

No one will ever understand what made his parents name him Lloyd.

There's no time to dash off stage. He has a feeling Mayor Shivo would catch him anyway. The crowd has grown to a couple of hundred people. He plants a smile on his face and stays where he's told.

News cameras are rolling, phones are recording, and people are waiting for the big reveal. Mac just stands there like a sop, waiting for the action.

Wearing white fabric gloves, Jim gently lays the capsule down on the table next to the podium. The screw cap and gasket had already been unsealed by a team of helpers from Ace Hardware a few days before, but no one had looked inside (or so they told Jim). He wouldn't blame them if they had.

There's a hush over the crowd. Jim carefully reaches in with a set of pliers to pull the top item out. It's a thick roll of paper. There's no sign of water damage. He sets it down and looks inside again. Another roll. This looks like a newspaper.

Jim takes out the items and lays them carefully on the table next to them. There's a tall sheet of plastic to flatten and protect the rolled-up papers. The mayor, also wearing gloves, helps separate and lay out each one.

A metal object is at the bottom. A medal? It looks old, but then, of course, anything from this time would look old. It was stored away almost a century ago.

Another medal, this one less heavy but still substantial. A few photos, which he's excited to examine more carefully in a less public situation. And a railroad spike. He recognizes it instantly.

He peers into the canister. Everything's out, for the first time in decades. Jim walks over to the table. It's one of the most exciting moments in his life.

There are old editions of the *Cape May County Gazette* and *The Star*, former newspapers covering 7 Mile Island. An original bond from the Stone Harbor Railroad. The Stone Harbor Railroad cars were part of the Reading Railroad and Pennsylvania Railroad train systems, connecting passengers to Cape May Court House and other main shore points. Another bond, this one from the Risley brothers offering a free lot with the purchase of their "Beachfront Improvement" bonds.

Along with the bonds is a photo of the Reading Railroad Bridge, the first 96th Street bridge that was dedicated by then New Jersey Governor Woodrow Wilson before he became President.

The railroads were the reason out-of-town visitors to Stone Harbor were given the nickname "Shoobies." They would travel from Philadelphia and Camden on the trains, their lunches packed in shoeboxes, to enjoy the beach for the day. Tourists are still called "Shoobies" today.

It's not a compliment.

The first medal is a Victory Medal from World War I, given to servicemen after the war. The second is a Lifesaving Medal that was given to people who helped save sailors after their ships ran aground on the barrier island.

Faded photographs of former council members and the dedication of the Bower Memorial Pier, long gone after the hurricane destroyed the boardwalk and popular fishing dock. The first airmail flight in 1912, by a Wright Brothers plane, was between Ocean City and Stone Harbor. Pictures of the first lifeguard, Cleon Krause, as well as the first police officers and the volunteer fire department.

It's a treasure trove of the past. The value isn't monetary, but historical.

All the reporters are eating it up. You don't find a time capsule lying around every day. Or one that gets stolen and shows up weeks later.

Jim has a feeling it's going to be the final story for all the major newscasts that night. They like to end with a light-hearted, local news piece, and this one has plenty of heart and history.

He stops to talk to a few fellow residents, developers, and guests he knows. Now that the capsule is open, the mystery is gone, and so is their interest. They're all heading down to the fields to participate in 4th of July games.

Detective Shroud is standing nearby, eyeing the scene with interest. Jim is pretty sure he has zero leads. He doesn't envy the man.

"Are you ready to go?" he asks Mac, who nods gratefully. Jim has a feeling his mind is on other things. He keeps looking at the crowds for someone. Jim doesn't ask. He's just so happy with the way this day turned out.

Chapter 33

July 9

Things with Tyson have gotten worse. Margo hasn't seen him in weeks. He's avoiding her calls and texts. No response at all, not even a thumbs up emoji. When she asks Eddie, he shrugs and tells her Tyson must be busy. Eddie hasn't seen him around either, but he doesn't think anything of it.

Margo is beginning to think something between them has been irretrievably broken. Their connection was cut - the rope between two boats - and now they were adrift. Unable to be tied back together.

It's still so surreal and out of character that the scene had even taken place. Margo can barely wrap her head around the thought that she'd been about to sleep with one of her closest childhood friends.

Steady, uncomplicated, steadfast Tyson. The one who was with her through her teen angst years of high school crushes, petty arguments with her parents, and college admission anxiety. Who sat there and listened every time she had adult concerns over bills, worried about her art, or had drama with one of her friends.

Tyson has always been there. Never one to be the center of attention, but always in the fold.

And now he just… isn't.

Margo went to see the Fourth of July fireworks on the beach with Eddie and Tish last week. They were so adorable together that she didn't even mind hanging out with them. She noticed the little things Eddie did, like reaching for Tish's hand when a big firework went off or looking at her when they were having a conversation with other people.

Margo has never seen him like this. Hadn't even thought he could be like this; a devoted boyfriend who makes thoughtful gestures, picks up flowers, and remembers Tish's favorite ice cream flavor among the countless options at Springer's.

He's even doing his fair share of laundry. And waking up before noon.

It's been absolutely mind-boggling. Margo wishes her parents could see it for themselves, but they're not coming to visit until after Labor Day. She hopes it will last until then.

She's been pretty busy herself. Now that the hotel chandelier commission is back on the table, she's been working on it nearly every night after work. It's taking a huge chunk of her time. She's poured her heart into it.

Every little piece is being hand-carved and polished, then integrated together. She's trying not to use any hardware unless it's necessary. All tongue and groove connections. It's back-breaking work, but it's finally coming together. It's going to be her greatest piece of art yet.

It's finally Friday, and she's giving herself the night off. She's finally going out with Mac. Or rather, staying in. They're having dinner at his place in Cape May. Who knew he cooked? She's hoping to discover more about him after seeing where he lives.

The number of guests at the gym is slowly dwindling. The weekend is almost here, summer is halfway over, and clients have lost some of their willpower to work out regularly.

Hank pops in to say goodbye. "I'll be back bright and early Monday for my morning training sessions," he tells her. Hank and his husband are in a competitive pickleball league that travels around on the weekends. "You're sure you don't want to join?"

He's tried to get Margo into it multiple times with zero success. "You know I have no interest in team sports," she says with a laugh.

Chelsea left hours ago for a music festival in South Jersey. Something else Margo has little interest in. She doesn't like crowds or long lines of traffic.

Tish had her last client at 3 pm and left soon after, making sure she checked to see if Margo needed anything. Considerate to a fault.

And who knows where Tony is? Probably making out with a client somewhere.

Finally, the clock hits six, and she locks up and heads back to her place to change. She picks out a strappy white tank and colorful palazzo pants. A mix of casual and dressy.

It's about half an hour (with shore traffic) to Mac's house in Cape May. Margo pulls into his driveway and takes a moment to stare at the home. It's a stunning two-story historic home with a wraparound porch. Way too big for a single guy. She wonders what the backstory is. Did he use to live here with someone else? Have roommates?

Curiosity piqued; she rings the doorbell. Mac answers right away.

He seems nervous. "Wow, you look great," he says to her. He steps to the side and welcomes her in.

Margo takes a step into the foyer. It's even larger than she realized. There's a wide wooden staircase that makes a sharp left on its way to the second floor. He's added a dark wooden table with blue and white porcelain vases. Sconce lights add soft lighting. To her right is a dining area, and to her left is a living room that looks comfortable and well lived-in.

The house has a relaxed coastal vibe. The walls are mostly white, with brick accents and light oak floors. The rooms are a mix of faded rugs, comfortable couches, and traditional antiques. Some of them are family heirlooms from Newburyport; others are pieces he tells her he picked up from estate sales and former clients. His sisters had hung all the art.

"I still need to redo my yard and the patio in the back. It's a work in progress," he says.

"I'd imagine it is. Why don't you show me around? I'd love a glass of wine," she says, taking control of the date.

He leads her to the open kitchen and family room layout, which takes up the rear of the house. It looks bigger than it is, thanks to the row of glass doors opening to the outdoor patio area.

Mac tells her he splurged on tall cabinets with a second set of panel glass fronts on top of the wooden doors, along with wide crown moldings. A double-wide Aga oven that the previous owners bought is centered along the wall of cabinets.

In the middle, a pale green island is as large as the space will allow. "I need a lot of seats for my nieces and nephews to sit at when they're in town," Mac explains.

"Mm hmm," she murmurs non-committedly. She's too distracted with her mission to check everything out. See what kind of guy he is. Who would have guessed she was so nosy?

On the opposite side, low couches with thick striped throw pillows and a set of white fabric chairs flank a wide, light coffee table. There's a fireplace with bookcases on either side. They're filled with books and framed black and white photos.

Margo wanders over to look at the book spines. American history, architecture, and a good amount of World War II books. A lot of non-fiction works, but there are also novels by a range of authors, from Gabriel Garcia Marquez and Mark Twain to John Grisham. There's even a few Elin Hildebrand, the queen of the beach read. Some poetry and a few classics. An eclectic collection.

She sees something and stops in her tracks. There's an intricately carved wooden osprey on the mantle. It's made of Western white pine to mimic the feathers in its tail.

Margo turns around. "Where did you get this?"

Mac shrugs. "Some store in Cape May. I liked the look of him. He's got a personality."

"I carved this," she responds. "Its long beak gave me the most trouble, and of course, the wobbly legs it stands on." Then she gives him a huge smile.

This is her sign. To be with Mac.

He's standing in the kitchen, over by the counter. His hands are resting on his hips. She slowly walks over to where he's standing.

"I didn't realize. I guess I really like your work," he says as he gently brushes a strand of hair off her cheek.

He looks down – he has at least four inches on her – and stares into her eyes. He's waiting for her to make a decision. To decide on them.

It doesn't take long. Margo puts a hand behind his neck and pulls his head down to her level. Their lips are inches apart. She feels his breath. It's starting to become uneven as he takes in air.

Her lips curve. "I think dinner can wait. Want to show me the rest of your place?"

"Do you want the grand tour?"

"No," she says decisively. "Just your room."

Before she moves, Mac has her pressed against the wall. She arches back, giving him better access to her neck. His mouth moves to her ear, then across her cheek, before he finds her mouth.

Margo runs her hands up his neck and tugs at his hair. She pulls harder.

Mac nudges her legs so he's wedged between them, pressing against her. She feels him getting hard, which turns her on even more. Margo presses into him. Grabbing her wrist, he pulls her arms up and pins them against the wall. The whole time, he is doing incredible things to the spot below her ear.

Margo can barely think. He's all over her, his hands roaming and dipping, giving and getting.

"Whatever you're doing, don't stop," she begs.

"I don't plan to." Taking Margo's hand, Mac leads her up the stairs to the last door in the hallway, the master bedroom.

Margo pulls her shirt over her head and she's standing there in a light purple lace bra that sets off her lean, tanned skin. Her hair is highlighted from the sun. It's still light enough that some sun is shining through the window.

"My golden girl," he says.

Hardly able to believe his luck, he cups her breasts and pulls her to his chest. She helps him pull off his shirt. It's not easy, since he can't stop kissing her mouth.

Flames mount as Margo shimmies out of her pants, then pulls down his shorts. They're skin to skin. Warm and wet, hot and bothered, licking and tasting.

They fall down to the bed. She opens for him, and he slides into her, picking up the pace until they're both breathless and sweaty.

They're in too much of a hurry to slow back down. When she comes, it's with a deep and throaty moan that's so sexy Mac can't stop himself from falling over the brink with her.

When they finish, he rolls over to give her time to catch her breath. She's practically purring, stretching her back as she lies on his sheets, naked.

"That was incredible," Mac tells her.

"Mmmmm hmmm." Margo curls up to his side and he extends his arm so she can lay in the crook of his shoulder. "Why did we wait so long?"

"I still owe you dinner. Can you stay?" It seems like he doesn't want her to leave, to break the magic. Go back into the real world where everyone seems to get in the way.

"I have the day off tomorrow. I can stay."

Content, he pulls her closer. She fits.

They both smile.

Chapter 34

July 12

This past month has to be one of the hardest times Sabrina has ever gone through. Her father is so angry that he's barely speaking to her. She doesn't talk to her two older brothers often, so he's the only close family member that she has left.

She doesn't return their phone calls or answer many of their texts. What's the point? They don't have much in common.

Her siblings are much older and live on the West Coast. Both of them are *obsessed* with their families. It's so annoying to hear their stories about things she cares nothing about: potty training, teething, or spring sports.

Who cares?

She has bigger issues to deal with, anyway. They wouldn't understand. The situation has gone completely out of control, and now she's dealing with the repercussions. She shouldn't have made her anger and animosity so obvious to everyone involved. It had been a big mistake.

Of course, Mac would realize she was the one who made the phone calls to mess with his business. He'd just broken up with her. And with Margo, she shouldn't have used her real name when she called the accountant.

She'd been so pissed off that she hadn't thought straight. It was dumb of her; she has to admit. But she's learned her lesson. She won't be making those mistakes again.

She's Sabrina Elliot. She can turn this around. And she knows just how to do it.

Looking down, Sabrina realizes her drink is nearly empty. She frowns. Their servers should be better than this. She's not going to have to track down one of the pool boys to get a drink, is she? Wave them over like she's at a motel chain? This is the Seven Mile Hotel. They should know how to anticipate her needs.

She's been so busy working *around the clock* as her punishment that she'd decided to escape purgatory and take a break. In her opinion, they have the chicest poolside hotel situation of any spot on the island. Laid out in white travertine marble with a pool shelf for lounging, it's surrounded by custom cabanas that can be rented for the day.

Sabrina spotted an open cabana at lunchtime and helped herself to it, along with her cocktail. She requested a poolside massage and a scalp facial. No food. She doesn't eat. But she could really use another drink.

One of the pool servers walks past. What luck. It's Benjamin! She knows him well.

"Yoo hoo!" she calls out. "Benjamin!" He turns at the sound of her voice and heads over to her spot.

"Hi Ms. Elliot," he says bashfully. He's such a doll. Her favorite employee. The only one who actually listens to her.

"Could you be a dear and get me another drink? And see where my masseuse is?"

He's so sweet. Just graduated from college and filling in gaps at the hotel as a porter, valet attendant, and waiter. Benjamin always does whatever she asks of him. And that means *anything*.

"I'll see to it," he answers Sabrina, dashing into the lobby to get her the care she needs.

Sabrina sighs happily and settles back into her chaise. This is more like it. She feels better already.

Chapter 35

July 17

Any beach day is a good beach day. The weather is gorgeous: high 70's with a nice ocean breeze pushing off the early morning humidity. Bright and sunny, with just a hint of cloud cover. The perfect kind of day for a group of friends to spend the day at the beach.

Want to go to the beach?

Eddie starts a text conversation with a group of friends to get together by the 80th Street beach entrance. There's plenty of parking, and when they eventually decide to come off the sand for a drink, the Icona Windrift restaurant and bar is right there waiting. With multiple levels of indoor and outdoor bars and dining areas, it has enough space to accommodate their whole crew.

The initial text string has grown and expanded to a group of more than 20 friends. Margo recognizes most of the names in the thread. She invites Mac. She hasn't seen him since their date, although they have sent flirty texts with plenty of innuendos.

I won't be able to make it, Mac texts. *One of my high school friends is getting married back home in Newburyport.*

Well, she tried. Now, she's going to enjoy the weekend and a perfect beach day with her friends. She packs a cooler with gourmet food: mozzarella, basil, and tomato ciabatta sandwiches; grilled chicken and smoked gouda pasta salad; frozen watermelon; bags of chips; and cans of beer and spiked seltzers.

Eddie brings his bocce set because he always plays bocce on the sand. She used to find it annoying, and now she finds it nostalgic.

On the way to the beach, they pick up Tish, who jumps into Margo's car with a huge beach bag that takes up most of the back seat. She's wearing a wide, floppy hat and a bright cover-up.

"I can't believe it's mid-July and I'm finally going to my first beach bash!" Tish exclaims. Her excitement is endearing. Margo still can't get over how much Tish has changed in just a couple of months.

Everyone Eddie texted must have had the same idea to invite more people. There must be thirty or forty of their crew on the beach. It's a mix of local surfers, bartenders and servers, retail workers, and other people who keep the town running during the season.

She's not surprised. Eddie put the party together. He has a knack for knowing just about everyone in the industry.

The group sets up chairs arranged in a wide half-circle facing the ocean. Someone has a portable speaker. Margo gratefully accepts a drink and casually pops it open. The sun is shining brightly, guaranteeing cases of sunburn to anyone not piling on the sunscreen.

It's freaking perfect. Exactly what she needed.

Margo recognizes a few friends from grade school that she hasn't seen in years. Some are back home on vacation or living with their families for a few weeks of the best season of the year.

"Margo! Come sit with me," her childhood friend Melanie calls out as she offers Margo a chair. Melanie is sitting with Andrew and Liam, who she adores. They were two of the funniest and friendliest guys from their class.

Margo sits with them to catch up. The stories grow more and more outrageous as the drinks flow.

"Stop! Stop!" She yells, laughing. She can't handle it anymore. They were discussing all their adventures over their summers in high school. Some of it she doesn't believe.

"That never happened," Margo answers.

"It's absolutely true," Andrew says as he takes a long pull from his drink. "You weren't there to see it. You were always off somewhere with Tyson."

"She usually was," Melanie agrees. "You guys were always together. Speaking of, where is Tyson today?" She looks around.

Margo shrugs nonchalantly. "I have no clue."

Her comment is met with skepticism. "You guys always come in a package. What's wrong? Did something happen?"

Margo feels her cheeks flushing. She has no poker face. "Nothing. I just don't know where he is today." To deflect, she takes a sip from the can she's holding. "We don't keep tabs on each other."

Melanie and both guys nod, although they don't look convinced. A few more people join their group, and the rest of the afternoon and early evening is spent jumping in the ocean, moving chairs around, and yes, even playing bocce.

Around six, a group decision is made to head to the Windrift to grab some tables and listen to an acoustic guitar player. Margo has a pleasant buzz as she sits at one of the high-top tables. Melanie is dancing at the front by the stage with some of the other people they came with. Margo met them but can't remember their names anymore.

It doesn't matter. Everyone is happy; everyone is friendly. Eddie has officially introduced Tish as his girlfriend, to a lot of good-natured ribbing. Margo thinks this is the first time Eddie has ever put a label on a relationship.

Margo's phone buzzes on the towel, and she reaches down to check it. A text from Mac: *Hope you're having a great beach day. Really wishing you were here with me instead.*

Smiling, she's about to respond when she notices Tyson. He's at one of the tables further away from her, doing that back-slapping thumping thing with Liam that guys do. It's never made any sense to her.

Margo is so taken by surprise to see him that she doesn't know how to react. She just freezes as she watches him smiling and talking with the guys.

Did Tyson get better looking?

The past few weeks have been one of the longest stretches of time that Margo and Tyson have ever been apart. Now, as she stares at him, he looks familiar and yet different at the same time. His summer tan is in full effect, and his hair has grown longer. Margo is usually the one to remind him to cut it.

She doesn't know what to do. Should she approach him? Wait for him to spot her? What if he doesn't, and then she misses her chance to talk to him? This is so *frustrating.*

Margo is standing there frozen, holding her phone in mid-text and watching him chat it up with the guys, when he lifts his head and makes eye contact. She can tell from the look on Tyson's face that he knew she was there the whole time.

Tyson doesn't look angry. Or frustrated with the situation between them. Did Margo say that she was? *Because she really was.*

She doesn't send Mac the text he's probably waiting for. She's too busy eyeing Tyson.

A couple of minutes pass – it feels like hours – and he makes his way over to her table. In what may go down as one of the most awkward hugs in the history of mankind, Tyson leans forward and gives her a soft pat on the back.

"Hey," he says quietly.

Margo looks up at him. "Hey, yourself. It's been a while."

"I know." Tyson's face is unreadable. *What* does he know?

"I miss you," she says quietly.

Tyson sighs. "I'm sorry. Things just got weird. I needed some space."

She takes a deep drink from her hard seltzer. Anything to keep her hands busy. "Do you still need space?" she asks, though she's not sure what she'll do if he says yes.

"No, Margo. I'm good. We're good."

"Can we talk about it?" He never wants to talk about anything. She puts her hand on his arm.

"There's nothing to say. It's all good." Tyson looks at the singer wailing away. "Who is this guy? He's flat."

She laughs. This is so awkward. "Yeah, he is." She doesn't know what else to say.

Eddie walks over and puts an arm around Tyson. The moment is over. They stay there for a while, having drinks and listening to the out-of-tune acoustic guitar player belting out *Don't Stop Believing* and *Brown-Eyed Girl*. He's so terrible that it lightens the mood.

Everyone decides to head to The Princeton, sandy suits and all. In the mob of people, Margo gets separated from Tyson. There are just too many of them, and The Princeton is packed.

She never gets a chance to be next to him again. Eddie and Tish invite her to have a pizza with them before grabbing their car and heading home.

The next day, Margo wakes up wondering what else she could have said. Something better than the lame words that came out of her mouth. And if last night meant they were friends again.

She also has to wonder if Tyson possibly wanted more. With her. More than friendship.

Which was silly, because she's dating Mac. Right?

That's when she realizes she never even responded to his text.

Chapter 36

Today is the Stone Harbor Triathlon, a day when the super athletic residents of Seven Mile Island challenge themselves to a quarter-mile open-water swim, 11-mile bike ride, and 5K run. It's been held for more than 20 years.

Early Sunday morning, Quinn and other volunteers are putting down cones and road barriers along the bike and run course. It's super early. The majority of the prospective triathletes have already picked up their race bibs the night before at the firehouse, but a few early risers should be arriving to pick them up between 5:30 and 6:30 AM.

The swimming portion will take place first, in the Snug Harbor bay area surrounding the yacht club. Then, the triathletes will bike three loops on Second Avenue before switching over and running back along First Avenue, the beach block.

The race sells out each year, which boggles Quinn's mind. Who knew 350 people wanted to get up at the crack of dawn on a Sunday morning to push themselves to the limit?

Not Quinn. He's only doing this shift for overtime. Their crew of police, fire, and EMT members can pick up some extra money during the race. And all the proceeds from the event support the Stone Harbor Volunteer Fire and Rescue Squads, so it's a win-win.

Quinn's on 122nd Street and Second Avenue, the southernmost part of the island and halfway point of the race, when he notices something missing.

Up here on the Point, where the houses fade away and the dunes come into focus, the large electronic billboard timer is gone. The timer is critical for the triathletes to see where they are in the race, especially as they make the turn for their next lap.

Maybe someone forgot to haul it up to the parking lot? The huge piece of equipment isn't anywhere to be found.

He saw the other timer earlier at the club, over by the start (and end) of the race. But there's nothing here, on the other end of the island.

He figures it must have been an oversight, so he takes out his walkie-talkie and calls headquarters. The race organizers have been doing this long enough that missing something so vital to the triathlon seems out of character.

Nick Romanski is in charge of the event. He's usually competent, calm, and reliable. When Quinn gets him on the line, though, Nick panics.

"What do you mean, the timer isn't up there?" he yells. "We installed it last night!"

"I'm not seeing anything. I can't imagine it could have gone far." The thing has to be nine or ten feet tall. It isn't hiding behind a bush.

"I'll be right there," Nick replies. "Over."

122nd Street ends abruptly, with a guardrail to turn bikers around. On the other side of the guardrail is a parking lot where visitors park their cars and bikes before going on a walk up the Point.

Curious, Quinn walks around the lot to see if he missed anything.

With no overnight parking, the lot is mostly empty. It isn't hard to do a quick scan and see that the timer isn't there. Takes two seconds. It's not on the street either.

With nothing else to do, Quinn wanders over to the beach ramp and crosses the sand towards the ocean.

And there it is. Lying on its side, just past the post railings. It's been pushed over onto its side, but it's still intact. Quinn breathes a sigh of relief. This is salvageable.

There's no way he can move it by himself, though. Within a few minutes, Nick pulls up in a truck. Quinn trots over.

"Good news is I found it. The bad news is that it's been knocked over. And the wheels are in the sand."

"Lucky there's two of us," Nick answers. See? Competent.

Quinn sighs as he walks back with Nick to the beachfront entrance. There's no one there this early in the morning, so Nick lets some of the air out of his tires, and they slowly drive the truck onto the sand.

In less than ten minutes, they have the timer up and loaded on the truck's bed. They back up, steadily driving backward down the ramp they'd just come up.

Panting heavily, Quinn and Nick move the timer onto the pavement of the Second Avenue turnaround lane. Then comes the moment of truth: will it actually work?

Nick sets it up and switches it on. Miraculously, the thing is still operational. It's solar powered, so it's been getting plenty of charge.

Quinn breathes a sigh of relief and pats Nick on the back. "We got lucky."

"Yeah," Nick agrees, although his eyes are narrowed. "But what kind of asshole did this in the first place?"

The heat from the boats and break-in has fallen off, since nothing else has happened, and the police never identified any suspects. Even the time capsule is back at the museum. They were all feeling safe again. But now there's this.

Could it be a bunch of teenagers fooling around? Or is it the same person who trashed the store and damaged the sailboats? How can anyone tell?

"Are there cameras up here?" Quinn asks.

Nick shakes his head. "None that I know of. We could check to see if anyone caught it on their home security systems."

"Let's do that. I'm getting tired of cleaning up after this guy."

Nick radios back to the yacht club headquarters to let them know they're back in action. It's only 6:30 AM, but Quinn feels like he's already put in a full day.

"I better call Detective Shroud to let him know about the latest."

"You think it's connected to the other things that happened?" he asks.

"It definitely could be." Quinn is now wishing he hadn't put his hand prints all over the aluminum posts, ruining the evidence. But what was his other option? They have to make sure the race could go off.

Quinn is going to see that the police department steps it up a notch. They don't need one more incident.

Quinn jumps into Nick's truck, and they slowly drive back to the starting line. There, he's given high fives and pats on the back by the race organizers, who would have been in trouble if the triathlon didn't go as planned. He and Nick accept the praise, as well as the jokes that go along with it. It's all in good fun.

Inside, though, Quinn is getting more and more angry at whoever the culprit could be. He hopes he's there when they find out who's causing all this chaos. Because Quinn is really getting sick of this shit. And he will make sure whoever is doing it is held accountable for what they've done.

Chapter 37

July 27

Mac is in the discussion and planning stages of two historic home renovation projects – one in Cape May and one in Spring Lake – where he's ready to start ordering materials and doing demo work.

He can't nail down a date to begin the projects, though. The house on 53rd Street is taking twice as long as it should have to wrap up.

Any idea why? If you guessed Sabrina Elliot, you were right.

She's driving everyone crazy. They'll have a room almost finished: lighting installed, trim painted, even the wallpaper is hung. And then, she'll change her mind. Show up with a completely different "mood board" that brings them back to square one. They have to rip everything up, order new materials, and start all over.

Sabrina doesn't compromise either. If Mac tells her his team has already installed the custom bunk beds in the room and painted them light blue, she doesn't give a damn. She makes them tear them out and build a different configuration.

Custom. Bunk. Beds.

They take five days to build. That's a whole week they're now behind schedule.

Yesterday, his flooring guys almost threw her out of the house when she tried getting them to redo the kitchen floor. After the cabinets were in place and the radiant heating floor was installed underneath the tile. That's right, she decided wood planks were better after they had already put in custom tile. Three hundred square feet of it.

His guys are fed up. And it's starting to cost him a lot of money in overtime, which Mac doesn't want to pass on to his client. Even if she has the money to pay for it, it's not the right thing to do. He has a reputation to uphold.

Still, it's time to make a move. Things keep getting worse. So, against his will, Mac makes a call to his client's manager, Lucky. Everything goes through Lucky.

The homeowner of 53rd Street is so famous that she can't be reached without going through a representative. He knows they're in Europe, so he makes the call early Tuesday morning and leaves a message.

Mac waits for a call back. Two hours later, he gets on a Zoom call with Lucky, where he reviews all the changes and delays with the manager. Even on the computer screen, Lucky is intimidating.

"I'm trying to work with all the changes your client gave Sabrina, but it's going to delay the project by a few weeks, at minimum," Mac says.

"What changes?" Lucky asks as he chews on the end of a cigar. "She's been happy with everything you guys agreed to do."

Mac goes over the list. "Wood planks over the custom tile pattern? New bunk beds? Ripping out the recently hung wallpaper in the music room?"

Lucky blows his lid. "Are you crazy? That designer was only called in to add decorative accents to the home and pool house. She's not supposed to mess with any of the woodwork, electric, or plumbing. And definitely not that wallpaper."

"Damn it," Mac answers. "I should have known." Sabrina was clearly enjoying making their lives miserable.

"My client really likes the birds in that wallpaper," Lucky continues as he takes the cigar in and out of his mouth. "You better not have taken it down." The threat in his voice makes Mac uneasy.

"No, no," Mac reassures Lucky. "We haven't touched the wallpaper." He grabs his phone and holds it under his desk to stealthily text his foreman, Silas to stop work immediately.

"I don't like this," Lucky says. "We let her in as a favor on behalf of her father. I know Roger from way back. But his daughter is bad news."

Mac is visibly sweating but trying to appear calm. *Please respond, Silas,* he thinks.

Lucky stares at Mac without speaking. For such a sweet name, he's a terrifying guy. Mac can see the background of their luxurious hotel suite as he gets reamed out by his client's manager.

"If she finds her birds damaged, I'm going to have to take you out back for a talk," Lucky tells him. "It reminds her of her tour in Brazil. The birds. Parrots."

Mac feels like he's in the middle of a mob movie. He's assuring Lucky that everything is back on track when SHE suddenly appears and walks over to the camera. She's as stunning on a Zoom call as she is on magazine covers. Mac holds his breath. He hadn't expected to actually talk to her.

"Oh Lucky, give him a break. It isn't his fault," she says in a *sotto voice.* "We're going to have to fire the designer. I'll get one of ours from the penthouse remodel to go down and finish up."

Mac gives her the sappiest grin. There's no way he can help it. He's a big fan. Huge. "Thanks a million," Mac says. "If we can keep moving forward with the original plan, we should be done in a few weeks."

"That sounds great. I can't wait to see it." And she flits off camera.

Lucky glowers but nods. "You dodged a bullet with this one."

Mac wants to say, "Did you mean I got *lucky*?" but he doesn't dare. The call had gone much better than he'd hoped. He should have handled the situation earlier, instead of letting things get to the point where he was risking losing Silas and his crew. And then where would he be? He owes them an apology.

Silas had responded that the wallpaper was still up. Mac shuts down his laptop and gets in his car to drive to the job site. It's time to fire Sabrina from the project. He wonders if 8 AM is too early for tequila.

Mac checks in at the gate house and goes up the steep drive to see the house humming with contractors. Cowardly, he's relieved not to see Sabrina's Porsche there. It gives him time to tell the guys the news (to much applause) and stop any more Sabrina-sanctioned work from getting started.

Everyone is suddenly in a good mood. Mac hasn't realized how much of a drain she's placed on his crew. It's something he should have recognized earlier.

Lively music is now playing on paint-splattered speakers as the team moves efficiently throughout the house. One of his crew members is even whistling, and the guy *never* whistles.

They're all chugging along, even humming as they get shit done, when Sabrina appears. She's in another one of her getup's: fancy blazer, silk tank, high-waisted white linen shorts with espadrilles.

She saunters into the front hallway with its three-story sweeping staircase and bank of windows. Her arms are loaded with idea books, mood boards, and fabric samples. Mac can tell she has a long list of things to redo.

He can't believe he used to sleep with her.

It's time for his second confrontation of the day, and it isn't even lunchtime.

Mac walks up to Sabrina and gives her an encouraging smile. "Can we talk?"

She frowns. "Mac, I don't have time for you today. I have a list of things we need to change." As if he's the one holding the job up. She's too much.

"I think it's worth your time." Mac looks behind him. The entire team has stopped working and is avidly watching their interaction. "Please," he adds.

"Oh, fine," Sabrina grumbles. "Five minutes."

Mac leads her into the butler's pantry. It's one of the more private spots in this house that's always teeming with carpenters, electricians, and painters.

"The homeowner has terminated your contract," Mac tells her. He's trying not to look like he's enjoying it. Keep it professional.

Sabrina raises an eyebrow.

The crew hears her scream, then Mac yells. He says something they can't catch, but it sounds like he's in pain.

Nobody moves.

A moment later, she storms out of the pantry. She's heaving so hard that all the men scatter.

"Fuck you and fuck this place!" Sabrina yells. "I was only doing it as a favor. You guys don't know what you're doing. I can't wait to see how badly you fail."

She crosses the foyer and flings open the front door. One of her binders falls, but she doesn't pause to pick it up.

"You'll regret this!" Sabrina shouts again. As if they didn't hear the first time. Then she's gone.

Silas goes to check on Mac. Make sure he's still alive. Breathing.

He walks back to the pantry area, where Sabrina had most likely gutted her victim. He finds Mac at one of the island's double sinks, rinsing his arm under the water.

"You okay?"

Mac sighs as he dabs at his arm. "Yeah, I'm fine. She just scratched me a little." He waves his hand towards the direction of the pantry. "She broke a window, too. She was trying to hit me, but missed and hit the glass instead."

"We'll take care of it," Silas assures Mac. He looks down at Mac's bloody arm. "Man, she has a temper."

"I know," Mac answers with a sigh. "She always has."

Chapter 38

July 29

Chelsea is having so much fun at the front desk that she doesn't even want to leave for college in a few weeks. This is *way* more interesting than her sorority mixers.

There's so much to talk about right now in Stone Harbor. It's a virtual treasure trove of gossip items, ranging from the stolen (misplaced?) triathlon timer to Sabrina Elliot's dramatic firing. Who would have thought that was possible?

Eddie St. James has a serious girlfriend, for the first time anyone can remember. Kirby Bennett and Jacob Martinez have been separated since last year and are on the path to divorce. Tony is still sleeping around with married women (no one's surprised by this).

Liz the realtor just sold an $18 million dollar home on the island. And it wasn't even beachfront! Prices have gotten out of hand, but every homeowner is thrilled at the bump in their property values.

It's one of the best summers so far. Absolutely scrumptious. Different sides are being taken with each person's story. Some feel bad for one party, some are happy to see another getting their just dues. It all depends on who you talk to.

Each day, Chelsea gets to see Margo, Tish, Hank, Tony, and their gym regulars walk in the door. She knows who is willing to gossip (Liz) and who keeps a tight ship (Hank and Tina). Personally, Chelsea is happy to talk to anyone.

There's still a full month left until Labor Day. In her opinion, anything could happen.

Chelsea is simultaneously scanning a key card and looking for a water bottle in Lost & Found when a big man walks in. He must be six foot four and well over 250 pounds. She's never seen him before.

He's positively brimming with angry energy. She can totally tell by the sight of his tight jaw and the way he clenches his fists.

"Hi," Chelsea says brightly. "How can I help you?" This is exciting. He's not wearing workout clothes, and he doesn't seem like the type to go for a lavender facial. Not with that shaggy beard. She wonders what he's so *mad* about.

The man doesn't answer her. He just stands there, his narrowed eyes scanning the front area. A few people are having drinks in the café. Nothing interesting to see there.

Chelsea tilts her head and tries again. "Are you interested in a Plank membership?"

"No," he finally answers brusquely. Okay, so he's definitely not here for a skin treatment. "I'm looking for someone."

"What's their name?" Chelsea isn't quite sure how to deal with him. He doesn't seem like a serial killer, but then again, she's never met one before. His strained button-down shirt and khaki pants don't show any obvious places to hide a weapon. Still, she's not letting him past her. Plank protocol. And it's obvious he's not happy about something.

She waits for him to answer, her head cocked in question. She's not budging.

Finally, he relents and gives in to her request. She has that kind of effect on people.

"I'm looking for my wife. Sara DiCecco?"

Chelsea can hardly breathe. This guy is Sara's HUSBAND. After months of seeing Sara and Tony together, it had almost seemed normal to Chelsea for them to be a couple. But not to this guy. And now he was here. To confront them.

Unfortunately for Sara and Tony, they are at The Plank right now. Chelsea knows they're in an active training session at this very moment.

She doesn't know what to do. Should she tell him? Will he make a scene? Attack Tony?

Time to get Margo. "Just a minute," she says and runs to the back office as quickly as she can.

This is way above her pay grade.

Luckily for Sara and Tony, Margo is walking around the training area when Chelsea spots her.

"Mayday," Chelsea whispers under her breath. "Sara's husband is here. And I don't think he wants to sign up for a membership."

"Thanks, Chelsea," Margo tells her. "I'll be right there." She strides over to the front reception area.

"Hi, I'm Margo. I manage the Plank. Chelsea tells me you're looking for Sara?"

"I need to talk to her. I'm her husband."

Ouch, this could get ugly. Chelsea sips her latte at the desk as she watches Margo take over. She can't wait.

"I'll let her know you're here. Why don't you take a seat in the café? I can offer you a smoothie. On the house."

He doesn't want a smoothie. "Why can't I go back with you?" Charles argues. "I want to talk to her."

"I'm sorry, it's club policy," Margo says with a shake of her head. She gives him a sympathetic face, like she wishes she could let him, but she'd get in trouble if she did.

Chelsea is impressed. He's got a hundred pounds on her boss if he decides he's not taking no for an answer.

"I'll get her right now." Margo shoots Chelsea a look under her lashes to let her know to keep an eye on him, then rushes back to the gym area.

"Sara, your husband is here. Can you wrap up and come out front?"

Sara and Tony instantly stop their reps. They both look terrified. "Charles is here? He was supposed to be on a work trip," Sara responds weakly.

"Well, he's not. And he definitely wants to talk to you." Margo looks at Tony. "You stay here."

He puts a hand to his chest. "No problem." Of course, Tony causes all the drama but takes none of the blame.

Charles DiCecco doesn't look happy. His arms are crossed over his chest as he scowls at everyone who walks in to scan their key card. Chelsea tries to keep a poker face, as if this were normal. Husbands come to the gym looking for their wives every day.

Sara walks over to where they're standing in the reception area. She looks wary. Chelsea doesn't think this is going to go over well.

"Charles, what are you doing here? I thought you were in Vermont," Sara says.

"I'm sure you did," he answers. "I was until I logged into our iCloud account. And saw some *messages* on your account."

Wow. Chelsea's ready to get out the popcorn.

Sara flushes. "Let's not do this here. I'll get my bag, and we can go talk."

"Oh, we're going to talk," Charles responds. He still hasn't uncrossed his arms.

Chelsea feels even worse for Sara. The guy is kind of a prick, acting like a parent coming to take his kid home from an underage party.

She stands there, uncomfortable being so close to him as Sara heads to the locker room. They wait in tense silence. No one says a word.

She feels like he's blaming the peeps at The Plank for the affair. It's not her fault that his wife started sleeping with the trainer.

Then again, Chelsea doubts she'd be in a good mood if she found out her partner was sleeping around. She should probably give him the benefit of the doubt.

Sara's back in under a minute. She hasn't attempted to change; she's just clutching her gym bag and purse.

"See you later, guys," Chelsea says with an awkward wave. Margo nods goodbye as well.

Sara gives them a sheepish smile. She and Tony have been snogging all over the island. What did they think would happen?

The DiCeccos walk out the door. Chelsea doubts she'll see them again soon. She has a feeling Sara's membership is about to be put on hold.

"Let's not talk about it," Margo says.

Chelsea nods in return. "Absolutely."

"You know, speaking of relationships … seeing Charles just made me realize there are a lot of families who share the same account," Margo draws out, a frown on her face as she thinks out loud. "I brushed off Tina needing a new card before because Rafael had one as well. But what if their children use the same card too?"

Chelsea nods. "Yeah. That happens all the time. I scan a lot of different people on the same account."

"Are Jacob and Kirby still on their account? Tina told me she was missing a card. It's all the same number on their keycards."

Chelsea squints, checking the computer. "Yes, they are. But Kirby hasn't used it for a while."

"Since they're getting divorced and living separately, we should let them know they aren't eligible anymore."

Chelsea nods. "Kirby hasn't been here for weeks. It's August. I can send her a notice in the mail. I have all the mailing addresses in the system."

Just then, Mac walks in. He greets them with a smile. "What's new?"

"You don't want to know," Margo answers. "Drinks later?"

"Works for me." Whistling, he heads over to the weight area.

Chelsea sighs as she watches him walk away. "He is so damn cute. You're seriously lucky."

"Get back to work," Margo tells her.

Margo is no fun, but Chelsea isn't going to let that bother her. This morning was one to remember. She can't *wait* to tell everyone what happened!

Chapter 39

August 3

Detective Nate has been furiously working on breaking the case of the damaged sailboats, Quinn's assault, the store break-in, the stolen time capsule, and the hidden triathlon timer. If he does, he'll be a hero. A town legend. On the fast track to promotion.

But he hasn't gotten anywhere.

It doesn't make sense. The targets are all different people and organizations. Who has a vendetta against the members of the yacht club, volunteers at the museum, shoppers, and triathletes?

It's too wide a range of individuals. He can't find one person who overlaps every category. The only connection is that they're all local.

Each incident is a minor crime that isn't particularly threatening. No one has been seriously hurt or injured besides Quinn, and that seemed more like someone trying to get away than setting out to hurt the firefighter. But taken together, all these incidents have caused a great deal of trouble for the residents of Stone Harbor.

Nate has been getting pressure from the mayor and town council to find a break in the case. Something to show they're getting closer. But he can't find a single thing.

There are no fingerprints. No video footage. No hard evidence of any kind. His witness interviews have turned up zilch.

He's only one year out of the police academy. This lack of experience, combined with the fact that he's the first full-time detective on the island, makes Nate eager to prove himself to the department.

He took this job as a summer hire and worked up to a full-time position. Growing up in nearby Wildwood, he's always wanted to crack a big case. Get the bad guys. Be the hero. He was never a standout athlete; he wasn't ever particularly smart or gifted with music. But he does notice things. Small things that other people don't.

Nate learned early on that if you just sat still and let people talk, sometimes you'd learn more watching their mannerisms than by hearing what they were saying. He'd done well in the Police Academy, and his instructors had told him that he was a natural for detective work.

And now this, he has his first big case. The one everyone's talking about. *And he's not getting anywhere.*

He's pulled background records on every employee at the local clubs and businesses. The only one who's had a similar type of trouble is Richard Banks (known as Banksy), who had a previous conviction in Queens.

He can't help but notice that the issues started when Banksy arrived in town. Still, there's no evidence to tie him to any of the incidents.

That doesn't mean Nate isn't keeping an eye on him.

There have been some people who've become known for being particularly critical of the town leadership. They've sent nasty emails and shown up to council meetings to protest certain policies.

Roger Elliot is widely considered to be a major pain in the ass. But it's all small potatoes. Nothing major.

As far as he's aware, none of the council members or the mayor have ever felt threatened. Most of these issues are just the squeaky wheels in the normal course of small-town politics.

There is less than a month left of summer and most of the homeowners will begin trickling back to their more permanent homes. If he can solve even one of these crimes, it will be a major win. A potential promotion.

Maybe Nate should give Banksy another look. He's one of the newest transplants in town, with a background in mechanics and a keen interest in sailing. He also has first-hand knowledge of how The Plank operates. And there's his prior conviction. Maybe he has a grudge against all the rich people enjoying their perks of wealth while he has to work two jobs.

His decision made, Nate decides to make a few calls into Banksy's past. Talk to people he worked with, and find out who he's hanging out with. Nate needs to come up with something soon. And right now, it looks like Banksy is his best bet.

Chapter 40

August 9

It's early morning at the Stone Harbor Yacht Club. The steam is still coming off the water. Steady puffs of air rise and disappear as the temperature begins to warm. The surface of the water is glassy.

Most of the boats aren't out yet to make wakes with their motors. It makes the marshy bay side much quieter than the oceanfront - the gentle hum of water lapping the docks over the roar of crashing waves.

Tyson is rinsing off the docks with an industrial-sized hose, getting rid of the slime that seems to build up overnight. It's a mindless job, which is just what he needs. He doesn't want to think about anything right now.

He's been in love with Margo since they were kids. The feelings have always been there, a part of him that he'd never thought to act on. She's kept him firmly in her friend bubble. And he's never been brave enough to pop it.

When Margo's not there, Tyson looks for her. It's as if he needs to know where she is. She fills in his empty spaces, her positives filling his negatives. Making him whole. A better person.

Tyson knows he's an idiot. No one has to tell him that. He's handled it badly, and he has no one to blame but himself.

He should have talked to Margo instead of running off; he should have answered her calls instead of avoiding them like a petulant child. But he couldn't help it. The feelings that had been unleashed when he and Margo finally kissed had been overwhelming.

After years of pushing his feelings down, he didn't know how to deal with them, so he just…. didn't. Then, he didn't know how to turn it around.

Tyson pulls out a small carved wooden duck Margo made for him years ago. Just a few inches across, it is one of the first pieces she ever made. She'd been so proud of it, finishing the carving with her grandfather.

He's kept it in his pocket for good luck. All these years. And she never asked why.

It's all his fault. Tyson knows this. So now Margo is dating the developer, Mac. The hero. The one who "found" the time capsule and "saved" the Fourth of July. If Tyson didn't actually like the guy, he'd punch him in the face.

Tyson wants to sock Mac anyway, because he's lucky enough to wake up in the morning next to Margo St. James.

The bastard.

His thoughts are interrupted by Banksy's arrival. The man is as noisy as a bear, shuffling his large frame down to the dock. He's making so much noise that the seagulls scatter, honking as they fly off to search for more crumbs of food.

Tyson gives him a curt nod but doesn't say anything. He's not in the mood for small talk. Banksy is a known chatterbox.

"What a morning, right? It's so beautiful," Banksy says without breaking stride. He's already securing drifting boat lines to metal cleats, whistling cheerfully as he works.

He was right. Tyson nods non-committedly. He's hoping Banksy will take the hint that he doesn't want to wax poetic about the sunrise.

It doesn't happen. "I'm dating a real dame," Banksy tells Tyson. "We're planning on going out to Black Cactus tonight, then going dancing at the Windrift."

Tyson doesn't bother to reply. It does little to dampen Banksy's good mood.

"She's amazing. I can't believe she's into me." He keeps telling him about his new girl.

They have plenty to do. The club has a popular sailing regatta this weekend, followed by a member party on Saturday night. And then they have to prepare the boats for this morning's sailing campers. It's a busy time. They have a lot to do to get everything prepped.

The pair work together in a comfortable routine, each familiar with what needs to be finished. Banksy has come a long way from the Shoobie who arrived in town with zero sailing experience. Tyson could tell him that, but he still feels too moody to grant him a compliment.

Banksy is still amiably chatting away, telling Tyson about the party over the weekend. "I heard there was almost a fight between two guests in the second-story bar," he says.

Tyson is only half listening, but that's fine with Banksy.

"I tell you, the women around here are so happy to go out," Banksy continues. "So many beautiful, divorced, and wealthy ladies are looking for company. And generous! Sometimes they try to pick up the whole tab!" He shakes his head. "I tell them I've got it."

Tyson has a feeling Banksy is going to be sticking around for a while. And might be getting a sugar momma in the near future. Good for him.

The sun rises above the marsh as they continue getting everything ready for the youth campers. The campers will be taking the Mates and Optis out for a sail, so Tyson and Banksy make sure each boat has appropriate life jackets and safety gear.

Teaching the kids how to sail is one of his favorite duties at the club. The young sailors start out the season weaving all over the bay, but eventually develop a knack for changing the sails with the direction of the wind.

Around 8 am, a car pulls into the parking lot next to the boat ramp. Tyson looks up, shielding his eyes against the sun. It's still too early for any guests or campers. The marked police car bears the logo of the Stone Harbor PD.

Tyson and Banksy watch as two officers get out and head towards them.

It's strange for the police to be out here, especially so early in the morning. Are they doing a security detail? Or do they want to talk to someone in charge?

"Richard Banks?" one officer asks Banksy, who's been standing next to Tyson watching them approach. Tyson recognizes Detective Shroud.

"That's me," Banksy answers cautiously. "I talked to you before."

"Yes, about that. We'd like to take you into questioning for an incident that occurred here on the night of May 2."

Detective Shroud doesn't sound friendly, even though he looks about 12 years old. It's hard to take him seriously with that baby face.

Tyson doesn't like the sound of this. *Why is Banksy being singled out? Because he is a newcomer to the town? Because he isn't a trust fund baby? Isn't one of "them"?*

He trusts Banksy implicitly. Tyson throws the ropes down on the dock. The hell with his job right now. He needs to be there for his friend.

"I'm going with you," Tyson tells the police officer. Surprisingly, the young detective doesn't put up a protest. Shroud just nods and steps aside to let them walk past. The officer follows behind the pair, bringing up the rear.

Tyson throws an arm around Banksy, who looks queasy.

"Don't worry about this. I know you had nothing to do with it."

"Ah man, then why are they bringing me in? I haven't been involved in anything that would get me in trouble. Not anymore."

Tyson shakes his head and walks with Banksy up to the car. They get in the back seat. The cops climb into the front.

"We'll figure it out," Tyson assures Banksy. He pulls out his phone to start making some calls.

Chapter 41

August 10

Margo walks into The Plank early Tuesday morning. Liz is already there, deep in conversation with Chelsea at the front desk. She tries not to make a face when she sees their heads huddled together, whispering about something she knows she's not going to want to hear… but is pretty sure she'll have to anyway.

Liz is always at the gym now, but she barely sees her sweat. She's not there to work out. She just comes to compare notes with Chelsea. The two of them have found a similar affection for sharing tidbits of gossip.

Margo nods a quick hello and tries to walk past them. She really isn't in the mood, but they stop her before she can squeak by.

"Margo!" Chelsea bubbles, grabbing her by the wrist. "Did you hear the latest? Banksy was taken away in handcuffs and ARRESTED."

Margo *knew* she was going to learn something she didn't want to hear about. This is different, though. Personal. The news stops her in her tracks.

Banksy has been working there for months and is more reliable than the majority of her staff. There's no way he did anything that would get him in trouble with the law.

"What could he possibly have been arrested for?" Margo asks. This is ridiculous. The guy wouldn't hurt a fly.

"They think he's the one causing all the terror around here," Liz says as she shudders. "Just think, the suspect has been next to us all along."

Margo rolls her eyes. None of them - especially not Liz - has ever been in any real danger.

"I wouldn't be too worried if I were you. But why are they accusing Banksy? Did they find any proof? Fingerprints? Catch him in the act?"

Chelsea snaps her gum, squinting. "Well, I don't know exactly what happened," Chelsea backtracks. "Only what I heard. They took him in for questioning yesterday."

"So, he wasn't arrested. He was just questioned. That's different."

At least Liz and Chelsea both have the decency to look sheepish. "Right," Chelsea says. "But they did take him into the station."

"That doesn't make sense." Margo shakes her head. "Banksy has no reason to do any of those things. He loves it here."

"Maybe he got in trouble in Queens, and he ran away," Liz offers. "Decided to hide out in our town."

She can tell Liz is relishing the news. It's the first big break in the case, and she's one of the first ones to know about it.

"I checked his references before I hired him. Everyone loved him. Banksy did NOT run away from New York," Margo counters, pissed. "He was just trying to get a change of scenery."

Margo doesn't want to hear any more. Liz and Chelsea are sitting there enjoying the terrible news about someone they know. She can barely look at their faces. She turns on her heel and heads to her office.

Almost immediately, there's a call from Sandy, The Plank's owner. She's not happy to hear one of their newest employees was taken in for questioning. And that an angry husband showed up to confront one of their trainers.

"Margo, you know this is not the time for things to blow up," Sandy says in a clipped voice. "I'm counting on you to enhance the reputation of the Plank. Please don't make me change my mind about bringing you into my next investment."

Margo assures Sandy she has it handled. "Don't worry about a thing," she says. "The rumor mill is running rampant. Everything is taken care of."

"I need you to keep your ears open and let me know if anything else comes up. We have a meeting with investors in September. You'll need to put your share in then," she reminds her. She tells Margo to keep on top of the gym.

Margo gets off the phone and squeezes her eyes shut. The call from Sandy has made her feel antsy and agitated. She has less than three weeks to finish all the details of her art installation for the Seven Mile Hotel.

With the commission and every last drop of her savings, she's just barely going to make it to 30 grand. And even then, it might be close. She's counting on sales of her art in the stores that carry it. She just hopes people like her work this summer.

And now poor Banksy. And Sara. All these people are gossiping without even knowing any of the details. So quick to judge.

There could be a million reasons why Banksy was at the police station.

Margo needs to talk to someone level-headed. The only one around here is Hank, who's training a male client. She heads over to his spot on the training floor.

"Can I talk to you for a minute?" she asks.

Hank nods. "Give me ten." He doesn't ask why, but that's Hank. He's low-key drama.

Banksy and Hank have been hanging out a lot after work. Hank might know more about the situation. Something more than word-of-mouth, behind-the-back rumor mongering.

On the way back to her desk, Margo spots Tony training a young female client. His hands are holding on to her hips as she does dips from the overhead bar, her body shaking as she pulls her full weight up top. "And three…two…one. Nice job!"

The young woman beams under his praise. Another potential victim. Margo shakes her head.

Margo logs on to her computer and responds to a few messages, but she can't concentrate on anything. Her throat is tight, and she catches herself picking at her nails.

Poor Banksy. She's worried he's going to get into big trouble for something she is sure he didn't do.

Hank heads into her office exactly ten minutes later. He's always like that. Steady. Reliable.

"Can you shut the door?" Margo asks. She tells Hank about Chelsea's news. What Liz accused him of. She feels dirty even repeating the words.

"Do you know if Banksy ever talked about New York? Did he have to leave for any reason?"

Hank shakes his head. "No, not that he ever told me. But he didn't talk about it much." He smiles. "And you know how he likes to talk."

"Yes, I do." How well does she know Banksy? Margo has to admit, not too much. Banksy only works there ten hours a week, helping maintain the machines and fixing any issues they might have. When he was there, she was friendly, but she never engaged him in deep conversation. Never asked about his family, his opinions, his hobbies.

Margo has been too caught up in her own drama to consider if Banksy had any problems of his own. She feels a sense of shame that she'd overlooked him as more than just a part-time employee.

She has Banksy's cell number but doesn't want to call him and let him know they're all talking about him at The Plank. He might want to keep the entire incident private. If she can trust anyone to keep silent about the rumors, it's Hank.

Turns out Hank already knows. He confirms that Banksy was questioned at the police station, but that he wasn't put under arrest. Then Hank drops a bomb.

"Banksy has an alibi, but he doesn't want to name the person."

"Why not?" Margo asks.

He raises an eyebrow. "Why else? Because she's married."

"Oh God, save me from all this action around here. Fine. Let me see what I can do."

Hank looks at Margo. "Banksy was with Tyson when the police came to talk to him. I'm sure Tyson has all the details." He doesn't say anything more. His face is a careful blank slate. No expression at all.

"Got it. Thanks for telling me. I know you'll keep this on the down-low, but just have to ask you anyway."

"Absolutely. Although I doubt it's going to help much. Chelsea should keep a screen running on the front of her desk with fresh updates. Would save her the trouble of telling every person who walks through the door."

"Ugh, I know." Margo needs to talk to Chelsea about it. The situation is getting out of hand.

Is she allowed to discipline an employee for gossip? She needs to go back and read the employee handbook.

Margo walks Hank to her office door and then sits down at her desk, lost in thought. The only person who knows where Banksy is and what's going on is Tyson. Does she dare call him? He's avoided all her calls and texts for weeks. Margo doubts he's going to answer now.

Still, this is about their mutual friend and co-worker. Maybe he will. Because she's *positive* that Banksy is innocent. He's not the right person for these accidents.

In her opinion, the perpetrator has to be a townie. Someone who wants to wreck the season for the people who enjoy it. The acts are too personal. It's like they have a grudge they want to punish someone for. Or maybe it's just a bunch of teens? But not Banksy.

Margo grabs her phone and, without pausing to think about it any longer, she dials Tyson's cell. It rings a few times, and then he picks up.

It's been so long since they've spoken that she's caught off guard. She'd fully expected to be put through to voicemail.

"Ty?" Just saying his name gives her jitters. Margo feels like she should apologize, but isn't even sure what to say she's sorry for.

"Margo," Tyson answers calmly. As if it hasn't been weeks since they've talked to each other. The longest they've gone since grade school.

"I was calling to see if Banksy needed any help. I heard what happened, and I know he didn't do anything." Margo leaves everything else unsaid.

"He's going to be fine." Tyson's voice softens. She doubts he even realizes it, but she's so familiar with him that she hears the difference in tone.

"They just brought him in for questioning. In my opinion, it's because they're at a loss for any breaks in the case, so they want to make it look like they're doing something."

An ache in her throat that she hadn't even noticed she had begins to ease. Banksy is going to be okay. And Tyson is finally talking to her. Things aren't so bad.

"Can we meet up? I haven't seen you in so long," Margo asks. She knows it sounds like she's pleading. She doesn't care. Anything to get things back to how they were. She can't take the frosty distance anymore.

"I don't think that's a good idea." Tyson's voice has lost its warmth.

"But why? What did I do wrong?" She's getting even worse. Now she's whining. But she can't help it. She misses him so much it's painful.

"Nothing, Margo. I just have so much going on right now. I'm glad you're happy." Tyson clears his throat. "Listen, I gotta go. I'm sure we'll run into each other soon."

Tyson disconnects before she can respond. What in the actual fuck? He dismissed her so easily.

Telling herself the point of the call had been Banksy, Margo puts her phone down on the desk. She stares at the wall of her office blankly. This summer is different than any other she's had in 29 years of living at the beach. The whole thing is a mess, a terrible emotional mess that she can barely figure out.

Margo needs to talk to someone, get out of here. Grabbing her jacket off the back of the chair, she pulls her hair back and walks to reception.

"I'm going to run out for a few. I'll be back in an hour."

Chelsea holds up her hand. "Wait, Margo. I need to tell you something about that key card."

But Margo is already out the door, too caught up in her own turmoil to hear anything that Chelsea says.

Miffed, Chelsea goes off to find Tish. She'll listen. She always does. And the mystery of the key card is too big to keep to herself.

Chapter 42

August 10

Eddie is home when she walks in the door. He's also alone, which she
is happy to see. Even though she adores Tish, right now she needs her
brother's full attention.

He's making himself breakfast in their tiny kitchen while he hums,
buttering bread and frying bacon. Funny, it feels like the day is almost
over, with everything that's already happened. But it's only ten in the
morning.

She's actually surprised to see him up. This is early for Eddie.

"Hey sis, what are you doing back here?" he asks as he turns from
the stove. He's wearing a pair of board shorts, flip flops, and a cutout
muscle tank. His surfer uniform.

Margo doesn't bother to answer. She runs over to him for a hug. He
jolts for a sec, surprised by the contact, but then leans in and squeezes
her back. He smells the same as he always does: a mix of sea salt and
Tide detergent. It's exactly what she needs. She holds on tight.

"Margo. Is everything okay?" He lets go to turn back to the stove
and shut the flame off. His eggs will be ruined, but she knows he won't
care. That's the best part about Eddie: his generosity extends to his

time, not just his wallet.

"I could really use someone to talk to," she answers. Without any further questions, he makes her a cup of coffee (the way she likes it, skim milk, no sugar) and they sit down at the kitchen table.

Eddie doesn't say anything, giving her time to collect her thoughts. He sits there patiently waiting for her to explain.

It all pours out: Banksy's police questioning. Distrusting and then sleeping with Mac. Making out on the dock with Tyson. Sabrina canceling the commission. The Plank's surprise visit exposing an extra-marital affair. Trying to manage the club and all its personalities. Sandy's barely veiled threats that she'll fire Margo and keep her out of the Avalon branch. Working frantically to catch up with her commissions and replace the damaged inventory to make enough seed money for the Avalon location. Feeling like she's failing.

Through it all, Eddie just sits and listens without interrupting. Some of it sounds melodramatic even to Margo's ears – it's not as if anything is life-threatening – but it's become too much for her to handle by herself. She needs to unburden herself to someone. And who can she trust more than her big brother?

A little while later, she's spilled everything. Wrung dry. Eddie is looking at her with a mixture of awe and disbelief, but in an encouraging way.

Eddie reaches out and puts his hand on Margo's shoulder, rubbing it in comfort. "You've had a hell of a summer. I had no idea."

Margo shakes her head. "You've had enough on your plate."

"Not really. And you know there's never been too much on my calendar. But I appreciate the nod." Eddie laughs. "Honestly, I didn't think it was possible for my little sister to juggle two men."

She glares at Eddie. "It's not like that. Tyson made the move on me. I simply responded. And he's ghosted me ever since." She stares into her coffee moodily, wishing Eddie had thought to add some Baileys.

"Well, it sounds like you have two things to take care of. Getting control back at your gym and deciding who you want to be with."

Margo shakes her head. "I'm with Mac now. I just want Tyson to be my friend again. Go back to how it used to be."

Eddie stretches. "Yeah, as for that? I don't think it's going to happen."

Margo knows Eddie is right. Something has shifted in her friendship with Tyson, and they can't pretend like nothing happened. Margo had never felt that kind of crazy "I need to have more" desire before. Ever. And then Ty goes and makes everything awkward, and now there's another distance between them she can't bridge.

"Do you miss him?" Eddie asks.

"Every day," Margo replies.

Eddie grins. "I didn't ask which one."

He is such a pain in the ass. But then Margo thinks some more. Is Eddie right? Have her feelings for Tyson been hidden all this time? Always there but never noticed?

"It's like one of your pieces of wood," Eddie says. "There's a block of material that's overlooked by everyone else. And you notice it for what it is. What's underneath. Tyson doesn't show that side of him to most people."

"Or maybe it's too late. I did it all wrong, and now whatever possibility we could have had of being together has passed." Like when she makes a bad cut and the block is ruined. You can't get it back once it's been chipped off.

It's already almost 11 o'clock. Margo has to get back to The Plank and take charge of her staff and scheduling. There's a big museum benefit in four days, and the spa is booked solid with facials, eyelash extensions, and other treatments early in the week. Everyone wants to peel their summer skin and be all "glowy" by Friday.

"Thanks for the help. I'm feeling a lot better now," she lies.

She gives Eddie a kiss on the cheek and gets up from the table.

Feeling foolish, she turns around. "I didn't even ask how things are going with you."

Eddie grants her one of his movie star grins, the one that charms half the island. "Great. Did I tell you I'm staying? Hanging around here. All winter long."

Margo can't believe it. "Really? Are you sure?"

"Yep. I've been offered a full-time job at the Surf Shop. They need someone to manage inventory, take reservations, and handle hiring seasonal staff. I said I'll do it."

"Wow. Mom and Dad are going to be excited. Both of us in one place."

"And I'm going back to school. The Rutgers branch at Atlantic Cape."

Now Margo is stunned. What happened to her brother, the drifter? He's going to work full-time AND go back to college? It's mind-boggling.

"That's amazing news. I couldn't be happier for you."

"Yeah," Eddie says agreeably. "I'm happy here, being near the water. Being with Tish. And you. It's time I put down some roots."

This is definitely a summer for the books. Margo says goodbye to Eddie and heads back to the spa, feeling lighter. It's time to make some moves. If her brother can do it, so can she. Right?

Chapter 43

August 14

Every year, the Seven Mile Hotel hosts the museum's annual fundraiser. It's always an elegant affair. The boutique hotel hosts luxurious weddings and events year-round, but the museum gala is a highlight of the season – one of the last big parties before all the Swells leave town again.

The event features a sunset cocktail reception with live music, a silent auction, an open bar, and tables full of catered food. It's black tie only.

Many of their clients are attending the party. Tish has been working overtime for the past few days getting clients ready for the fundraiser: nails, facials, eyelash extensions, you name it. Their spray tan booth has never seen so much action. Margo even hauled in some of Chelsea's local friends to pitch in with extra help organizing schedules and running supplies.

It's been a busy time. Margo has taken Tish's suggestions and has been interviewing potential candidates to come on board so they can offer more serious, medical-grade procedures. New Jersey is one of the strictest states for medical spa regulations. For the spa to offer

Botox and Juvéderm injections, IPL, and intense peels, they'll need someone with a medical license. There's definitely interest from Plank members about adding more services to the spa menu.

It's time. Tish is ready to ramp up her business. On to the next stage in her career.

She already knows which types of services will be an instant hit and give the spa a nice boost in new clients. As an added plus, it will give her some extra money in the winter, when business normally slows down.

Tish is also planning to take additional training courses so she's up on the latest in skincare trends. And she's going to talk to Margo about expanding their product lines, something she knows Margo has been looking to do to help with sales.

Everything is looking up. Last night, Eddie told Tish he loved her, and she said it back. Moving to Stone Harbor has been the best decision she's ever made. Her life in Hoboken seems a world away. A different world of pressure and anxiety, not knowing who she was, feeling like everyone else was doing something special.

It's amazing what happens when you take charge and change the way you're living. She wishes she could go back and tell the old Tish how to find the courage to change. To get out of a bad cycle of self-doubt.

But that Tish needed to learn it herself. She wouldn't be the person she is now without going through the hard patches.

The new Tish is currently enjoying a glass of wine at the St. James house as she waits for Margo to finish getting dressed. She's wearing a maxi dress that she and Margo picked out together. They had gone shopping for new outfits to celebrate their successful week.

Margo began selling a new line of serving bowls and tiered platters to The Gables boutique in Avalon. It will feature animals specific to the region that visit the Stone Harbor Bird Sanctuary. The line will be an exclusive offering only available at the store. She's hoping it will help the owner recoup the loss to her business.

Tish can't help admiring how Margo juggles her art and her day job at the same time. The woman is a *boss*.

Eddie looks smart in a light gray checkered suit with cigarette pants. In keeping with his surfer identity, he's pairing it with tan moccasins. Tish is pretty sure he doesn't own a single pair of shoes with laces.

Margo floats down the stairs. The jumpsuit fits her slender frame to perfection. Her hair has been worked into a thick side braid with tiny tendrils of hair framing her face. She pairs the look with big earrings and platform wedges.

"Ready?" Margo asks as she pulls a set of gold bangles over her wrist.

Tish nods, finishing her last sip of rosé. "Is Mac coming with us?"

"He has a big meeting with a potential client, so he'll meet us at the fundraiser." Margo grabs her purse off the counter and gives Tish a wink. "We have plans for later. I'm staying over at his place."

At this bit of news, Eddie shoots Tish a guilty look, and Tish can immediately tell he's done something he shouldn't have.

Tish sidles over to Eddie and whispers, "What haven't you told me yet?" Then she braces for the answer.

Eddie has the decency to look sheepish. "We're waiting for one more."

Of course. Tish knows who it is without having to ask. Eddie told her a little about his conversation with Margo, without getting into specifics. Tish suggested that he shouldn't interfere with whatever was going on with his sister and one of his best friends. *Twice.* But of course, he hadn't listened. Men.

Margo shoots Eddie a wary look. "Who else?"

Her brother shrugs. "Who do you think?"

Margo answers. "You invited Tyson."

"I totally did," Eddie responds. He looks smug.

They sit there in angry silence, as only brothers and sisters can do.

The tension is humming when Tyson walks in a few minutes later.

Tish can't quite put her finger on it, but Tyson looks different somehow. Sharper.

He must have gotten a haircut. It looks styled, the locks now falling over his eyes instead of below his ears. The five o'clock shadow is gone. He's wearing a slim navy-blue suit with an open collar button-down, no tie.

Tish has never seen him looking better.

Margo completely ignores him. Doesn't even acknowledge that he's there.

Tish isn't sure exactly why, but she can't help feeling sorry for the guy.

"Ready?" Eddie asks cheerfully, rubbing his hands together as if the situation isn't awkward at all.

No one responds.

Their Uber arrives, and they pile into the SUV. Margo hops in the front seat. Tish would bet money that Margo is trying to avoid sitting next to Tyson. Tish, Eddie, and Tyson jump into the back.

It's a short, uncomfortable ride, and before they know it, the car is dropping them off in front of the Seven Mile Hotel. Valets are waiting outside to help guests out of their cars and move vehicles.

Tish takes the hand of an attendant she recognizes and grants him a full smile. She's seen him working out at The Plank before. It makes her happy to realize she's getting to know people in town.

They head up the steps to the main entrance. Roger Elliot is standing at the front, welcoming guests. Sabrina is right next to him. He greets their group warmly. Trying to make up for his daughter being a brat, most likely.

Tish doesn't think Roger Elliot actually knows who she is, but she's with the St. James family, so he acts like he does. She shakes his hand.

Sabrina looks like she's sulking, but leans over and says hello after her father shoots her a look. Tish has given that face many times as a nanny to small children. It meant to behave. OR ELSE.

Tish tucks her chin to hide a smile and glances around. The space is gorgeous, with oversized windows offering stunning waterfront views. It's decorated with votive candles and large white cherry blossom stems arranged in tall vases. Items for the silent auction are arranged on tables around the perimeter of the ballroom.

It's like another world, one Tish suddenly has access to. She doesn't know if she should pinch herself or just appreciate it.

Definitely enjoy it. An intimate jazz trio is playing softly. The space is growing crowded, with most of the cocktail tables taken by guests.

She spots the Martinezes. They're huddled together with a few other members of the council: Burt Feldman, Mayor Chloe Shivo, Jim Trainor, and a few other township authorities she recognizes but can't name.

Liz the realtor is at one of the tables, her hands waving in the air as she tells her colleagues a story. Tish has had enough of the rampant gossip going around, so she avoids Liz, sneaking past as a caterer serves the table.

Kirby is there, too. That's surprising. Tish hasn't seen her at the spa in weeks. When Tish started at The Plank, Kirby was one of Tish's best customers, and then Kirby ghosted her. She hasn't been there since June.

Tish decides to go over and say hi. It hasn't been easy for Kirby, going through a tough separation from Jacob. During her skin treatments, Kirby had confided in Tish how hard it had been. He'd told Kirby she wasn't a fit mother. Threatened to take full custody of the kids.

Tish heard that Jacob moved out and hasn't even told Kirby where he's living. It's not a pretty situation.

"Tish! You look dazzling." Kirby is obviously thrilled to see her.

"I haven't seen you at the Plank in so long. You need to come by."

"Oh," Kirby answers. "I lost my key card. I've been meaning to call and get a new one made."

Tish is suddenly aware of Kirby's expression. She's giving the same look Eddie did when he knew he was surprising Margo with Tyson: guilt. And Tish realizes a few things.

One: Kirby is getting divorced from Tina and Rafael's son.

Two: Kirby lost her key card. But Chelsea told her that *Tina* asked about it. Maybe Chelsea had mixed them up?

Three: Kirby's relatives lived in the house on 80th Street where the time capsule was originally found.

What if *Kirby* is the one behind all the incidents happening in town? She's had access to everything that happened. She's a local through generations of 7 Mile Island families. And she belongs to their gym.

Bingo.

Tish needs to tell someone. But who? The mayor and head of the museum are literally talking to Kirby's soon-to-be former in-laws right now. That's not a great idea. She scans the room. The only person she trusts is standing there, watching her.

Eddie. Tish tries to hide her expression as she turns to Kirby. "Can you excuse me? I have to talk to someone."

Kirby is oblivious. "Absolutely. Nice to catch up, Tish. You're one of the good ones."

Uh huh. Tish nods before she says anything else. "I'll see you in a bit."

Tish hurries over, practically tackling Eddie and Margo. They're standing there silently next to the auction table. Tish doesn't have time for this. She grabs their hands.

"I need you guys," Tish says. "Now!"

Without questioning anything, they follow her out onto the outdoor patio overlooking the bay.

Tish whirls around. "I was just talking to Kirby Bennett. Kirby

Martinez. The daughter-in-law of Tina and Rafael."

Margo nods. Of course, she knows who Kirby is related to.

She pauses for a breath, panting. "And I put it all together. She's the one who did everything. The boats, the broken key card, the time capsule. Jeez, even the store break-in. She's behind it all."

Eddie raises his eyebrows. He looks doubtful.

Tish grabs his hand and tugs him towards her. "I'm serious. She did it."

"Let's back up a bit. What makes you think it's her?" Margo asks. She's pressing her lips together as she considers it. Tish knows Margo isn't just humoring her. She honestly wants to know.

"She just told me she lost her key card. Margo, remember when you told me you found one in the office on the night Chelsea forgot to lock up? And then Chelsea told me she came in looking for it? I bet she was trying to find out where Jacob is living."

Margo nods. "That makes sense. Okay, keep going."

"Well, then I realized her family owned the house with the time capsule. And she hates her in-laws. What better way to embarrass them - and the whole town - than to mess up their plans?"

Tish rakes her hands through her hair. "The storefront. The electronic race sign that was tossed on the beach. It all adds up. Together, it's bad press for the town."

"And embarrasses her in-laws, who sided with Jacob." Margo taps her bottom lip thoughtfully. "It's a win-win."

Eddie nods. "Okay. What are we going to do about it?"

Tish hasn't thought that far ahead. She crosses her arms. "I don't know."

"I think we need to tell somebody." Eddie looks around the room. It's full of people they *should* tell, but it's probably not the right time. And they have no proof.

"We have no proof," Tish adds.

"Same page," Eddie smiles. "That's why I love you. I can talk to Quinn. Maybe we tell him our suspicions? Have him check it out?"

"Yeah, let's not jump the gun."

"Hey, guys… Who are we talking about?" Chelsea appears out of nowhere and sidles up to their conversation. She's wearing a fluffy pink dress that poofs away from her frame like the top of a cupcake.

Tish hadn't even spotted her at the party. Of all the people to have overheard, it has to be gossipy Chelsea.

"No one," Tish says firmly at the same time Eddie says, "Kirby Martinez.'"

"Kirby Martinez? That's who I wanted to talk to you about!"

Margo's eyes narrow. "What do you mean?"

"I *told* Tish. About the membership card."

This gets Margo's attention. "What about it?"

"Kirby came in asking for a new one. And I remembered you said you'd found part of one in your office. Guess what? It was her card. So, she was in your office at some point."

Chelsea's face falls. "Probably that time I lost the keys."

Tish doesn't think this is a good time to lecture her. Especially when the culprit is right there, at the same party. Kirby might literally overhear them talking about her.

"Wasn't your fault. But yes, that's good info. Thank you. Can you keep that to yourself for now, though? Don't tell anyone about it."

"Absolutely," Chelsea responds.

"No one else," she repeats firmly.

"Got it," Chelsea says, and Margo sighs in relief.

Chelsea offers a big, sparkling smile. "So, who wants to dance?"

Chapter 44

August 14

The party is in full swing. A jazz trio has been replaced with a cover band playing classic dance hits. Guests are downing too many cocktails from the generous open bar, and everyone feels pretty loose.

This is it! The tail end of summer. The season they waited nine months for, only to see it fly by without taking advantage of every precious, sun-drenched minute. And they're determined to soak it all up.

Kyle and Ryan from Fourth & Bay are cutting the dance floor, jumping around, waving their hands in the air, and getting everyone fired up. And why shouldn't they? They had an incredibly successful opening season. Another fabulous restaurant to add to their real estate portfolio.

Margo recognizes a lot of people at the event - locals, Swells, and Shoobies. There are gym and spa regulars, business owners, government figures, and Stone Harbor regulars. Their community has shown up. She's grateful that she's a part of it.

Mac canceled on her, sending a text that he'd been stuck in his meeting and then delayed in traffic on the way back from Long Island.

He says he feels terrible doing it, but it's been such a grueling ride that he's going to call it a day.

Well, there goes her plans for a sleepover. She can't help being upset that she isn't going to see him. There's so much going on that he doesn't even know about.

Margo has also had a few too many drinks, and everything is getting to her. The stress of the season. All the long hours she's worked to restock her art. The pressure of creating such a large commission. Sandy's threats about potentially losing her shot at part-ownership in the new location.

People are going around spreading rumors about everyone without any regard for how they feel. And then there's the fact that she and Tyson are sharing their own secret, something that would definitely be considered a hot piece of gossip. She's still not sure what to think about their relationship either.

Did she mention how good he looks tonight? Literally every woman at the party is giving him side-eyes and appreciative looks. She's both annoyed and protective as she observes them. And she hates herself for it. She's with Mac, Margo reminds herself.

Oh, one more thing. Despite her promise, Margo is pretty sure Chelsea is going around whispering to *everyone* about Kirby being a potential prime suspect. She's just waiting for someone to overhear the news that isn't supposed to know about it, derailing the investigation.

Suddenly, Sabrina is right in front of Margo. As always, she's drop-dead stunning. Dressed in a slinky white gown that shows off her golden tan, she looks so perfect that Margo feels shabby in comparison.

She keeps a smile on her face. "Sabrina, hi. You look beautiful."

"And you, Margo." She seems friendly enough. But she's on edge. Her eye is twitching.

Margo takes a careful sip of her martini, waiting for the punchline. She's not going to indulge in small talk when she knows there's definitely a motive behind seeking her out. It's not a common occurrence, unless it's to cancel her commissions.

The reason doesn't take long to arrive.

"I heard that you've been dating Mac." Sabrina's eyes glitter.

She nods. "Yes, I have." She isn't about to give Sabrina any more than that.

"You know he's my ex, right? My former *lover*."

Margo wonders where this is going. She did nothing wrong. She and Sabrina aren't good friends. Dating Mac doesn't fall into the "friends don't date exes" category. But it's pretty apparent that Sabrina has a fight to pick.

"I do know that. I'm sorry it didn't work out," Margo says as politely as she can. She's just trying to get out of this conversation as soon as possible.

"So, you did know. But you went out with him anyway."

"I did." What else could she say?

Sabrina's eyes narrow. "I didn't take you for someone who went for sloppy seconds."

Okay. Now she's just being rude. "What are you angling for, Sabrina?" Margo asks.

"I just don't want you to make the same mistake I did." She crosses her arms across her chest, glaring at Margo. "He's not going to give you what you want. He'll dump you, just like he dumps every girl he dates. And then you'll be sorry you didn't listen to me and walk away now."

"Well, it's pretty obvious you're upset that he broke up with *you*. And I'm sorry it didn't work out. But that doesn't mean you need to come at me."

Sabrina flings her drink in Margo's face. And then she gives her a shove. The force catches her off guard, making her fall backwards.

Holy shit. Margo's lying there on the ground with her vodka soda dripping down her jumpsuit.

It had been a full drink, too.

"Whoa!" someone shouts. "That was nasty."

Tyson and Eddie come running over. Tish isn't far behind, but her high heels are slowing her down.

Eddie glares at Sabrina. "What's wrong with you? Leave Margo alone!"

"Why does everyone ADORE her?" Sabrina yells. "She's not that SPECIAL!!!" She looks unhinged. She starts to lunge towards Margo again.

Tyson grabs her arm, and Sabrina swivels back, her hand raised.

"Get off me!" she yells.

"Let's not make a scene. She's not worth it." Margo pulls herself up off the ground, trying not to slip in the puddle of vodka.

"You're about to see how worth it I really am." She pulls her arm away from Tyson's grip.

"Sabrina!" Roger Elliot strides over and grips Sabrina firmly. He's vibrating with anger. "I'm so sorry. I'll handle this," he says. He doesn't give them time to respond before he's marching away, his daughter in tow.

"I have a feeling Sabrina is going to get her allowance taken away," Tish says. She hands Margo a set of napkins. "Let's get you home and cleaned up."

Margo doesn't argue with her.

Chapter 45

August 19

"Are you kidding me?" Mac says the instant Margo picks up the phone. He's already heard the entire story before she had a chance to tell him. And he's *furious*. "She owes you an apology. And a dry cleaning."

"It wasn't that big a deal." She tries calming him down. "Just a little spill."

"It's my fault. She hates me, so now she resents you. I should have been there."

Margo convinces him to hold off. She doesn't need any more drama right now. And nothing was ruined that a little cleaning couldn't fix. She's mostly just embarrassed that she's the topic of conversation around town. She's not comfortable being on everyone's radar and having them all gossiping about her fight with Sabrina. Not to mention, she's still waiting for Roger to pay for the remainder of her chandelier commission.

"It's better to let it go," she tells Mac as she drives down Ocean Drive.

"I'll do it for you," he relents.

"Thank you. See you in ten." Margo is on her way to see the big waterfront house that Mac has been working on. The project is finally on the verge of completion. Without Sabrina around, the project delays and extra work have mysteriously disappeared.

It's about 40 blocks away from The Plank, so she navigates her car, admiring the spectacular houses lining the road, while dodging packs of teens weaving their bikes in and out of the bike lane. Everyone bikes around in Stone Harbor.

Mac has been eager to show her what he's been working on. She has to admit she has a little fangirl in her, getting to view this VIP estate that she would normally never have access to. It's incredible to think someone will spend all this time and money on a place they'll visit maybe two or three times a year.

After the home tour, they plan on grabbing a bite to eat in Avalon. She hasn't seen him in more than a week. So much has happened that she doesn't even know where to start. Or what she should tell him.

Don't go there, Margo. Just breathe.

The house is impossible to see from the road. The property is sheltered from view by tall trees and the curve of the drive. She's about halfway up the hill when she sees it up close. She gasps. It's magnificent, even by Stone Harbor standards.

The size of the estate is overwhelming. She can barely see all of it at once. It's a modern style, with black oversized windows, boxed angles, and sharp edges. Terraced boulder walls spread across the entire length of the property, leading up to three levels of beachfront living.

Mac's waiting for her. He trots down the front stairs and greets her with a long kiss. "Hey, gorgeous."

Margo stops herself from pulling back. She knows they need to talk.

Luckily, he doesn't seem to notice. He grabs her hand and takes her up to the main entrance. The doors are extra wide and open on a pivot.

"This was already here," he tells her. "We redid the main kitchen, exterior, and pool houses."

Pool houses? There's more than one?

There certainly are, as Margo discovers. In fact, there's more than one kitchen, too. They have a kitchen on each level, as well as a smaller one for the outdoor space (small being on a relative scale, since it has a double sink and stone walls incorporating a grill, wooden fireplace, and refrigerator). There's also a small kitchenette in each guest house.

The property is a showstopper, from the inlaid marble floors to the wide-open hallways dripping with modern brass lighting. The kitchen walls open accordion-style to let the outdoors in, making the patio seem like an extension of the home. Wide rattan swings are everywhere, hanging from nooks and rafters.

If you thought of something to put in a home, it's already there. Patios, decks, pools, saunas, spas, waterslides. There's even a paddleball court.

Mac leads her to the lower level of the outdoor living area, which has sweeping views of the Atlantic. It's both private and open. She can't explain how, but it is.

She sweeps her hair off her face. "Mac, you should be so proud of what you did. This is amazing."

He shoots her a happy grin. "It turned out better than I hoped. Even with all the issues we had."

That's right, Sabrina again. Margo frowns. Getting fired from this project just gave her another reason to hate Mac and Margo.

Mac pulls out a bottle of champagne, and they enjoy the setting sun on a set of loungers surrounding the infinity pool.

"You're sure you're allowed to do this?" she asks. His client isn't just anyone. She could probably order a hit on them if she wanted to.

"Absolutely. She's so happy with how it turned out that she gave me the house for the night."

She isn't sure how to respond. Eventually, the bubbly helps her relax, and she tells him all about the museum benefit and Kirby Martinez. Margo and Chelsea had both reported their suspicions to Detective Nate, and he was anxious to investigate the lead.

"Are they taking her in for questioning?" Mac asks.

She shakes her head. "I don't think they are yet. Her own mother-in-law is on the town council. They want to get all their ducks in a row before they bring her in."

Mac grimaces. "Unlike Banksy, who had no one to back him up."

"That's not true. I found out Hank, Eddie, and Liz all went to the station and told them they were on the wrong track." She laughs. "Even Tony. I didn't expect him to stick his neck out for anyone."

"That's incredible. I'm glad to hear it." He puts his arm around her shoulder. She doesn't feel any sparks when he moves closer.

This is the same Mac she's known for a few months now. He's met her brother and best friends, taken her to dinner, helped out with her gym, and shared her bed. She realizes he's a catch. *Anyone* would say he's a catch. Sabrina can't get over him.

What's wrong with her? Margo feels like she's doing something wrong. Missed a step. Even though he's what she's always wanted. And he clearly adores her. He's already talking about taking a trip up North in the fall to meet his parents and visit his hometown of Newburyport. Asking her to take time off so she can travel with him for on-site visits.

She decides to go with it. They can talk another day. Why ruin the magic of the moment?

He pulls her in closer for a kiss. She surrenders, letting him pull her down to the cushions of the deep seating. He makes quick work of her dress, and they're suddenly skin to skin.

They've already discovered how to pleasure each other. What turns each of them on. He enters her, and even though she's enjoying what he's doing to her body, she feels a part of herself separate from the entire interaction. Watching it from afar.

After he comes, she lies next to him quietly. Margo has never felt more confused.

Chapter 46

August 21

Mac is so damn proud of his girlfriend. Even though he's personally seen how hard Margo has worked on this project, it still blows his mind that she was able to create something this incredible.

The three-tiered chandelier is a massive eight-foot-wide hand-carved piece of art. Each level was sculpted to resemble an intricate maze of vines and branches. Perched throughout are colorful birds and animals native to the Jersey shore.

It's delicate but formidable, inspiring yet familiar.

She'd meticulously assembled and then disassembled the entire piece to bring it down to the hotel. Everyone helped out.

Eddie and Tyson, Chelsea and Tish, Tony, and Quinn. They all showed up. Even Jim from the museum came over to pitch in. Together, they brought pieces of the chandelier into the lobby and helped her wire it together. They do it because they all love Margo and want to be part of her big debut.

It took the better part of the day to pull it together. Mac watches Margo string the electricity and mount the first pieces herself. She's a better electrician than some of his crew members.

Friends and family come and go in shifts, taking turns to help out. Roger Elliot has the lobby cordoned off so they can do the installation in private. Guests have been rerouted through the back of the hotel.

"Baby girl, I didn't know you had this in you," says Tony. He slings his arm around Margo's shoulders. She bestows on him one of the biggest smiles she's given him all summer.

"Thanks, Tony."

Mac can see how happy Margo is. She's positively bubbling over with energy.

He spots Tyson standing on a ladder watching their exchange. Margo looks back at him, and they share a look. It's not one Mac can identify, and it reminds him that he hasn't known Margo very long. He's still learning about her friendships and previous relationships. He's not sure where Tyson falls in there, but even he can see they have a solid connection. A history of friendship.

He hesitates, uncertain, before walking over to hand Margo a beautifully carved plover. She secures it to a branch. "Thanks, Mac."

There's a large-scale rendering of how it should look that they keep trying to match up, but only Margo knows where everything goes. Eventually, they give up start handing her the pieces to attach.

Tyson walks over with a long-tailed duck. "This one's not fancy, but it's a true Stone Harbor native," he says. Margo accepts it from him. "Thanks, Tyson."

The other volunteers head out, and there's only Tish, Eddie, Mac, and Tyson left. After another half an hour, the chandeliers are fully assembled. They pull the ladders to the side.

Tish pulls out a couple of bottles of champagne from a cooler. She pours each one of them a glass.

"Are you ready, Margo?" she asks.

Margo exhales. "Yes, I finally am." And she flicks the switch.

The chandelier's hidden lights come on, illuminating the curves and beaks of each feathered creature.

The group stands still, admiring Margo's work and appreciating the attention to detail of every animal. It's stunning. A true work of art. Worth every hour of work she poured into it.

Eddie grabs his little sister for a hug. "You did it!" he yells happily.

Margo hugs each one of them. She's glowing. When she hugs Mac, he feels unsure. Unsettled. Like he doesn't know what's going on. But this is Margo's night, so he gives her a kiss and announces that he's taking everyone out for drinks.

They leave the hotel and head to 96th Street to celebrate. Later that night, as Margo lies in his bed, Mac can't sleep. He watches her, hoping his golden girl cares about him as much as he's begun to care about her.

Chapter 47

August 24

Quinn sees a call come in from Detective Shroud. He's pretty sure he knows what it's going to be about. He picks up on the second ring.

"Can you come into the police station? I need to go over a few things with you," Nate says.

Quinn is technically off the clock, having worked a double shift at the fire department the day before. That's information he'd bet money that the detective is already well aware of. But he's asking him to stop by anyway.

Despite himself, he's developing some respect for the guy. He's sharper than most people give him credit for.

"No problem," Quinn answers. "Give me half an hour."

When he arrives, he's shown into a conference room with a few other police officers and the Chief of Police. They're spread out around the table, which is covered under sheafs of paper and piles of notepads, cups of coffee, and empty water bottles.

No one is smiling. This must be a pretty big deal.

He's asked about the night the boats were sunk. What time the firefighters were called, who took the call, his first impressions. The people he spoke with. Then they ask him about the missing race timer.

"We've spoken with Nick Romanski." He had been there with Quinn when it was discovered. "He confirmed what you told us."

"Do you still have Banksy as a suspect?" Quinn asks. "Because there's no way he had anything to do with it. I know it for a fact."

Shroud waves his hand dismissively. "Not anymore. We have a different suspect." He doesn't apologize for targeting Quinn's friend.

Quinn lets it go. The guy doesn't have the best table manners. "Who do you have?"

"You know we can't tell you that."

"Give me a hint." This is getting interesting. He loves it.

One of the other officers gives him a look. "You're not privy to this level of security. You're just a firefighter."

"I'm pretty sure people like us more than you," Quinn offers. That's universally true. No one gives firefighters a hard time. Women love them. Dogs love them. Grandmothers love them. They even have hunky calendars. Have you ever seen a police calendar?

"More than likely," Shroud says as he continues his questioning. He asks Quinn to go through his memory, answering questions that seem completely off-topic but must somehow be relevant. The officers grill him on so many things that it's hard to remember all the details of each moment.

He answers as best as he can, responding to their line of questioning without understanding why they're asking some of the things they do. Some of the things seem completely irrelevant.

"Can I ask who else you've talked to?" Quinn looks around the table at the officers.

The same cop answers, perhaps not realizing the importance of what he's saying. "Tina and Rafael Martinez, the Bennett family, Jacob Martinez, Jim Trainor, Lloyd MacIntyre."

Nate shuts him down. "That's enough."

Interesting. Why Jacob Martinez? The only person all these people have in common is Jacob's soon-to-be-ex Kirby. Could she somehow be involved?

He gets through another hour, and they finally signal it's time to go. Quinn thanks them with a dazzling smile and gets in his truck to drive right to Mac's house. This can't wait.

While he's driving, he gives Mac a call to make sure he's home. That man could be in any town in the tri-state area right now, having meetings with clients or working on a project.

Turns out, Quinn's right. He's doing the final walkthrough of the house on 53rd Street with Robin, the township inspector. Mac tells him to stop by so they can talk when it's finished.

* * *

Quinn pulls into the famous singer's house and waits in the driveway while Mac finishes up with the permit inspector. Unfortunately for Mac, it hasn't been going well.

Someone has completely trashed the pool house. "We discovered two broken windows, a fuse box with the wires cut, and a broken pool drain," Mac tells him. "There's spray paint all over the glass double doors. We also saw pieces of glass and patches of drywall scattered across the stone pavers."

"Holy shit. Who do you think did it?"

"I'm not calling anyone out right now. Whoever did it wasn't able to get to the main house, probably due to the alarm system in place. But they were able to sneak around to the pool and wreak havoc there."

He takes out his phone to show Quinn pics. The sight of so much damage makes him sick. "Dammit. I know how much time and care you took with this project."

"We'll find out who it was." Mac nods as he takes some paperwork from Inspector Metcalf. She's not going to be signing off on any permits anytime soon. "You're going to have a lot of work to do to get the place back to regulation," she says.

"You're telling me."

Mac shakes her hand, then walks over to Quinn's truck and gets in, slamming the door.

"Did you call the police?" Quinn asks. He's never seen Mac so furious.

"Not yet. I can't believe that once again, another one of my projects is completely fucked. I'm telling you, when I find out who's behind this…"

Quinn cuts him off. "I think I know who it is."

Mac stares at him without saying a word. Should he continue?

Quinn does. "They think it's Kirby Bennett."

Mac doesn't respond for a beat. Quinn waits.

Finally, Mac says, "I know she's the lead suspect in the boats and the break-in, and potentially the time capsule. But not on this." He turns to face Quinn in the truck. "Why would she come after this project? It has nothing to do with her."

"I don't think they've decided on her motive yet," Quinn admits. "But they're pretty sure it's her. She's been in the area for each of the incidents. And she's really mad at her ex-husband and in-laws."

"You think she knocked you out?" Mac asks.

"It doesn't seem like her style; I have to admit. But anything is possible."

Mac shakes his head. "I don't know why she'd come after this house, but it doesn't matter. This client is used to being stalked by paparazzi and fans. She has cameras."

Quinn grins. "That means you finally have proof?"

"We do." Mac finally smiles back at him. "I have it all downloaded, and I plan to watch it as soon as I get home. And then we'll call Detective Nate."

"Can I join you?"

"Of course."

They drive directly to Mac's house in Cape May and settle in for movie night.

Chapter 48

August 27

Kirby Bennett has been arrested and charged with:

- 4 counts of NJSA 2C:17-3 for Criminal Mischief (Stone Harbor Yacht Club sailboats, the stolen time capsule, The Gables, and the race timer)
- 4 counts of NJSA 2C: 18-3 for Trespassing (Yacht Club, Stone Harbor Museum, The Gables, and The Plank)
- 2 counts of NJSA 2C 20-3 for Theft (The Gables and the time capsule)
- 2 counts of NJSA 2C: 18-2 for Burglary (The Gables and the time capsule)
- 1 count of NJSA 2C 20-31 for Wrongful Computer Access (The Plank)
- 1 count of NJSA 2C: 12-1 for Assault (Quinn)

She pleads not guilty to every one of the charges. She hasn't said one word without her attorney present.

Kirby is a smart lady. She was quick to get high-end legal representation as soon as she was taken in for questioning.

They're still not sure about her motives behind the incidents. They can understand why she wanted to get her ex's home address. But why sink the boats and trash the store? To get back at her in-laws?

One of the incidents of vandalism that she was being investigated for was dismissed because of Mac's video footage. It was not the small, slight Kirby slinking onto the beachfront home with a baseball bat and a pair of wire cutters.

It was the statuesque Sabrina.

No one knows about that piece of information except for Mac, Quinn, and Detective Nate. They're careful not to give her any advance notice that they're on to her before the police can make an arrest for vandalism.

The rookie police detective is in his element. He's been interviewed by several news channels ("No comment") and is getting praises from the entire Stone Harbor Borough Council, save for Tina, which is understandable. He's getting accolades from residents, high-fives from kids, and bakeries dropping off trays of cookies and donuts.

Nate has to admit, it's pretty cool.

Everyone is relieved that the department finally figured out who did it. Detective Nate Shroud closed the case.

What a day!

He's been so busy with Kirby's case that he hasn't had much time to get an arrest warrant for Sabrina Elliot. But he knows he needs to give it his attention, if only to keep Mac off his case. There's only so much time in the day.

Mac has been breathing down his neck, calling often for updates. Nate's afraid that if he doesn't get the warrant in the next day or so that Mac will take matters into his own hands. The guy is certainly taking it personally.

There's a clear video of the incident to establish grounds for issuance.

He just has to do all of the paperwork and place it in front of a judge for a determination.

This is his first search warrant. Did he mention he's only been on the job for a year? He really doesn't want to screw this up.

He decides to get to work on it. It's going to take hours.

The Chief of Police even comes over to help, as do the other members of the department. They go over his evidence and decide he has a clear case for issuing the arrest warrant.

Unfortunately, by the time he's finally checked and rechecked his paperwork, it's too late in the day to file it. The courthouse is closed until tomorrow morning.

Nate puts everything into a binder and clocks out for the day. Tomorrow is Friday the 28th, the date of the town's Festival of Lights. It's a big deal.

Boatloads of partygoers will travel among the basins and bays, their boats decked out in themes and lit up with strings of lights. Prizes are awarded for the best theme and costumes. Homeowners on the water also decorate their docks to take part in the festivities and compete for prizes. It's one of the biggest events of the summer.

He'd better get the warrant processed by then to make sure Sabrina isn't on one of those boats. That would be embarrassing.

The Seven Mile Hotel usually participates in the parade, sailing their 64' Sunseeker Yacht with guests from the hotel. It's a nice perk for their VIP's,

Nate knows he's stepping into a mire of controversy with this arrest. The Elliots are one of the town's most prominent families. But what else can he do? Sabrina did it. There's clear evidence she vandalized the home.

It's his duty to keep the public safe from her. And he's fully prepared to do so.

Chapter 49

August 28

The weather for the Festival of Lights is an ideal 74 degrees and partly sunny. Tyson's weather app says it's going down to the mid 60's after sunset. High visibility for parade goers to watch the parade of decorated boats travel down the waterway as they stand on bulkheads and docks to cheer them on.

A viewing party is being held at the Municipal Marina Lot, along with a set of food trucks and a beer and wine garden. This year's theme is "Famous TV Sitcoms." The rules are pretty clear-cut.

The festival was originally created in the 1960's by the Stone Harbor Yacht Club, but eventually the town took the event over. This year's Festival of Lights has 35 boats participating.

Each boat can take its pick from popular shows. After they settle on one, they decorate their boats and dress up as much as they can to resemble the show's characters. Obviously, the more outrageous the decorations, the better the reaction from the parade watchers. Prizes are given out for Best Dock Décor, Best Boat Décor, and Best Costumes.

Tyson outfits the yacht club's boat in the theme of *Schitt's Creek,* which won the most votes from their crew. They have a mix of guests on the boat: the Commodore, Vice Commodore, Rear Commodore, camp counselors, club members, and summer staff.

Eddie and Margo were invited, but there's not enough room for Tish and Mac, so they're having drinks with friends back on land.

It's easy to pick a Johnny Rose from one of the more dapper guests. A glamorous club member is the perfect Moira. Their manager is David. Tyson plays the part of Patrick, David's partner. The Commodore is Roland Schitt, and the female Rear Commodore is his wife Jocelyn. Alexis, Twyla, and Stevie are assigned to a few of the counselors and younger members.

Banksy and Tyson have been stringing ropes of white lights around the club's boat all morning. They have a decent size to work with. There's room for a wall of wigs, a huge mural of the town sign, and Rose Apothecary decor. Every plate, napkin, and cup is black and white striped.

The parade will begin at the yacht club and travel south around Paradise Basin, Sanctuary Basin, Carnival Bay, and Pleasure Bay. Then, they'll turn around and sail north to Shelter Haven and Snug Harbor before finishing up at the North Basin.

The boats will all return to the yacht club for the judges to vote on the best candidates. It usually wraps up around 10 at night, and then everyone heads to the bars to celebrate.

Margo teases and fluffs her hair to give it a "wig" vibe, then throws on a tweed jacket and turtleneck with black pants. It will get breezy on the water, even in August. She found some of her dad's formal clothes for Eddie to wear. They haven't seen the light of day since the 1990's.

I'm heading over to the yacht club, she texts Mac.

He's going to be watching the parade from the Seven Mile Hotel with friends. The outdoor bar is the perfect spot to watch the parade.

He responds with a thumbs up, and they plan to regroup after the parade back at Margo's place. It's implied he'll spend the night. Which will lead to sex.

It will be good sex, but not with the person she wants it to be with.

Margo wonders how she can keep doing this, sleeping with Mac when all she can think about is Tyson. But what can she do? She feels trapped. Everyone thinks they're an item. The whole town is happy about their relationship, saying they're perfect for each other.

Mac is kind. And thoughtful. And it's not like Tyson wants a relationship. He barely talks to her. He doesn't even want to spend any time around her anymore. He's made it clear their easy friendship is over.

Margo thinks about Mac sitting at the Seven Mile Hotel bar waiting for her to return. She reflects on what that will be like, having him as the person to check in with. The first one you call when you have a problem or celebrate a success. The last person to talk to before bed, who you reach for when you turn off the light. And she knows he's not that one.

She's felt torn about it for a while, but seeing Tyson in the hotel lobby solidified things. *He's* the one she wants to be with. Her anchor, the one that holds her and keeps her from drifting.

It's like she didn't realize what she was carving until the object showed itself to her. Recognizing the intended figure underneath that had been hidden for so long. Waiting to be revealed. Even if it wasn't what she'd expected when she first started out. It's even better.

Art is supposed to take a fragment of daily life and bring it up to the mirror, showing a little piece of yourself to the person viewing it, so they can connect with it. Draw out an emotion. Something pure.

Margo has experienced it before, when she finished a project she was surprisingly fond of. Pulled an emotion she didn't expect to have. It materializes when she's immersed in her art, but it's never happened in her personal life.

She knows Tyson is the one she wants.

Unfortunately, it's clear that he doesn't want her.

And that's okay. Tonight, she'll get dressed up and pretend it doesn't matter. Act like her heart isn't breaking in a million pieces every time Tyson gives her the cold shoulder. Smile and engage in polite conversation with everyone on Seven Mile Island.

The only good thing to come out of this fiasco is the amount of work she's getting in. Because she can't sleep, she stays up late every night carving and whittling, creating new pieces for her clients. It's been a boon to her business, replacing all the lost inventory from The Gables. Her pieces are selling out all over town.

It's time to go. She grabs her purse and grabs her brother. "Are you ready to head over?" she asks.

Eddie nods. He knows not to ask questions. The big brother who always used to tease her is now her best supporter.

Stone Harbor Yacht Club is a hive of activity, with people adding big signs, strands of lights, and anything that could be visible from the water. There are big boom box speaker systems blaring sitcom soundtracks on many of the boats.

They walk around the parking lot to the packed dock. She waves to people she knows and nods hello to others. Everyone's in a festive mood. Banksy is bent over loading a cooler onto the club's boat. He's sporting a denim jacket with metal studs and a pair of stonewashed jeans. She's not sure who he's supposed to be, but he's adorable.

"What can I help with?" she asks.

Banksy turns around, breaking into a grin. "Hey, Margo. You look great!"

She climbs on board and gives him a hug. "So do you. Now, what can I do?"

"Everything's mostly done. Just grab a drink and help me with the sound system. I can't figure out which Spotify station works with our theme."

It's only six o'clock and still sunny. They have an hour before they sail. As in years past, Tyson will drive and lead the parade, so he won't be drinking. He has to keep an eye out for all the other boaters as well, to make sure they keep a careful distance from each other and don't get into trouble. It's not technically his job, but Margo knows he considers it his responsibility. That's who he is.

Margo takes a long sip from a can of hard seltzer. It's time to end things with Mac. She's not looking forward to it. He's an incredible guy who would make anyone happy. He's just not the incredible guy *for her*. It's heartbreaking to realize that she'd rather be alone than be in a relationship with Mac.

At the same time that Margo is thinking about how to break up with him, Mac is at the Seven Mile Hotel with Quinn and some of their mutual friends.

He's still livid about what Sabrina did to Margo and to his project on 53rd Street. The spoiled brat doesn't care what happens to anyone else if she doesn't get her way.

Mac should have seen it coming. The way she acted when they first broke up, canceling orders and messing with building inspections. Why hadn't he thought she'd react the same way when she got fired and found out he was dating Margo? It's exactly the kind of petty bullshit she thrives on.

Only Detective Nate, Quinn, and Mac are aware that she's about to get arrested. He hasn't even told Margo. She has too much going on right now.

The Seven Mile Hotel's rows of tables and gas fire pits are packed with guests. It's standing room only. Mac takes it all in stride. He's leaning against the bar, making small talk, when he recognizes one of the waiters. He's bending over, wiping off the crumbs with a rag and spray bottle.

Mac is sure the waiter was in Snug Harbor the night the boats were sunk. He found the most badly damaged Sunny. What was his name again? He has to ask.

He walks over to where a young waiter is cleaning a table that has just finished dinner. "Hey, I remember you. You helped us locate the boats at the yacht club the night they were drilled with holes."

Mac is about to say thank you when the waiter looks up at him, and his mouth drops open. He comes to a full stop, standing there with a wet rag in his hand. "Oh shit." He seems like he's about to say something more when he stops and freezes, then runs.

He just takes off, leaving the table full of glasses and dishes. He's quick, too. Mac loses a few seconds before he begins to chase after the server.

The kid makes it past a few tables, bobbing and weaving around the crowd as much as he can. He knocks into a woman holding a martini glass, who screams. A chair is knocked over. They're attracting attention.

Quinn sees what's going on and rushes over, dropping his beer while he chases the kid. He comes from one angle and Mac from another.

Together, they manage to corner him against the back wall and a table.

He's young, maybe 20 years old, with the thick mane of hair in his eyes all the kids have right now. A young boy who looks absolutely petrified.

Mac holds up his hand, trying not to scare him any more than needed.

"Why are you running?" He's out of breath. The kid was fast. He's thankful he started cardio training at the gym, or there was no chance he ever would have caught up.

"I don't want any trouble," the kid responds. His eyes dart back and forth, looking for an escape. There's nowhere to go. He has his back to the wall, and a crowd has formed to stand behind Mac and Quinn.

"We weren't giving you any," Quinn says. "But now we have to."

One of Quinn's friends has managed to catch up with them.

"Stone Harbor Police Department," he identifies himself, showing the young waiter his badge. His eyes widen. The kid is absolutely petrified. "You're Benjamin Hall, aren't you?"

"It wasn't my idea! It was all hers!" Benjamin looks like he's ready to cry.

"Who? Kirby?" Mac asks.

The kid shakes his head. "Kirby? I don't even know who that is. Sabrina Elliot. My boss."

Holy shit. The puzzle pieces finally fit. It was Sabrina who sank the boats. Not Kirby. They'd been focusing on one suspect when there were two.

After all the time he's known her, Mac shouldn't be surprised, but he still manages to be. This wasn't the first time she caused destruction. Obviously, she's escalated from the boats to the beach house.

"Where is she?" Mac asks. He needs to find her. He doesn't blame the kid, and he knows the cop will take him in for questioning anyway. Mac hopes they take it easy on him. Benjamin wasn't the one behind it. He was just going along with Sabrina's master plan.

"I have no idea. She doesn't normally talk to me, except when she needs something."

Mac looks at Quinn. "We need to find out where she is. Before she does something else. She's out of control."

One of the managers comes over, followed by Roger Elliot. He's full of righteous anger.

"May I ask what's going on?" His voice is cold. "Why are you chasing one of our employees?"

Mac doesn't have time for this. "Because we just found out he damaged the boats at the yacht club. By your daughter's request."

To his credit, Roger doesn't flinch. He barely displays any emotion as they explain what happened, his arms crossed as he listens to Quinn and Mac. They tell him that they have Sabrina on video vandalizing the music star's house. And a confession from the young waiter that she paid him to sink the boats.

Honestly, after the summer Roger has had with Sabrina, he's probably not that surprised.

The kid has a handcuff on one hand from the officer and has already been read his Miranda Rights. His shift is over for the night. The cop leads him away.

"If what you're saying is true, I need to speak with my daughter," Roger says.

"Do you have any idea where she is?" They need to call Detective Shroud.

He shakes his head. "I haven't seen her for days. She's still upset with me about making her apologize to you and Margo."

Mac decides to get a hold of the detective to put out an APB on Sabrina. She's got to be around here somewhere. She can't get too far.

Chapter 50

August 28

Tyson steers the yacht club boat as he leads the parade of motorboats and yachts. They made a wide loop and are already heading back north after cruising past the docks of homes on Corinthian Drive along Carnival Bay. The crew of boats is moving slowly, letting partiers standing on the docks get a good view of their themed boats and cheer them on as they pass by.

There's plenty to watch. *The Simpsons, Golden Girls, Full House, Diff'rent Strokes, Friends.* There's even an *Alf* boat complete with Willie.

The boats are cruising past the bayfront homes of Sunset Drive when he spots something off. The main 96th Street Bridge covers the stretch between the mainland and the island. It's supposed to be up to let the larger boats pass.

But it's not. It's still down.

The usual clearance is only ten feet tall across the Great Channel. Not enough to let the larger boats go by. That's why an operator stands by to open the drawbridge via weights on either side. It doesn't take long, less than a minute and a half. Then it's down again so the cars can continue on their way.

Ten feet. That's it. Not even close to enough height to let the boats glide underneath. If the boats keep going, there's a risk of ramming their flimsy fiberglass right into the top of the steel bridge. In a contest, they'd lose every time.

It had been up when they left the club. Where was the bridge operator?

Tyson gets on the radio immediately, calling in a red alert that they need the drawbridge to be raised. NOW.

Sure, he can stall, but what if the other boats don't realize the drawbridge is down? They could slam into the steel, causing major damage. Or worse, major injuries.

There's no response. He radios again, then really starts to panic. His usually calm, peaceful nature is out the door. This is major.

Tyson grabs one of the club sailing instructors to man the wheel and goes to get Eddie, who's dancing on the top deck with the mayor.

"I need you. The bridge is down and we're about to run into it."

It's noisy from all the music blaring, but Eddie sees his face and snaps to attention right away. "Send out a message to the boats. We need to keep them away. I'll call the coast guard."

Eddie joins Tyson at the helm of the boat. They're both tense.

They don't have much time. Tyson idles the motor and lets everyone on the boat know what's going on (easier said than done). They begin to quiet down, recognizing the gravity of the situation with the bridge down. Picturing someone slamming their boat into it. A train of boats sinking into the water. The potential loss of lives.

Margo comes up and stands next to Tyson. She doesn't say a word, just grabs hold of his hand and presses her palm into his.

"I'm here," she says. "What do you need?"

Eddie has his binoculars up and scanning the drawbridge walkway. There's someone in the operator's cabin. He can barely make out who it is. As they sail closer, he begins to make out a tall female with bright blond hair.

"Sabrina," he shouts. He recognizes her instantly. Even though he has no idea what she's doing up there.

Tyson turns around and holds up his hands. What can they do?

Out on the water, without any way to get onto the bridge and raise it, they're stuck. What are their options? There's about to be a massive pileup of boats. It will be impossible to let them all know, with all the guests partying.

The drivers might be slow to act, surrounded by the noise and chaos. All it would take is one out of the 35 boats to keep going, ram into the steel bridge, and capsize.

Tyson spots a couple of people traveling the walkway over the closed bridge, oblivious to the danger around them. They're dressed in glitter jackets that sparkle as the setting sunbeams strike the sequins.

Kyle and Ryan. Wait. Kyle and Ryan!

He grabs his cell phone.

Ryan picks up right away. "Tyson, you naughty boy. What are you up to? Meet us at the restaurant?"

"Ryan, listen up. I need your help. It's *urgent.* Sabrina Elliot is in the bridge operator station. She put the bridge down, and she's not letting us through."

"Wait, what?"

There's no time to explain. "I NEED you to get the drawbridge up before 30 boats crash into it. Sabrina must have found a way to lower it. If we don't get it up, the bigger boats are going to hit the bridge."

"Tyson, is this a joke?"

"The Festival of Lights Parade. We're almost at the bridge. You need to get it back up before we crash."

"How do I do that?"

"You need to get to the operator station. Quickly."

Ryan doesn't hesitate. "Got it. The bitch is going down."

He disconnects, and Tyson doesn't hear anything.

Despite his radio and slowing down their speed, they're still nearing the bridge. It's hard to pull back against the current of the water.

They can't do anything but float slowly towards it. He's hemmed in by the parade of boats.

They need time for the bridge to rise high enough to pass underneath. If it were just one boat, he wouldn't worry. He could stop in time. But it's a parade of boats lit up with loud music and too many drinks. It's a disaster waiting to happen.

Tyson trains his binoculars on the bridge. No movement. He can't tell what's going on.

The boats keep approaching, despite Tyson's best efforts to slow them down and radio the drivers. Everyone is having fun. They're not paying attention.

"Fuck me," Eddie says softly.

Margo squeezes Tyson's hand. They watch in horror.

They're getting closer when he hears the bell clanking, closing the lanes of car traffic. Almost there….

The gate begins to rise. In a minute and a half, it's all the way up. Two big beams are sticking up in the air.

Their boat glides underneath in the nick of time. Their lead boat isn't that big, but the Icona's yacht would have been crushed. They were third in line.

He expels a huge sigh of relief. His saviors, Kyle and Ryan. Who would have thought they were good for more than epic parties?

He owes them big time.

The caravan of boats continues north, past Snug Harbor and the North and South Basins. The festival has been a huge hit. The crowds at the docks love the creativity of each boat, offering applause and shouts of laughter. They have no idea what could have happened.

A pileup of boats, maybe even a sunken one. A damaged bridge that's one of the only ways to get on or off the island. The official end of the season, for a long time.

His heart still hammering, Tyson steers the parade back to the yacht club. He pulls into the docks and ties the bow lines to the cleats on the dock. He's still sweating from their near miss. It had been close.

But they made it. The last hour feels like a strange dream, where the familiar backdrop of Stone Harbor became something different. What he saw every day transformed into something that almost killed him.

Their ship's crew is less animated, realizing how close they came to disaster. The commodores and their wives climb off, followed by members of the club. They're mostly quiet. The mayor walks by and shakes their hand.

"Well done," Chloe says. "You saved us."

They hug friends and family members who have been waiting at the club for them to sail back. Cans of drinks appear and are gratefully passed around.

Tyson finishes tying the lines and drops the anchor. He and Eddie help get most of the crew off the boat, holding them as they jump off to the dock.

Margo is one of the last to disembark. He stands there, waiting for her. As he's done for more than two decades.

She reaches for his hand and doesn't let go.

"Tyson," she says softly. Her lips curve. And he knows.

He doesn't hesitate. Doesn't allow himself to overthink. Tyson simply goes in for a kiss, giving her everything he's felt for the past twenty years of being her best friend who's been in love with her since kindergarten.

This time, she doesn't pull away.

"I knew it," Eddie says with a smile. "Welcome to the fam."

Epilogue

Guess what? There were TWO people causing chaos on the island. Kirby Bennett and Sabrina Elliot. They both had grudges against people.

Kirby was livid about Jacob moving out and not letting her know where he was living, and she held it against her in-laws, who were basically the mascots of the town. So, she did everything she could to embarrass them.

That meant sabotaging their season by breaking into Margo's office at The Plank for Jacob's new address, destroying The Gables, whacking Quinn on the head, and stealing the time capsule.

Sabrina was angry with her dad for cutting off her spending, so she paid one of the hotel's staff members to sink his treasured Sunny. The boat he started sailing on more than 30 years ago. Poor Benjamin Hall was just a young kid she talked into doing the damage.

To disguise who she was targeting, she had him sink a lot more than one. When Mac fired her, she vandalized his client's pool house. And then, of course, she tried to ruin the Festival of Lights Parade.

The race timer? Neither one of the women had any hand in that. It was just a bunch of kids. They thought it was funny to move it to the beach.

There's some sympathy for Kirby, who was going through a rough divorce. Sabrina? Not so much.

Both women are placed in custody. They're currently out on bail, waiting for their first hearing. Everyone in town is sure to be notified when that occurs.

Chelsea is BESIDE herself. She had to leave right when everything was getting juicy! But college beckons. She already told Margo she'll be back next year. Totes.

Rafael and Tina Martinez decide to take a long-awaited vacation to Europe. It also helps give them a break until the gossip in town dies down. Tina isn't sure if she's going to remain on the council. They're taking it one day at a time.

Banksy is sticking around. He likes Stone Harbor, and he has no hard feelings towards certain members of the Police Department. Well, at least not that much. He's also seriously dating the now officially separated Sugar Momma he's been seeing. Things are getting serious.

Sara and her husband Charles are back together. She's now doing home workouts at the new gym in her garage that Charles built. Tony has already returned to Florida, where he's training bodies for the Miami season.

Eddie and Tish are looking for a place to move in together. His new gig as a manager at the Surf Shop is a solid one, with major responsibilities he's happy to accept. They're currently looking for a condo to rent. They might take Tyson's.

Mac and Margo ended things on Labor Day weekend. She didn't have to get into much detail over why she was ending things. She didn't have to.

Ever the gentleman, Mac spared her from any hard feelings. She has a feeling he already knows why, but he's too thoughtful to press for details. She has a hunch that he'll find someone new in less than a month.

Sandy gave her a big bonus, and it was enough with her savings and sales commissions to purchase a share in the Avalon location. Margo's officially a small business owner. To celebrate, Tyson takes her out for a cruise on Quinn's boat, where they christen their new relationship. He doesn't ask Quinn for permission.

Kyle and Ryan were so excited about their "rescue" that they decided to venture into the sailing business. Their first investment is a charter boat business, run by Tyson Vandenbraak himself. He has some ideas about what the next season should look like.